I HEARD THAT SONG BEFORE
Peter seems like the perfect husband, until police
show up with a warrant for his arrest . . . for murder.

WHERE ARE YOU NOW?
Her brother vanished when she was a child . . .
now Carolyn's pursuit of the truth plunges her into a
world of unexpected danger and unanswered questions.

JUST TAKE MY HEART
Broadway star Natalie Raines accidentally exposes the killer of
her former roommate – but that's just the beginning of the story.

THE SHADOW OF YOUR SMILE
Eighty-two-year-old Olivia Morrow has a horrible choice: expose
a long-held family secret, or take it with her to her grave.

I'LL WALK ALONE
What do you do when you're falsely accused of
kidnapping your own child?

THE LOST YEARS
When a well-respected academic in possession of a
priceless artefact is found murdered, his wife becomes
the main suspect. But she has Alzheimer's . . .

DADDY'S GONE A-HUNTING
Two sisters' lives are under threat when a dark secret
from their family's past comes to light.

I'VE GOT YOU UNDER MY SKIN
A father murdered in cold blood – and his
widow intent on revenge.

THE MELODY LINGERS ON
Parker Bennett has been missing for two years –
and so has billions of dollars from his company. Did he
commit suicide or was his disappearance staged?

AS TIME GOES BY
A woman is on trial for the murder of her wealthy husband –
but is she a cold-blooded killer or an innocent victim?

ALL BY MYSELF, ALONE
A glamorous cruise on a luxurious ocean liner
becomes a nightmare when an elderly woman with a
fortune in jewels turns up dead . . .

I'VE GOT MY EYES ON YOU
Kerry Dowling is found dead at the bottom
of her family's pool. She threw a party the night
before, but no one saw anything . . .

The
Under Suspicion
series
(co-authored with Alafair Burke)

THE CINDERELLA MURDER
Laurie Moran investigates the murder of a college student,
where everyone is a suspect . . .

ALL DRESSED IN WHITE
A destination wedding goes awry when the bride
disappears the day before the ceremony.

THE SLEEPING BEAUTY KILLER
Casey Carter was convicted of murdering her fiancé
fifteen years ago. But Casey claims she's innocent.
Now Laurie must try and prove it . . .

EVERY BREATH YOU TAKE
The Met Gala: the world's most glamorous fundraising party.
People would *kill* for an invitation . . .

LOVES MUSIC, LOVES TO DANCE
A killer is on the loose, using personal ads to
lure his victims to their deaths . . .

ALL AROUND THE TOWN
University student Laurie Kenyon is accused of murdering
her English professor, but she has no memory of the crime.
Her fingerprints, however, are everywhere.

I'LL BE SEEING YOU
When a reporter sees a sheet-wrapped corpse,
she feels as if she's staring into her own face:
the murdered woman could be her twin sister.

REMEMBER ME
A killer turns a young family's dream holiday
into an unfathomable nightmare . . .

LET ME CALL YOU SWEETHEART
When Kerry McGrath visits a plastic surgeon, she
sees a woman with a hauntingly familiar face. On
her next visit, she sees the same face again –
on a different woman . . .

MOONLIGHT BECOMES YOU
With her stepmother brutally murdered and
the police stumped, Maggie Holloway decides
she'll have to solve the case herself.

PRETEND YOU DON'T SEE HER
While showing a luxurious penthouse flat, estate agent
Lacey is the only witness to a murder – and to the
dying words of the victim . . .

YOU BELONG TO ME
A radio talk show host tries to discover the identity of a
killer who is stalking and murdering lonely women.

WE'LL MEET AGAIN
They're best friends: but one has just been convicted
of murder, and the other may have committed it ...

BEFORE I SAY GOODBYE
A desperate wife searches for answers to her husband's death,
but the nearer she comes to learning the truth, the nearer she is
to becoming the next victim of a ruthless killer ...

ON THE STREET WHERE YOU LIVE
A young woman is haunted by two murders that
are closely linked – despite the one hundred
and ten years that separate them.

DADDY'S LITTLE GIRL
Seven-year-old Ellie's testimony put a
man behind bars for the murder of her sister.
Twenty years later, the murders start again ...

THE SECOND TIME AROUND
A wealthy man disappears but his wife seems
bafflingly unaffected. Is he in hiding, or dead?
Or is something more sinister going on?

NIGHT-TIME IS MY TIME
High school reunions: the perfect time to catch up
with old friends ... and enact vengeance against
the women who once humiliated you.

NO PLACE LIKE HOME
Ten-year-old Liza Barton accidentally shot and killed her
mother while trying to protect her from her violent stepfather.
Twenty-four years later, she's the target of a ruthless killer.

TWO LITTLE GIRLS IN BLUE
When her twin daughters are kidnapped, a mother's
nightmare is about to become her reality.

MARY HIGGINS CLARK

& ALAFAIR BURKE

YOU DON'T OWN ME

**SIMON &
SCHUSTER**

London · New York · Sydney · Toronto · New Delhi

A CBS COMPANY

First published in Great Britain by Simon & Schuster UK Ltd, 2018
This paperback edition published by Simon & Schuster UK Ltd, 2019
A CBS COMPANY

1 3 5 7 9 10 8 6 4 2

Simon & Schuster UK Ltd
1st Floor
222 Gray's Inn Road
London WC1X 8HB

Simon & Schuster Australia, Sydney
Simon & Schuster India, New Delhi

www.simonandschuster.co.uk
www.simonandschuster.com.au
www.simonandschuster.co.in

A CIP catalogue record for this book is available from the British Library

Paperback ISBN: 978-1-4711-6766-9
Export Paperback ISBN: 978-1-4711-6844-4
Ebook ISBN: 978-1-4711-6765-2
Audio ISBN: 978-1-4711-8164-1

Printed and bound by CPI Group (UK) Ltd, Croydon, CR0 4YY

MIX
Paper from
responsible sources
FSC
www.fsc.org   FSC® C020471

For my firstborn great-grandchild,
William Warren Clark
Welcome to the world, Will!
—Mary

For David and Hiedi Lesh,
Cheers!
—Alafair

YOU DON'T OWN ME

Prologue

Sixty-year-old Caroline Radcliffe nearly dropped one of the saucers she was carefully stacking in the overstuffed sideboard when she heard a bellow from the den. She immediately felt guilty for turning her eye from the children for even a moment. She had been looking out the window rejoicing at the fact that now, in late March, she would be able to spend more time outdoors with the children.

As she made her way toward the cry, four-year-old Bobby scampered by, an excited giggle escaping his open mouth. In the den, she found two-year-old Mindy wailing, her blue eyes focused on the tumble of building blocks scattered around her legs.

It wasn't difficult for Caroline to see what was going on. Bobby was a sweet little boy, but he took pleasure in devising small ways to torment his baby sister. On occasion, she was tempted to warn him that girls have a way of balancing the scales eventually, but she figured they were typical siblings who would work it all out in the end.

"It's okay, Mindy sweetheart," she said soothingly. "I'll help you put them back, just the way they were."

Mindy's pout only deepened, and she pushed a nearby stack of blocks away from her. "No more!" she cried. The next sounds out of the girl's mouth were an unmistakable request for *Mama*.

Caroline sighed, bent down, and hoisted Mindy to her hip, wrapping her arms tight around the toddler until she quieted and her quick, upset breaths returned to normal.

"That's better," Caroline said. "That's my Mindy."

Mindy's father, Dr. Martin Bell, had made it very clear that he wanted Caroline to stop "babying the kids." In his view, even picking Mindy up when she cried was "babying."

"It's simple reward and punishment," he liked to say. "Not to compare them to dogs, but—well, it's how all animals learn. She wants you to hold her. If you do it every time she pitches a fit, we'll have tears flowing day and night."

Well, for starters, Caroline didn't like comparing children with dogs. And she also knew a thing or two about raising them. She had two grown children of her own and had helped raise another six of them in her years as a nanny. The Bells were her fourth family, and, in her view, Bobby and Mindy deserved a little extra TLC. Their father worked all the time and had all his little rules for everyone in the house, including the babies. And their mother— well, their mother was clearly going through a rough patch. It was the whole reason why Caroline had a job in a house with a stay-at-home mom.

"Bobby." She had heard his footsteps charging up the staircase. "Bobby!" she called out. She had learned by now that she and the children could make plenty of noise as long as Dr. Bell was gone. "I need to have a word with you. And you know why, young man!"

Even though Caroline had a soft spot for these little ones, she wasn't a complete pushover.

Caroline placed Mindy down to greet her brother at the bottom of the stairs. With each step, Bobby's pace slowed, trying to postpone the inevitable. Mindy's gaze moved hesitantly between Caroline and Bobby, wondering what was going to happen next.

"Cut it out," Caroline told Bobby sternly. Pointing at Mindy, she said, "You know better than that."

"I'm sorry, Mindy," he muttered.

"I'm not sure I can hear you," Caroline said.

"I'm sorry I knocked your blocks down."

Caroline kept waiting expectantly until Bobby gave his sister a reluctant hug. A still angry Mindy was having none of the apology. "You're mean, Bobby," she wailed.

The moment was interrupted by the rumble of the mechanical door rolling open beneath them. Of all the homes Caroline had worked in, this one was arguably the finest. It was a late-nineteenth-century carriage house. What once served as a horse stable had now been renovated with every modern amenity, including the ultimate Manhattan luxury—a ground-floor, private garage.

Daddy was home.

"Now maybe the two of you can pick all that mess up in the den before your father sees it."

Pop! Pop! Pop!

Caroline's scream scared the children, who both began to cry.

"Firecrackers," she said calmly, even as her racing heart told her that her first instinct had been correct. Those were clearly the sounds of gunfire. "Go upstairs until I find out who's making that racket."

When they were halfway up the stairs, she hurried to the front door and then ran down the front steps to the driveway. The dome light inside Dr. Bell's BMW was on, and the driver's-side door was halfway open. Dr. Bell was slumped over the steering wheel.

Caroline continued moving until she stood outside the open car door. She saw the blood. She saw enough to know that Dr. Bell wouldn't make it.

Terrified, she rushed inside and called 911. Somehow she managed to tell the dispatcher the address. It wasn't until she hung up the phone that she thought about Kendra, upstairs in her usual groggy state.

Dear God, who is going to tell the children?

1

Five years later, Caroline was still working in that same carriage house, but so much had changed. Mindy and Bobby were no longer her little babies. They were nearly finished with the first and third grades. They rarely cried anymore, even when the subject of their father came up.

And Mrs. Bell—Kendra, as Caroline often called her now—well, she was an entirely different woman. She no longer slept away the days. She was a good mom. And she worked, which is why it would fall to Caroline to pick the children up from their twice weekly visit to their grandparents' apartment on the Upper East Side. It was a task that neither of them enjoyed. Dr. Bell's parents made their son look like a free spirit compared to them.

Caroline had made it out of the apartment and halfway to the elevator when she heard the children's grandmother call out behind her. She turned to see both grandparents standing side by side outside their door. Dr. Bell was thin, almost to the point of being gaunt. His wispy hair was combed sideways across the dome of his head. As chief of vascular surgery at prestigious Mount Sinai Medical Center, he had grown accustomed to getting his own way. Nine years into retirement the scowl he had brought to the hospital every day had not diminished in the least.

Cynthia Bell, now in her eighties, showed little sign of the beauty that had once been hers. Her long hours in the sun had left her skin wrinkled and dry. Her lips were turned down at the corners, giving the impression of a permanent pout.

"Yes?" Caroline inquired.

"Did Kendra even *try* to get that television producer interested in Martin's case?" Dr. Bell asked.

Caroline smiled politely. "It's really not for me to say who Mrs. Bell speaks to—"

"You mean *Kendra*," he said sternly. "My wife is the only Mrs. Bell. That woman is no longer married to my son, because my son was shot to death in his driveway."

Caroline continued to force a pleasant expression. Oh, how she remembered the drama that had unfolded in the living room six months earlier over the subject of that television producer. Robert and Cynthia had asked to come to the house following Mindy's after-school dance recital. They told Kendra all about *Under Suspicion*, a television show that reinvestigated cold cases. Without notifying Kendra, they had sent a letter to the studio asking them to look into Martin's unsolved murder.

The official Mrs. Bell, Cynthia, interjected. "Kendra tells us that the producer, a woman named Laurie Moran, passed on the case."

Caroline nodded. "That's exactly what happened. Kendra was at least as upset about it as you are. Now, I need to get your grandchildren home before my shift ends," she added, even though she was never one to watch a clock.

As the elevator made its way down from the Bells' penthouse apartment to the lobby, she had a feeling that the couple wasn't going to let this subject drop. She was going to hear the name Laurie Moran again.

2

Laurie Moran was doing another round of "up . . . and down . . . and up . . . and down" to the beat of eardrum-piercing techno music in a room lit like a late 1970s disco. The man in front of her let out another enthusiastic "Wooooh!" which Laurie was certain provided no additional health benefits.

To her right, her friend Charlotte—the one who had suggested this morning's spin class—grinned mischievously as she wiped her brow with a small towel. Her voice couldn't overcome the music, but Laurie could read her lips: "You love it!" On her other side Linda Webster-Cennerazzo looked as exhausted as she did.

Laurie most certainly did not, in fact, love it. She felt a moment of relief when the music changed to a song she recognized, but then the perfectly tanned and toned instructor ruined it by yelling, "Turn those knobs, people! It's time for another hill!"

Laurie reached down to the frame of her stationary bike as instructed, but snuck in two quick rotations of the knob to the left instead of the right. The last thing she needed was to increase her resistance, especially if you counted the psychological type.

When the torture finally ended, she filed out with the rest of the winded students and followed Charlotte and Linda to the locker room. It was unlike any gym Laurie had ever frequented, complete with eucalyptus-soaked towels, fluffy robes, and a waterfall next to the saunas.

Laurie's beauty routine took less than ten minutes, thanks to her wash-and-wear shoulder-length hair and a quick application of tinted moisturizer and one coat of mascara. She rested on a cedar recliner as Charlotte attended to her own finishing touches.

"I can't believe you put yourself through that agony four times a week," Laurie said.

"Neither can I," Linda said.

"And I cross-train the other three, don't forget," Charlotte added.

"Now you're just bragging," Linda said, an edge in her voice.

"Look, I finally decided I have to exercise like this, because most of the time, I'm sitting in a chair at work or going out to dinner with clients. The two of you run around plenty enough in your regular lives."

"So we do," Linda added as she headed for the shower.

Laurie also knew that it was practically in Charlotte's job description to be in tip-top shape. She was the New York head of her family company, Ladyform, one of the country's most popular makers of high-end workout attire for women. "If I come back here again, I'm going to sit in the hot tub next to that waterfall and leave the *wooooh*-ing to you."

"Laurie, suit yourself. I think you're perfect just the way you are. But you're the one who said you wanted to get in better shape before the big wedding."

"It's not going to be *big*," she protested. "And I don't know what I was thinking. Those wedding magazines pollute a woman's brain: designer dresses, thousands of flowers, and so much tulle! It's too much. I've returned to my senses."

As she thought of her impending marriage to Alex, a surge of joy swept through Laurie. She tried to keep her voice even as she concentrated on what she was saying to Charlotte. "Once Timmy's done with the school year, we'll do something small and take a family trip together."

Charlotte shook her head disapprovingly as she tucked a tube of hair gel into her black leather Prada backpack. "Laurie, trust me. Forget about a family trip. You and Alex are going on your *honeymoon*. It should be just the two of you. Toasting each other with champagne. And Leo would be happy to take care of Timmy when you're away."

Laurie noticed a woman at a locker in the next row eavesdropping and lowered her voice. "Charlotte, I had a big wedding when Greg and I were married. I just want to have a quiet wedding this time. What matters is that Alex and I are finally together. For good."

Laurie had originally met defense attorney Alex Buckley when she recruited him to serve as the host of her television show, *Under Suspicion*. He became her closest confidant at work, and then more than that outside of the office. But when he stepped back from the show to return full-time to his legal practice, Laurie hadn't been entirely sure how Alex fit into her life. She had already found a great love in Greg and, after losing him, had forged ahead by juggling the demands of her career and being a single mother. She thought she was perfectly content, until Alex finally made it clear that he wanted more from Laurie than he believed she was ready to give.

As it turned out, she realized after a three-month hiatus that she was miserably unhappy without Alex. It was she who had called and asked him to dinner. The moment she hung up the phone she knew she had made the right decision. They had been engaged now for two months. She had already become accustomed to the feel of the platinum ring with a solitaire diamond that Alex had chosen.

She honestly couldn't recall whether she had even once asked Alex what *he* wanted.

She tried picturing herself walking down a long aisle in an elaborate white gown, but all she could see was Greg waiting for her at the front of the church. When she pictured herself exchanging vows

with Alex, she saw them somewhere outside, surrounded by flowers, or even barefoot on a beach. She wanted it to be special. And
different from what she'd had before. But, again, that was what *she*
wanted.

She was almost to her office door by the time she realized that
her assistant, Grace Garcia, was trying to get her attention. "Earth to
Laurie? You in there?"

She blinked and was back in the real world. "Sorry, I think the
spin class Charlotte dragged me to made me dizzy."

Grace was looking at her with wide, dark eyes lined in perfect cat
style. Her long, black hair was pulled into a tight *I Dream of Jeannie*
topknot, and she was wearing a flattering wrap dress and knee-high
boots—only three-inch heels, practically flats by Grace's standards.

"Those spin addicts are a cult," Grace warned dismissively. "All
that hooting and hollering. And people wearing crazy outfits like
they're in the Tour de France. Girlfriend, you're in a gym on Fifth
Avenue."

"It definitely wasn't for me. You were saying something when I
was in la-la land?"

"Right. You had visitors waiting for you in the lobby when I got
in this morning. Security told me they arrived before eight and were
adamant about waiting until you arrived."

Laurie was grateful for the success of her show, but could do without some of the ancillary benefits, such as fans who wanted to "pop
in" to the studio for selfies and autographs.

"Are you sure they're not fans of Ryan's?" As popular as Alex had
been with viewers, apparently the current host, Ryan Nichols, was
considered "crush-worthy" by the younger generation.

"They're definitely here to see you. Remember the Martin Bell
case?"

"Of course." A few months earlier, Laurie had thought the case would be perfect for *Under Suspicion*—a renowned physician shot to death in his driveway while his wife and children were just yards away inside the house.

"His parents are in conference room B. They say the wife is a killer and they want you to prove it."

3

What Grace had referred to as "conference room B" was now officially known as the Bernard B. Holder conference room. The studio chief, Brett Young, had christened it as such upon Holder's retirement last year. Holder had been at the studio even longer than Brett, overseeing shows as varied as soap operas, hard-hitting journalism exposés, and a new breed of reality television that seemed anything but realistic.

Grace, however, continued to refer to the room by its original, generic name. So many times, Laurie had wanted to lecture Bernie for the off-color jokes he often made at Grace's expense, but Grace had insisted on smiling politely. "I'll be here long after him," she liked to say. And so it was.

Laurie could hear raised voices from inside the conference room as she approached the door. She paused before turning the knob. She heard a woman say something about moving on and peace for the sake of the children. "I hate the family name being involved in a scandal." The man's voice was clearer and bitterly angry. "I don't give a damn about preserving the family name. She murdered our son."

Laurie waited four beats before finally entering the room. Mrs. Bell sat up straight in her chair, and it appeared as though her husband had already been standing.

Laurie introduced herself as the producer of *Under Suspicion*.

"Dr. Robert Bell." His handshake was firm but quick.

His wife's grip was barely a squeeze. "Call me Cynthia," she said quietly.

Laurie could see that Grace had already played hostess. They both had paper cups with cardboard sleeves to protect their hands from the hot liquid.

"My assistant said you were here first thing this morning."

Dr. Bell's eyes were icy. "To be honest, Ms. Moran, we assumed it was the only way we could be assured of a meeting with you."

She could tell that at least one half of the couple was already treating her as the enemy, and she had no idea why. But the only thing she knew about Robert and Cynthia Bell was that they had lost their only child to a homicide, which meant that she would go out of her way to be kind to them.

"Please, call me Laurie. And, Dr. Bell, have a seat if you'd be more comfortable," she added, gesturing to the unoccupied chair next to his wife. He looked at her suspiciously, but Laurie had always had the kind of demeanor that put people at ease. She could almost feel his blood pressure begin to lower as he got settled into the leather conference chair. "I assume you're here about your son. I'm familiar with the case."

"Of course you are," Dr. Bell said, sniping, and drawing a disapproving glance from his wife. "My apologies. I'm sure you're a very busy woman. But I would certainly hope you'd at least know my son's name, and the circumstances surrounding his horrific death. After all, we were the ones who contacted you. We wrote the letter to you ourselves, side by side, each word coming from both of us." He reached over and held his wife's hand on the table. "It wasn't easy, you know, recounting that terrible night. We had to identify our only child's body. It's unnatural. We weren't meant to outlive the next generation."

"We were childless for years," Cynthia added. "We assumed it was never going to happen. And then, when I was forty years old, there he was. He was our miracle."

Laurie nodded but said nothing. Sometimes listening in silence was the most compassionate thing to be done for a murder victim's loved ones. She knew that from personal experience.

Cynthia cleared her throat before speaking. "We just wanted to hear it for ourselves: Why won't you help us find our son's killer? You've helped so many other families. Why isn't our son worth the effort?"

One of the hardest parts of Laurie's job was wading through letters, emails, Facebook posts, and tweets from the survivors. So many unsolved homicides. People who just went missing. Their friends and families sent Laurie detailed timelines of the cases, complete with stories about the lives lost. Graduation photos, baby pictures, descriptions of the dreams that would no longer be fulfilled—sometimes it was enough to make Laurie cry. She had decided that it would do more harm than good to contact families personally when she wasn't moving forward with their stories. But sometimes, like now, the families wanted to hear from her directly.

"I'm so sorry." Laurie had delivered this news so many times, but it never got easier. "It's not a question of your son's value. I know he had young children, and was a highly regarded physician. We only take on a few investigations per year. We have to focus on the ones where we really believe we have a chance of making progress where the police did not."

"The police made no progress," Robert said. "Not even a named suspect, let alone an arrest or a conviction. Meanwhile, we have to watch Martin's killer raise his children."

He didn't need to use the suspect's name for Laurie to know that he was talking about their former daughter-in-law. The details of the case were fuzzy now, but Laurie remembered that the wife had been unhappy in the marriage and appeared to be withdrawing money for unexplained purposes.

"That's actually the very worst part of it," Cynthia added. "It's bad enough to live with the fact that Kendra killed our son and got away with it. But grandparents basically have no legal right to see their grandchildren. Did you know that? We've had lawyers look at it from every angle. Until some court of law holds her responsible for Martin's death, she has complete say-so over the kids. Which means we have to be nice to that woman, just to keep Bobby and Mindy in our lives. It's sickening."

"I'm so sorry," Laurie said again, feeling like a broken record. "It's never an easy decision for us."

The mail through which Laurie routinely waded had taught her that the country was home to thousands and thousands of unsolved cases. Mysteries waiting to be solved. But many of them were mysteries with no leads. No loose threads to be picked. No holes to be dug further. For Laurie to do her job, she needed clues to follow. Laurie had pulled the Bells' letter about their son's case because it had seemed promising. It also had the added benefit of being a local case. She tried to travel as little as possible during Timmy's school year.

But, unfortunately, the case turned out not to be a good match after all. *Under Suspicion* required a suspect or suspects who were willing to go on camera and attest to their innocence. On television, there were no police around, no defense lawyers, and no Miranda rights, only tough questions. Not every suspect was willing to go along.

"As the title of the show suggests," Laurie tried to explain, "we can't make much headway without cooperation from the people who have been living under the shadow of suspicion in the years that have passed since the crime."

"What other suspects are there?" Robert demanded to know.

"That's the type of thing we explore once we believe we might be moving forward with production."

"But you just suggested that was the reason you couldn't use our son's case. You needed cooperation from the people under suspicion, so to speak."

"Yes."

"So who are the other people? Maybe we can get them on board."

"We never got to that point, I'm afraid." Laurie felt as if they were speaking in circles, like a bad version of "Who's on First." It had been obvious to Laurie, both from the Bells' letter and a cursory review of press coverage, that any reinvestigation of Martin Bell's murder would require the cooperation of his widow, Kendra. Had she been willing to participate, Laurie would have worked with her, the police, and other witnesses to identify alternative suspects and attempt to gain their participation as well. But once Kendra Bell made it clear that she was adamantly opposed to appearing on *Under Suspicion*, Laurie had moved on to another case. She did not understand why the Bells were so confused by this.

"Kendra was our one and only suspect," Robert said. "The police never named her as a suspect, but they certainly led us to believe that she was the leading contender. What more do you need?"

The fog suddenly lifted, and Laurie got a tickle in her stomach. She realized the source of the confusion in the room.

"And you think Kendra's still willing to participate?" Laurie asked, testing her theory.

"Absolutely," Cynthia blurted, her eyes brightening with hope. "She was very upset that you took all these months to make a decision, only to turn her down. Oh, please, tell us that you'll reconsider."

Laurie smiled politely. "I can't make any promises. But let me take another look at the case, just to make sure I didn't miss anything."

Laurie hadn't taken months to make a decision, and she certainly had never turned the case down. Kendra Bell had lied to Robert and Cynthia, and Laurie was determined to learn why.

4

After Laurie walked the Bells to the elevator, she made her way back to her office, eager to refresh her memory about the details of Martin Bell's murder. She remembered how excited she had been when she first came across his parents' letter in the backlog of accumulated fan mail. The case seemed so perfect for her show. Martin, by all accounts, was a doting young father and brilliant physician from a renowned New York family. His father had served as the head of surgery at Mount Sinai, and his grandfather had been the state attorney general. The Bell name was on more than a handful of buildings across New York State.

And then the beloved son, Martin, was shot dead outside of his beautiful Greenwich Village home.

A brilliant young doctor—a father—killed out of nowhere by gunfire in downtown Manhattan. Of course she had thought about her Greg at the time. How could she not?

The similarities to Greg's case ended there, however. Laurie's own son, Timmy, had witnessed his father's murder. Only three years old at the time, he'd been able to provide his version of a description, based on the gunman's eyes: "Blue Eyes shot my daddy . . . Blue Eyes shot my daddy!" Martin Bell's young children had been inside the family home under the watchful gaze of their nanny, and no one else had observed the shooting outside in the driveway.

And unlike Kendra Bell, Laurie had never been treated as a suspect in Greg's murder. Sure, she had felt a suspicious gaze here and there during the five years when Greg's murder had remained unsolved. To some people, a spouse is automatically presumed guilty. But Laurie's father, Leo, had been the New York Police Department's first deputy commissioner at the time of the shooting. No officer would have dared speak of her in an accusatory tone without cold, hard evidence to back it up.

Kendra, on the other hand, had been churned through the machine that was the New York media's tabloid-style crime coverage. Even before his murder, Martin Bell had been something of a celebrity. He had been a rising star in NYU's Neurology Department when he left to start his own, bold practice specializing in pain management. He was the author of a best-selling book emphasizing homeopathic remedies, stress reduction, and physical therapy as a means to reduce physical pain, advocating prescription drugs and surgical intervention only as last resorts. Laurie remembered Greg saying he'd have far fewer patients in the emergency room if more physicians heeded Bell's advice. As Bell's celebrity grew, some people started referring to him as a miracle worker.

After his murder, the juxtaposition between his public image and the woman to whom he was married could not have been more stark. Photographs emerged of Kendra looking confused and disheveled. It came out that she was a regular at a dive bar in the East Village and had been withdrawing large amounts of money from the couple's savings account. Reports leaked that she'd been so passed out at the time of the shooting that the nanny couldn't wake her after calling 911.

Front page headlines dubbed her the "Black Widow" and, more colorfully, "Stoner Mom," based on a rumored substance abuse problem.

After her preliminary online research, Laurie had contacted Kendra in the hope that she might appreciate the help of a major television studio to present her side of the story. Laurie liked to think that her show helped a crime victim's family and friends find closure. It also helped those whose lives were left in limbo, never arrested or charged with a crime, but always viewed with a suspicious eye. As Kendra's children got older, wouldn't she want them to know who killed their father? Wouldn't she want them to be absolutely certain that their mother had clean hands? Laurie knew how desperate she had been for answers about Greg's murder.

But when Laurie arrived at Kendra's house four months ago with a participation agreement for her to sign, Kendra had made it clear she wasn't interested. She gave all the reasons Laurie had grown accustomed to hearing. She didn't want to upset the police by suggesting that a television show might do a better job with the investigation than they had. She had finally been able to find a job and a new life without Martin, and feared that renewed attention would only trigger another wave of public scorn. And, perhaps most compellingly, she said that her children were now old enough to know if their mother was on television. "I don't want to put them through that unless you can absolutely guarantee me that you'll find my husband's killer."

Of course it was a promise that Laurie couldn't be certain that she could keep, which meant it was a promise she couldn't make.

It all sounded perfectly reasonable.

But now Laurie had a new piece of information.

She found Grace inside Jerry Klein's office, adjacent to Laurie's. Sometimes Laurie forgot that Jerry had once been a shy, awkward intern, when he first started working at the studio. She had watched as his confidence grew with each new accomplishment. Now he was Laurie's assistant producer, and it was hard for her to imagine going to work without him.

"Grace was just telling me that Martin Bell's parents showed up this morning," Jerry said.

Apparently Laurie wasn't the only one who remembered the case.

"It was certainly an interesting meeting," Laurie said. "They seem to be under the impression that Kendra was eager to do the show. Apparently, she told them *I* was the one who declined the case."

As usual, Jerry and Grace were her biggest defenders, immediately recounting Laurie's enthusiasm about the investigation at the time.

"Why would she lie about that?" Jerry asked.

"That's exactly what I intend to find out."

For the first time, Laurie noticed that the show's host, Ryan Nichols, was lingering beyond Jerry's door. He always had a way of showing up just in time to interject himself into any situation. He also had a way of getting under Laurie's skin.

True to form, he asked, "What are we about to find out?"

Laurie constantly had to remind herself of his credentials, which spoke for themselves: magna cum laude from Harvard Law School, followed by a Supreme Court clerkship and a coveted stint as a white collar prosecutor at the U.S. Attorney's Office. Unfortunately for Laurie, however, Ryan had decided his undeniable legal abilities meant that he could launch a media career with no further experience. Laurie had trained as a print journalist for years and then worked her way up to her position as the producer of her own show.

Ryan, in contrast, had only a few talking-head gigs on cable news before landing a full-time position at the studio. In addition to serving as the host of *Under Suspicion*, he acted as a legal consultant to other shows and was already pitching ideas for his own programming. In the world of television, his good looks were certainly an advantage. He had sandy blond hair, wide green eyes, and a dazzling smile — and of course all of his ideas involved him in front of the camera. But what really irked Laurie was Ryan's inability to see that his career's largest boost had come from his uncle's close friendship with Laurie's boss, Brett Young. Brett was usually impossible to please, but in his eyes, everything Ryan touched was magic. Despite Ryan's job description of "host," Brett had made it clear that he expected Laurie to involve Ryan at every stage of the production.

"We were just talking about the Martin Bell case," Laurie said. "The doctor who was shot in his driveway in Greenwich Village."

Laurie had not involved Ryan when she had conducted her preliminary research into the case last fall.

"Oh, right. Had to be the wife, right? That case would be perfect for us."

He said it as if he were the first one to think of it.

Laurie noticed Grace and Jerry exchange an annoyed glance. Their irritation with Ryan had grown over time, while Laurie had slowly come to accept Ryan's role—as outsized as it had become.

"I had some conversations with Kendra—that's the wife—around Thanksgiving, but she was a hard pass."

"Because she's guilty," Ryan said smugly.

Laurie wanted to ask him how many times he needed to be wrong about one of their cases to begin keeping an open mind. "Well, at the time, it seemed as if she was primarily interested in protecting her children's privacy. But now it looks like she gave her in-laws a different impression." She quickly explained the conversation she'd had with the Bells. "My plan is to try to catch her off guard when she comes home tonight from work. Want to join me? You can be the good cop."

"What time?"

"Five at the latest. We can't run late." Alex's induction as a federal judge was scheduled for six-thirty, and Laurie was not going to let anything cause her to miss one single minute.

"Sounds good," he said. "I'll read up on the case a bit before."

When Ryan was gone, Jerry and Grace were looking at Laurie as if they'd just seen the Hatfields and McCoys share an embrace.

"What?" Laurie said with a shrug. "If my instincts are right, Kendra lied to me the last time I saw her face-to-face. Having a former prosecutor there can't hurt."

As Laurie returned to her own office, she realized she'd been holding one other thing against Ryan: he wasn't Alex Buckley, the show's
original host. Now that she and Alex were engaged, she no longer
missed him at work. She was going to be with him forever. She could
deal with Ryan's imperfections.

5

Caroline told Bobby that the five-minute warning she had given him on his after-school "screen time" had passed. He snuck in a few additional moves on the cart-racing game he was playing, but otherwise complied with the unspoken request of her outstretched hand.

He handed her the tablet and then joined his sister, who was content to sit on the sofa and work on a puzzle she had successfully put together dozens of times before. They had always been so different. Even as a toddler, Mindy seemed to live inside her own thoughts, while her brother Bobby was always seeking outside entertainment.

As she passed the front bay window, Caroline spotted a handful of tourists clustered on the sidewalk below, appearing to examine the unoccupied driveway intensely. Their tour guide was lanky and had his long hair pulled into a "man bun" on top of his head. He wore his usual uniform of baggy black clothing and bright orange tennis shoes. He'd been coming around twice a week for almost four months now. He called the excursion the "Big Apple Crime Tour."

Caroline had tried to reason with him once, reminding him that a seven-year-old girl and nine-year-old boy called this place home. The site did not belong on a list of infamous scenes such as mafia hangouts, the spot where a woman had fallen to her death from the

Empire State Building, or the hotel where a punk rock star had murdered his girlfriend.

The tour guide had responded by reminding the tourists that Caroline was the nanny who called 911 after Martin Bell's murder, at which point they began asking her for autographs and selfies.

Now Caroline drew the curtains whenever she spotted the tour. She allowed herself a tiny bit of pleasure that the size of his groups seemed to be dwindling. Once, she had even gone online to a popular tourist website to post a devastating review.

I am nothing if not loyal to you children, she thought to herself as she looked at Bobby and Mindy disassembling the puzzle, only to start it over.

She was slicing an apple to pair with string cheese for their afternoon snack when the phone rang.

Her throat felt hot when the caller identified herself. Caroline had known that she hadn't heard the last of Laurie Moran.

"Is this Kendra?" the producer asked.

"No. Mrs. Bell is at work right now."

"I see. I don't suppose this is Caroline Radcliffe?"

"It is."

"You may not remember me, but we met briefly about four months ago. I came over to the house to meet with Kendra."

How could I forget? Caroline thought. Her heart had been racing as she stood at the top of the stairs, eavesdropping when she was supposed to be monitoring Bobby and Mindy as they completed their homework.

Don't do it, don't do it. She had repeated that mantra over and over, her fingers crossed, as if she could send a telepathic message to Kendra in the living room. She had felt such a wave of relief when Kendra gave all her reasons for declining to participate.

"Of course. Yes, I remember. Is there something I can help you with?" Caroline asked.

"I'm afraid not. Do you know how I can reach her?"

"Mrs. Bell can't be disturbed while she's working. Even I don't call unless it's an emergency."

"When do you expect her home then?"

"She works until five today. But then she'll want to have supper with the children and spend time with them before bed. She's very busy. Why don't you tell me what you need, and I can see if I can help."

"No. It's important that I speak to Kendra directly."

The Bells were never going to let this go. Of course they wouldn't: their son had been murdered. For months, she had heard Kendra fend off their questions. *Are they doing the show or not? What's taking them so long to decide?* Buying time over the holidays had been easy enough, but they'd grown increasingly insistent over the past two months. Finally, last week, Kendra had told them—falsely—that the producers had decided the case wasn't a good fit for their show.

Now the actual producer was calling again. This wasn't good.

"I can take your number and let her know that you called," Caroline offered.

When Caroline hung up the phone, she peered out the front window. The tourists were gone. Even so, she kept the curtains drawn, terrified in her heart that she couldn't keep the outside world from creeping into this house forever.

Kendra was in such a bad state back then. Pray God, please tell me she didn't do it.

6

The carriage house was precisely as Laurie remembered it from last fall, save for the addition of pale pink peonies blooming from the planter boxes outside the windows.

Ryan let out a little whistle as they stepped out of the black SUV Uber they had hired for the ride downtown. "Nice house," he declared. "Their own private garage and everything. If I could swing a sweet place like that, I might actually get the Porsche I've always wanted. No point having a dream car when I'm constantly getting dings in my parking garage."

Laurie smiled to herself. She made a nice salary that was enough to cover a perfectly suitable two-bedroom apartment for her and Timmy, and Greg's life insurance had helped her run a New York City household as a single mother. But now that she and Alex were getting married, they'd been talking about finding a place large enough for them to live together. She had a feeling that whatever they chose might qualify as "sweet" by Ryan's definition.

The nanny did not hide her disappointment when she answered the door.

"I told you I would give Mrs. Bell your message," she said sternly.

Laurie would have bet money that Caroline had not, in fact, delivered the message yet. She guessed that the woman was in her early to mid sixties, but she wasn't a youthful kind of sixty. She wore her grayish brown hair in tight pin curls, and hid her large frame beneath an oversized blue housedress. "We're about to put out supper."

The wonderful scent of butter and garlic was wafting from inside. "It smells delicious," Laurie said. "I don't want to keep Mrs. Bell long. But, as I said, this is important. I've brought my colleague, Ryan Nichols. You might recognize him from our show."

Laurie had hoped that the sight of Ryan inside the Bell home might impress Kendra's obviously protective nanny. Most people became giddy in the presence of anyone who remotely qualified as "famous." Caroline Radcliffe was clearly not "most people." She gave Ryan a cold stare, obviously unimpressed.

"Caroline, is everything all right?" The voice came from the back of the house.

"Nothing to worry about—"

Caroline had started to close the door when Laurie spotted Kendra Bell walking toward them. "Kendra, it's Laurie Moran. Your in-laws came to see me today. There's clearly been a misunderstanding."

Caroline shook her head as Kendra joined her at the front door. "I already told you I'm not interested," Kendra said.

"I know," Laurie said. "And I accepted your decision. But apparently you've told Martin's parents that I was the one to decline his case for our show. I'm perfectly happy to tell them the truth—that you were adamantly opposed months ago—but I thought I owed it to you to give you a chance to explain."

Laurie could see the calculations playing out quickly in Kendra's head. She didn't want Laurie and Ryan in her living room. But she definitely didn't want Laurie to go back to Martin's parents with the truth.

She opened the door to let them in.

Kendra was still in her uniform from work—dark blue hospital scrubs over a black turtleneck. Her shoulder-length dark brown hair was pulled into a neat ponytail at the nape of her neck. Kendra had been thirty-four years old at the time her husband was murdered, which made her thirty-nine now. Somehow, she seemed older than that, as if she had lived two other lives before this one. Stress lived in the lines on her forehead, and a sadness lurked behind her dark eyes. Even so, she was far more attractive than the disheveled figure that had been portrayed by the media. Laurie wondered if she had looked like that in the years after Greg's death, before she had finally allowed herself to be happy again.

Once Laurie had introduced Ryan, Kendra led them to the living room and asked Caroline to finish the dinner preparations in the kitchen. Laurie knew the nanny would be listening in, no matter where she went in the house.

"Someone's letting you work as a doctor?" Ryan blurted out.

Laurie and Ryan had gone over the broad brushstrokes of Martin Bell's murder during the car ride to the Village, but she had not updated him on the current state of his widow's life.

"Most certainly not," she said defensively, "most likely because people react as you just did. But thank you for remembering that I actually did go to medical school. The news coverage after Martin died—well, I'm sure you're aware of the tone. They talked about me as if I were some kind of drug addict off the street."

Laurie gave Ryan an urgent look. He was supposed to play good cop tonight, and he had not gotten off to a good start.

"You met each other when you were in med school, didn't you?" Ryan asked, his tone softening.

"Indeed," Kendra said with a sad smile. "Martin used to love to tell everyone our 'meet-cute' story, as he called it."

Laurie knew that Kendra loved the story, too, because she'd told it to Laurie the first time they spoke on the phone. Laurie had been the one to suggest that Ryan ask Kendra. She had expected him to introduce the subject more gently.

"I was in my final year of med school—at Stony Brook University School of Medicine," Kendra said, "on Long Island. Martin was a guest lecturer in my Physical Medicine and Rehabilitation class. Halfway through his lecture . . . flatline! His PowerPoint slides go totally dead. The famous doctor who was always full of answers on the *Today* show and *Good Morning America* was suddenly without words. He and the professor were fumbling with the computer. As Martin told it, he was in a total panic, knowing that he barely had enough time for the rest of his lecture, and that it required complex data that he had summarized in two charts that he desperately needed. According to him—and I seriously doubt this part—I 'confidently and gracefully' walked down the middle aisle of the lecture hall, calmly took the slide controller from his hand, and swapped out the batteries with fresh ones. I knew they were stored in the lectern cabinet. Then back to my seat I went. It was nothing, really, but Martin decided right then and there that I was something special."

She suddenly looked down at the coffee table as if she were watching some other scene play out in front of her. "Look where it got me," she said sadly. "No, I'm not a doctor. I finished school, to be sure. And I started my residency—a good one, too. Pediatrics at NYU. But Martin was so eager to start a family, and I was almost thirty. I should have listened to people who told me it would be too much to handle. It felt like such a rush at the time, but now I realize how young I was. Once Bobby was born, I felt so . . . exhausted. All the time. And distracted. It must have been clear at work, because, the next thing I knew, I was being 'encouraged' "—she made air quotes with her fingers—"by the supervising physicians to take what was supposed to be a one-year leave of absence from my residency. And then, before I knew it, I was pregnant again. Once Mindy joined Bobby, Martin decided that the children would be better off if I remained a stay-at-home mother. As my mother-in-law liked to say, 'One very busy doctor is more than enough for one family.'"

Laurie knew from their previous conversations that Kendra blamed her decision to give up her medical career for her subsequent decline, but none of that would matter unless Kendra changed her mind about working with *Under Suspicion*.

Laurie stole a glance at her watch. They'd been there for nearly ten minutes already and hadn't even gotten to the matter at hand. She could not be late to Alex's induction.

"So you're still working with your friend's practice?" Laurie asked, rushing the story along.

"Yes," Kendra said. "I doubt I'll ever find anyone willing to take me on as a resident so I can become a practicing physician, but thank God for my one remaining med school friend, Steven Carter. The rest of them act as if I never existed, but he went out on a limb and hired me as a physician's assistant. It's good for me to have a job to go to every day. Good for the kids to see me working, too."

By the time Martin died, Kendra had been anything but a hard worker. According to Martin, his parents, and even her own friends, Kendra "was never the same" after she gave up any plans of working as a doctor again. What had seemed like a temporary rut as she adjusted to motherhood became a complete personality change, especially after her mother was killed in a car accident when she was driving back to Long Island late one night, after coming into the city to help an overwhelmed Kendra with the babies. Kendra had stopped showing up with her husband on their social and academic scenes. When people did see her, she seemed confused, irritable, and disheveled. There were loud whispers among their friends that Kendra had become a serious alcoholic. "Poor Martin" and "he has to stay for the children" were phrases that often accompanied the *tsks* that were commonly offered when the subject of Kendra was raised.

In fact, the night Martin was murdered, the nanny said she had to shake Kendra to wake her from her nap as she desperately called 911 for help.

"I know you're eager to get on with dinner," Laurie said, her own time constraints pulling at her patience. "I'll be blunt about why we're here. You told Martin's parents I was the one who declined your husband's case. That's patently false. It makes it look like you have something to hide, Kendra."

"I don't. You know I don't. I'm just trying to move on with my life. Raise my kids. Go to work. Digging it all up again for the cameras is more than my kids and I can handle. I explained all of this to you."

"Then why can't you tell that to your in-laws?"

"They'd never understand. They tried for years to have Martin, so he was always their miracle baby, and then he was gone. They have no empathy for me. They look at me and see a murderer. Do you have any idea how horrible that is? My own parents are dead. Martin and his family were the only family I had. And now they hate me. And they're obsessed with getting custody of my children. It's relentless."

Her shoulders were beginning to shake. She was seconds away from tears. "Please," she implored, "don't tell them that I'm the reason you're not doing the show."

Bad cop, Laurie reminded herself. *You're playing the bad cop. And you can't be late for the most important night of your fiancé's career.*

"I can't *not* tell them," Laurie said. "They're the ones who wrote me that letter about Martin's case in the first place. I respect your wishes, but I have to respect theirs, too."

"They'll use it against me that I misled them. They're champing at the bit to get custody of the kids," she said, lowering her voice.

"They have money. And influence. They'll find a judge who favors them. Please tell me what I can do."

"That's not my call," Laurie said. "But you went and dragged my name into the deception. I'd be lying to them if I didn't correct their misunderstanding. I'll call them in the morning to explain why we're not moving forward."

"Or," Ryan said, "you could just do the show."

Kendra looked at him, blinking.

"If you do the show," he explained, "they won't ever have to know that you misled them. We'll move forward with production, and that will be that."

Kendra looked past him, clearly weighing her options. Then she reluctantly said, "I'll do it. I told you I have nothing to hide. But I don't want my kids on camera."

"Of course," Ryan said, placing a comforting hand on her shoulder.

"Or where I work," she said. "Steven stuck his neck out hiring me. I don't want him getting harassing phone calls or worse."

They assured her that would not be a problem, but Kendra asked for both promises in writing. Laurie jotted them down on the bottom of their standard participation agreement and gave it to Kendra to sign before she could change her mind.

"Oh, by the way," Kendra said, handing back the piece of paper, "I just read about the new federal judge. The news article mentioned that he was recently engaged and gave your name. Congratulations."

"Thanks," Laurie said, caught off guard by the comment. "I'm actually off to the courthouse right now. He's getting sworn in tonight."

As Laurie hopped into an Uber, she felt a pang of guilt. Maybe Kendra was telling the truth about being worried for the sake of her children's privacy. But then she reminded herself that Kendra had already proven that she was willing to lie when it served her interests.

And Kendra wasn't the only person who had lost a family member. Cynthia and Robert Bell had lost their only son and had pleaded with Laurie to help them get justice for Martin.

There was only one way for Laurie to help. Find out once and for all who had killed Martin Bell and why.

7

Kendra had barely finished turning the lock on the front door when she heard Caroline's footsteps behind her.

Oh, how Kendra had resented Caroline's presence when Martin had hired her. First, it was as if the decision for Kendra to quit her job and become a full-time stay-at-home mother had been made without her participation. It wasn't even a *decision* in any meaningful way. It had simply . . . happened. One day, she was leaving her residency with contractions—probably a false alarm, she told herself at the time. Then she was receiving flowers at the maternity ward from her fellow residents. *See you in twelve weeks, Mommy!* the card had read. She returned as planned, but didn't even last a month. She told herself that the leave would only be for the rest of the year; she'd return in the fall with the next class of residents. And then she became pregnant with Mindy, and the idea of practicing medicine seemed impossible.

When Mindy turned eighteen months, she called the residency coordinator and asked about going back. At that point, she thought the grueling hours of a medical resident would be a piece of cake compared to the demands of two young children. But by then, it turned out her medical education was out of date. She'd have to take more classes to re-enter the residency program. And meanwhile, Martin and his parents kept reminding her that Martin the "miracle baby" had been raised by a stay-at-home mother. She hated the way Cynthia would pat Martin on the arm, gaze at him adoringly, and say, "One very busy doctor is more than enough for one family."

No wonder you expected me to idolize you, Kendra thought. God knew she had tried her hardest to please him.

At first, her life with Martin had felt like a fairy tale come true. She had been walking out of the classroom with Steven after Martin's guest lecture when Martin caught her attention to thank her for fixing his computer glitch. "I think the good doctor's smitten with you," Steven had said afterward. She told Steven he had a wild imagination, but she knew he was right. Martin's words to her had been perfectly appropriate—modest, thankful, professional—but he had spoken them with a sense of wonderment, as if he knew that they were having an encounter that would change both of their lives.

Martin would tell her later that he even checked with the university to make certain that there was no prohibition against his dating a bright, young, aspiring pediatrician he had met as a visiting speaker. By the time he contacted her to accompany him to a medical lecture in the city, she was expecting him to call. By the time they finished dinner that night, he told her that she absolutely had to accept a residency in New York City. "It will be much harder to get you to fall in love with me if you move halfway across the country," he said.

She had tried so hard to make him happy. He wanted to get married as soon as she graduated, and then start a family, and then have a second child, and so she went along with all of it, every step of the way. And then he wanted his bright, young, aspiring pediatrician to stay home.

She had expected her mother to take her side. Kendra's father had been a plumber. He made a decent living by Suffolk County standards, but her mother worked as a hairdresser to help pay the bills. Then he died of a heart attack just as Kendra was completing her junior year in college, leaving behind her, her mother, and a mountain of student loans. Her mother had worked at two different hair salons—one days, one nights—to make sure that Kendra finished school.

Instead of telling her that she had to live out her dream of being a doctor, her mother told her to do whatever she thought was right. "Don't you see how lucky you are to have that choice?" her mother had said. "I never did. I would have loved to have stayed home with you. You only get one life, sweet girl. Whichever path you pick will be the right one."

So she gave in. She told herself there was no real reason she *needed* to work. Bobby and Mindy would enjoy all the advantages she never had—private schools, a New York City upbringing, Martin's parents' substantial connections. All she had to do was stay home and raise them.

I tried, Kendra thought now. *I tried to be what Martin wanted me to be. But it turned out that the confidence and grace he thought he saw in me in that classroom didn't translate to this house—to being a wife and a mother.*

The kids had exhausted her in a way that medical school had not. In hindsight she realized she had had postpartum depression. Her mother would drive two and a half hours each way, trying to help on her occasional days off. And then came the car accident. That's what they called it anyway. An accident. But Kendra knew what had happened. Her fatigued mother—sleep deprived from trying to help a fatigued daughter—had fallen asleep at the wheel.

Kendra had slipped further into the darkness. Martin hadn't even given her an opportunity to meet possible hires before he brought Caroline into their home.

"This is happening," he had announced. "You're a train wreck. Train wrecks don't get a vote." How she had wanted to kill him in that moment. She had wanted to be free of him.

Now, five years later, the woman she had resented so deeply was practically a member of the family.

"That woman was preying on your worst fears," Caroline said. "I'm sorry, I couldn't help overhear."

Kendra knew how soundproof this old carriage house was. Of course Caroline had been eavesdropping.

"Maybe Bobby and Mindy can start bringing their grandparents some extra unhealthy treats," Kendra said. "Those two fossils can't stay alive forever."

She wouldn't make such a dark joke in front of anyone else, but Caroline had seen for herself how horrible the Bells were to her. She had also grown accustomed to Kendra's morose sense of humor.

"You don't need to worry about anything, Caroline. It's just a TV show. Let me change out of these scrubs, and I'll come down for supper."

Upstairs, alone in her room, she closed her bedroom door and then went into the bathroom and ran the water. She didn't want anyone to overhear, not even Caroline.

She pulled up a phone number from her cell phone, stored under "Mike." That wasn't his name, at least not to her knowledge. And she knew this wasn't his real number, just a temporary one he'd given her for temporary purposes. It seemed he gave her a new one every time she saw him. He was too good to have a traceable phone. She knew that by now.

She never should have mentioned the television show to him last November. But she was terrified that he would find out about the letter the Bells had written to the studio and punish her for not telling him. He always seemed to know more than he should. She had promised she would get rid of the producer, and she had, until tonight.

There was a pickup after two rings, but no greeting.

"Hello?" she said nervously.

"What is it?" he asked.

She told him that the producer had shown up at the house unannounced and pressured her to sign a release.

"Call her tomorrow and say you've changed your mind. You can't do the show."

She told him that the Bells were never going to let this drop. That if she didn't go along with the show, they'd make good on their ongoing threats to take her to court. "If we went to court, they might find out about you."

"Don't threaten me. It won't go well for you." His voice was ominous.

"That's not how I meant it," she said. He was the scariest person she had ever encountered, simultaneously in complete control but completely unpredictable. "I'm just saying that I can do the show and not ever mention you. I swear on my life."

"On your *children's* lives?"

She felt a dagger of ice at the base of her neck. "It's been five years. If I were going to tell anyone about you, wouldn't it have happened by now? Please, I'm not trying to cause trouble."

"Fine. Do the show. But remember what's at stake. It would be a shame if something happened to Bobby and Mindy. Now, tell me every single thing you know about that television producer."

She did as he instructed. Her hand was shaking as she hung up the phone.

Martin had been dead for five years.

She would never be free of him, not really. Since she realized he had been feeding her drugs, that question was always on her mind. He of all people should have recognized she had postpartum depression. Being on drugs was not the way to recover from it. Or was it that he and his parents wanted her to have children, and after they were born, they didn't need her anymore?

8

As Laurie's cab inched its way from Kendra's home to the courthouse, she checked her watch, reassuring herself that she had time to spare.

Since today was such a special day, she had chosen to wear an outfit that Alex had never seen. It was a deep blue pantsuit. It was a color that suited her well, one that Alex always remarked on.

Laurie checked her makeup, then touched up her lipstick. On impulse she pulled her hair out of the ponytail and brushed it loose over her shoulders. She knew that Alex liked it better that way.

She was wearing her mother's single-strand pearl necklace and the small diamond earrings that had been hers as well. *How happy she'd be for me*, Laurie thought, as the taxi stopped in front of the courthouse. Because of the traffic she had arrived only ten minutes before the ceremony. She was sure that Timmy and her father would be there already.

As Laurie expected, they were sitting on a bench outside the courtroom of Chief Judge Maureen Russell. Timmy jumped up when he saw her. "Grandpa was afraid you'd be late."

"Never today of all days," she said, smiling at her father.

Leo had always been concerned to a fault about being late for anything. There was a sheepish expression on his face. "I was just concerned about the traffic."

"Uh-huh," Laurie said. "Anyhow, where's Alex?"

"Inside. The courtroom is filling up. Ramon brought enough hors d'oeuvres for the party in the conference room to feed the pope's standing army."

Ramon was Alex's assistant, chef, and trusted confidant and insisted on calling himself the "butler." He was also a gifted party planner who was bursting with pride over Alex's nomination to the federal bench. Laurie had witnessed the whirlwind unfolding in the kitchen last night and could only imagine the extensive selections he would have prepared for today's reception.

"God help the person who tries to get between Ramon and the perfect party," Laurie said.

"I testified in front of Judge Russell once in a case that went federal, and she's formidable," Leo told her. "It will be interesting to see her in action today. She's coming to the reception."

The courtroom was already standing-room-only by the time Judge Russell came out of her chambers. Laurie knew that many of them were Alex's fellow lawyers. He would miss the day-to-day interactions with them.

Alex's younger brother, Andrew, had come up from Washington. He had been chosen to welcome everyone to the main event. Laurie knew how close he and Alex were. Their parents had been killed in an automobile accident when Andrew was nineteen and Alex twenty-one. Alex had become Andrew's guardian, and he had taken that responsibility seriously. Laurie knew that Andrew's remarks would be warm and personal. And they were.

When it was time for the swearing in, Laurie stepped forward to hold the Bible as Alex, his voice clear and solemn, took the oath of office and became a federal judge. When he finished, he leaned forward and kissed Laurie. After he thanked the judge, he said, "I am so grateful for this honor. But I must share with you the fact that no honor would have any meaning unless I was sharing it with my fiancée and soon-to-be wife, Laurie Moran."

Five minutes after they left the courtroom, the family members and close friends who had been invited to the reception had filed into the conference room. The cocktail party was in full swing.

Laurie was chatting with several of the lawyers who had shared office space with Alex when one of them, Grant Smith, brought up a sensitive subject.

"I have to admit I was shocked when a criminal defense attorney went sailing through the confirmation hearings. I guess none of the senators lost money in the Newman scandal," Grant said.

Laurie knew that Alex had been concerned that the public's lingering anger about the case could have derailed his judicial confirmation. Alex had some regret that he'd managed to get an acquittal for Carl Newman, who had stood trial for bilking investors out of millions of dollars. But the detectives had mishandled the investigation. He had been doing his job as an attorney when he got key pieces of evidence thrown out. Even he was surprised when the jury acquitted Newman. In any case she thought it was unnecessary for Smith to bring it up now.

He's jealous of Alex, Laurie thought. Afterward she would ask Alex if he thought the same thing.

9

Despite Judge Russell's firm demand that her clerks clear the room after an hour, Laurie noticed that when seven-thirty rolled around the judge appeared to be enjoying herself. She had spent most of the evening talking to Leo, and Laurie couldn't help but notice that Leo seemed to be enjoying the conversation, too. She also noticed that Leo turned back to look at the judge as they were all saying their good-byes when the party died down.

She's really very attractive, Laurie thought. She guessed the judge was about sixty. Her white hair and youthful face belied her stern expression when she smiled.

"A new friend?" Laurie asked when she and Leo found each other in the hallway outside the courtroom. "A little bird tells me she's formidable."

"Stop it."

"Now you know how I've felt for the last year." It seemed as if he had asked her about Alex nearly every day.

"But I turned out to be right, didn't I?"

"And who says I'm not right about this?"

"Stop it," he said again, but she made a mental note of his small grin. She spotted Alex walking toward them, Timmy at his side.

"Where to next?" Alex asked, rubbing his palms together. She could tell he was energized from the induction.

"This one still has homework to do." Laurie grabbed Timmy and gave him a little tickle on his shoulder.

"Now that Alex is a judge, he can write my teachers a letter telling them to go easy on me."

"Better to save that for when you're in really big trouble," Leo joked.

Timmy nodded his agreement. "Good thinking, Grandpa."

Andrew could not join them for dinner because he had a case going to trial the next morning. Leo offered to take Timmy back to the apartment to finish his homework so Laurie could go out to dinner with Alex. As she watched them get into a cab, Laurie realized how eager she was to find an apartment suitable for their entire family. Alex's Beekman Place apartment was large enough for her and Timmy to move in, but it would be a thirty-minute commute each way to Timmy's school, and her father would need to relocate, too, if he wanted to continue to live a few blocks away. Besides, she liked the idea of them starting their new life together in an entirely new place.

Once they were in the car, Alex asked where she wanted to go for dinner, noting that Ramon also had plenty of food waiting back at the apartment. Ramon quickly nixed the latter option. "I'm afraid that the Marshals Office didn't finish installing the security equipment today. It's a bit of a mess with all the wires and cameras."

As a federal judge, Alex was now required to have a top-grade security system that was connected directly to federal law enforcement. He had told them to save their money and wait since he'd be moving in a few months anyway, but that apparently wasn't how the system worked.

"How about Gotham then," he suggested.

"Whatever the judge desires," Laurie said as Ramon started the engine. "You have a lifetime appointment to your dream job. Does it feel different now that it's official?"

"Honestly?" He reached over for her hand and touched the ring on her finger. "I already have the lifetime appointment that really matters."

10

On the opposite side of Pearl Street, a man watched the courthouse from behind the wheel of a white SUV. Forty-five years old, his hooded eyes incongruous in his chubby face, he spotted the group he was waiting for as soon as they walked outside.

The five of them all looked so comfortable together, he thought angrily. The older man and the little boy hailed a taxi. The smaller man opened the back door of the black Mercedes for the woman. He knew that she was the television producer. Her name was Laurie Moran. She had lost her first husband under such tragic circumstances.

She looked happy now, though, as the new judge climbed into the backseat and sat next to her. Against the back light of the street lamp, he could see them looking at the engagement ring on her finger.

She is actually quite a lovely girl, the man thought as he pulled into traffic to follow them. *I'm sure she's going to be missed.*

11

As Laurie entered the lobby of her 94th Street apartment building, she gave a quick wave to Ron, the nighttime doorman.

"How're you doing, Primo?" she asked, using his self-appointed nickname. He had previously explained that the word literally meant "cousin" in Spanish, but was also used to describe a close friend.

"Primo's doing pretty good. I hope you weren't stuck at work all this time. This is late for you."

Laurie had moved to this building shortly after Greg was killed. It made sense to be near her father since he was helping so much with Timmy, but she had also been eager to leave downtown, where it seemed every day she had to pass the park where her husband had been shot.

"Not a work night," Laurie said cheerfully. "I was out celebrating with my fiancé. He got some happy news."

"*Fiancé*," Ron said with a pleased smile. "I like the sound of that for you. I noticed you've had a little spring in your step lately. I hope he doesn't take you and Timmy from us, though. We'd miss you around here."

"No changes for now," she promised, even as she realized how much she was going to miss the people who had helped make this place a home after she unexpectedly found herself a single mother.

Once she was inside her apartment, she kicked off her heels and slipped off her blazer, tossing it onto an unoccupied hook on the hallway coat rack. She could tell from the silence that Timmy must have gone to bed for the night.

She found her father in his favorite spot—leaning back in the leather recliner, the *Time* magazine resting on his lap, the television on ESPN, the volume muted. She had a feeling Timmy wasn't the only one who had drifted off to sleep.

He must have sensed her presence, because he suddenly pulled the recliner upright. "How was dinner?" he asked.

"Don't hate me, but I ordered your favorites—the seafood salad and steak."

"Rare?"

"Just as you would."

He grinned and flashed her a thumbs-up. "You've got a good life, kid. Speaking of which, your Realtor came by with that." He gestured to an inch-thick binder on the coffee table. Laurie could tell it was another batch of real estate listings. "She said she happened to be in the neighborhood. I guess she just happens to walk around with your personalized listings." The tone of his voice was sarcastic.

Charlotte had been the one to refer Laurie to Rhoda Carmichael. "She's like the Energizer Bunny of real estate," Charlotte had said. "She won't stop until she finds a place that's perfect for you, Alex, and Timmy."

What Charlotte hadn't told her was that Rhoda expected the same level of commitment from her clients. Last week, she had called Laurie at five in the morning to tell her about a place in the hours before it officially hit the market.

Laurie would flip through the documents at her office tomorrow, she thought, even though she knew Rhoda would be calling her first thing for her feedback. Laurie already had Brett Young's impossible expectations to meet at work. She didn't need a second boss in her personal life.

Her father started to stand, ready to make the three-block walk to his own apartment.

"Have you got a second?" she asked.

"Of course." He eased back into the recliner.

She told him about the visit she'd had from Robert and Cynthia Bell, followed by her drop-in at Kendra's townhouse. "I spent most of the day reading up on the case again. The press was scathing. I couldn't find a single sympathetic article about Martin's wife. But I didn't see any official indication from the police department that she was actually a suspect."

"But let me guess: The NYPD didn't say anything to clear her name, either."

She shook her head.

"Don't quote me on this, but let me teach you how to read between the lines. The Martin Bell case was one where the newspapers were doing enough on their own to gin up public interest in the investigation."

"There was no need for the police to hold press conferences and the like," Laurie said, following his logic.

"Yes, but it's more than the *amount* of coverage. It's the *angle*. When I was working homicides, I had a case—a bad one. Kids were involved." He frowned at the memory. Leo had loved his work as a police officer, but Laurie remembered the way certain types of crimes would zap her normally upbeat father and rob him of his smile. "One of the reporters got it in his head that the nanny did it. Something about being jealous that she couldn't have children of her own. But here's the thing: we knew she had an ironclad alibi, and we could see with our own eyes how much she mourned for those kids. So we put out a statement that made it clear that we considered the nanny to be a secondary victim of the crime. It shut down the negative press coverage about her in an instant." He snapped his fingers for emphasis.

"But the NYPD didn't do the same for Kendra Bell," Laurie noted.

"Exactly."

"So she's a suspect."

He shrugged. "I heard some things at the time."

"Such as?"

"Remember how the press was calling her a druggie or whatever?" Leo asked.

As much as the public seemed convinced that Kendra had killed her husband, the sensational coverage didn't appear to have been backed by facts. All the articles boiled down to one basic observation: Martin Bell had been a superstar with a big public career, married to a recluse who had failed to live up to the potential her husband had once seen in her. There were anecdotes about her appearing intoxicated the few times she'd been spotted with him socially in the months before his murder. And a couple of anonymous sources alleged that she'd been withdrawing more cash than a stay-at-home mom was likely to spend. But Laurie hadn't seen anything close to a smoking gun.

"Stoner Mom," Laurie said, recalling one of the headlines. "One of the neighbors—anonymous, of course—said Kendra seemed *out of it* sometimes. But other people made it sound more like she might just have a tendency to drink a little too much. Maybe if she was a drinker, she was hungover sometimes."

"I think it was more than that," Leo said as he gazed toward the ceiling. "It was never disclosed to the press, but word got out around the department. Her behavior was apparently very strange the night of the murder. She acted like she was in a daze. The responding officers weren't even sure she was processing what was going on. In short, they asked if they could do a blood draw to make sure she wasn't under the influence of anything. Her husband had just been shot in cold blood and she was throwing a fit about taking a drug test without a search warrant."

"Wanting privacy doesn't make someone a murderer," Laurie reminded him.

"Yes, but then they started looking into the finances."

"The cash withdrawals," Laurie said. Kendra had been using her ATM card to make frequent cash-machine withdrawals from the couple's joint savings account. "I wonder if the police leaked that to the press."

"It was more than just the cash," her father continued, getting a second wind. "After Martin was killed, the police got a tip that Kendra was a regular at a dive bar in the East Village."

"I suppose it makes sense if she had a drinking problem. But she didn't strike me as the dive bar type. . . ."

"Exactly. It raises the question why she'd be going there. Turns out that, in the days before Martin's death, Kendra had met a tough-looking guy three or four times at the same spot. Even more suspiciously, neither of them went back to that fine establishment after the husband was shot."

"So who was the tough guy?"

He shook his head. "They couldn't trace him. Like Kendra, he always paid cash. And, from what I heard, Kendra wasn't especially helpful when the police asked her about him."

Laurie frowned, processing the new information. Kendra was in bed at the time of the shooting, so clearly she hadn't committed the murder personally. Her detractors speculated that she had squirreled away cash from her frequent ATM withdrawals to pay a hit man. If Laurie could prove that Kendra had been meeting with a strange man prior to the killing, she'd have more than mere speculation for her television program. "Do you remember the name of the bar?"

"Not sure I ever knew it. But I'm sure I can find out."

"Of course you can," she said. Leo Farley had retired from the NYPD after Greg was killed, so he could help Laurie raise Timmy, but years later, even rookie police officers stood up straighter when he entered a room. Last year, he had accepted an invitation to join the department's anti-terrorism task force on a part-time basis. As long as Leo was around, his reach within the department would remain wide.

She walked her father to the door and gave him a good-bye hug.

"You got what I meant about reading between the lines?" he asked.

"I did. Thanks for the tutorial, Professor. Maybe the chief judge of the Southern District of New York would find it an interesting subject over dinner."

"Oh, don't get any ideas. But I'm serious: Just because Kendra was never named a suspect doesn't mean the whole NYPD doesn't think she's guilty." His tone suddenly became troubled. "Her husband was killed while she had young children. It's only natural that you'll connect with her on some level. But she's probably a killer. Be careful, Laurie."

12

Exhausted from the day, Laurie cracked the door to Timmy's bedroom after her father was gone. She could barely make out his silhouette on the bed in the pitch dark. Her little boy was well beyond any need for a night-light. He wasn't even a little boy, she supposed, but she would choose to think of him that way for now.

Once she had crawled into her own bed, she pulled out her phone, which had been turned off during dinner, to send Charlotte a quick text message. *Still aching from spin this morning. Why didn't you warn me?* She pulled up the emoji menu and added tiny pictures of a bicycle and a happy face with devil horns.

Charlotte quickly replied with a flexed muscle, followed by a kiss sign, followed by *Zzzz* to signify sleep.

Laurie was still smiling about the note when a new voicemail alert appeared on her screen. The phone number looked vaguely familiar, but she couldn't quite place it. She hit the play button.

"Ms. Moran, it's Kendra Bell. You caught me off guard today at the house. I didn't even have a chance to tell you my side of the story. Can I meet you tomorrow afternoon? I looked at the patient schedule at work, and I can leave a little early. Would three o'clock work? And, please, you must keep your promise to keep my kids out of it." Her voice was shaky.

Laurie replayed the message, making sure it wasn't her imagination.

No, she was certain. Kendra's concerns had been apparent earlier that night, but now she sounded different. She wasn't simply anxious or nervous. She sounded rattled. Shaken. Absolutely terrified. And yet she was agreeing to do the show.

Why are you so scared? Laurie wondered. *What are you afraid I'll find?*

13

When Laurie arrived to work the following morning, she found Grace in Jerry's office. Both of them were huddled over the phone in Grace's hand.

"He hates dogs?" Jerry was saying.

"What kind of person *hates* dogs? What's wrong with him? That's an automatic *swipe left*." Laurie heard a little beep as Grace swept a perfectly manicured index finger across her screen.

"Browsing for boys again?" Laurie asked, interrupting their latest online matchmaking session. She had been spared the now common practice of online dating, but knew that "swiping left" on someone's profile was the virtual equivalent of slamming a door on him. Laurie marveled at Grace's carefree attitude about dating. She was perfectly content as a single woman, but obviously enjoyed the butterflies that came with meeting new people.

Grace sheepishly tucked her phone into the pocket of her fitted black blazer. "Sorry about that. We were both in early, but I guess it's officially work time."

Laurie waved a hand. "Don't worry." As much as she thought of Jerry and Grace as her "work family," she realized that ultimately, they also saw her as their boss.

"We can't all be as lucky as you and Alex," Grace said. "You found the right guy at work. Meanwhile, I'm out kissing a bunch of frogs from the Internet."

"What about Ryan?" Jerry pointed out. "When he first started working here, all you talked about was how *fine* he was."

"Yeah, and then I got to know him," Grace said, rolling her eyes. "No, thanks. Speaking of the ever-confident Mr. Nichols, he came by your office just a few minutes ago, Laurie. He wanted to know when Kendra Bell would be coming in for an initial interview. Excuse me for speaking out of turn, but sometimes I think that man forgets who literally runs the show around here."

"To be fair," Laurie said, "I'm the one who asked him to go to Kendra's with me yesterday."

"And how did that go?" Jerry asked.

"It worked," she said, reaching into her briefcase to produce Kendra's signed participation agreement. "She agreed to do the show. It's weird, though. She called me after we left her house last night, and she sounded absolutely petrified."

Jerry crossed his arms, mulling over the observation. "Well, you did put her between a rock and a hard place. Either she had to do the show, or her in-laws would have realized that she was the one holding it up."

Laurie nodded. "But that much was already true when we were at her place. When she called, it was different—as if something had happened in between that really rattled her."

"Maybe she looked into our track record," Grace said. So far, *Under Suspicion* had solved every case they had selected for production.

"Maybe," Laurie said, thinking again about the unknown man that Kendra was supposedly meeting at a dive bar shortly before the murder. If Kendra had hired a hit man to kill Martin, she had more than Laurie's investigation to be afraid of. The man who pulled the trigger would not want her talking to a television producer. She remembered her father's warning from last night and found herself wondering where this case might take her.

Laurie found Ryan in his office, practicing putts on a strip of green Astroturf. He was just about to hit a ball when she said, "Grace said you were looking for me."

The ball went careening to the right and rolled onto the office carpet.

"Sorry," she said.

"Good thing it didn't count." He held out the putter to her, offering her a try, which she declined.

"Trust me. I'd somehow find a way to send it through the windows." She told him about the frightened phone call from Kendra Bell the previous night. "She can leave early today, so we'll meet at three. My guess is she won't want us at her house because of the children, so I'll see if she's willing to come up here."

"I can't do three. I've got an appointment with my trainer."

"I'll let you know how it goes. I'll be interested to hear any alternative theories she has about the murder. The only public speculation has been about her."

"You're not going to reschedule it?"

"No. She works full-time and has two kids, and this was the time she had available. But have a good workout."

Laurie had carefully worked her way through half of the real estate listings that Rhoda Carmichael had dropped off at her apartment the previous night when the Realtor called her cell phone. "So don't leave me hanging," Rhoda said. "Give me your list of must-see's so I can line up some viewings."

Laurie flipped through the binder and realized she had only

dog-eared two pages so far. The properties were all stunning by any reasonable definition, far beyond anything Laurie could ever afford on her own. But they were all so . . . cold. Almost *too* pristine. She couldn't picture herself and Timmy in any of them.

"The one at Eighty-sixth and Lex would be a great location for us," she said halfheartedly, wondering why the listing included only two photographs. "And the apartment on Ninetieth has a good setup for Ramon to have a separate living area from us, but it's a little too far east."

"Well, don't forget the new Second Avenue subway," Rhoda chirped. "What used to be the boondocks is now prime neighborhood real estate."

"It's more about being close to my father and the school. We have our routines."

"I swear, Laurie." Supposedly Rhoda was born and bred in Queens, but somehow she had a slightly Southern accent. "Sometimes I get the impression you don't want to move at all."

And you're right, Laurie thought to herself. *I want to be married to Alex, but I don't want to upend everything else about my life.* "Maybe we can bribe the Hollanders next door to move and just combine two apartments," she said whimsically.

"Good luck getting your co-op to agree to that. And then where are you going to live during a year of construction?" Laurie's trial balloon was quickly deflated. "The Eighty-sixth and Lex property won't last long. Let me get you in there today. Does noon work?"

Laurie sighed. She was available, and Alex should be, too. "Sure, set it up." At least she'd have an excuse to see Alex in the middle of the day.

14

The smell of Rhoda Carmichael's perfume filled the elevator, a combination of lilies and baby powder. Rhoda held her ubiquitous cell phone in her right hand and a handbag the size of a small child in her left.

Alex flashed Laurie a smile with his eyes as they watched the floors tick upward. She knew he was sharing her thoughts: *Rhoda is going to ask us to sign a contract on sight*.

Rhoda hadn't slipped the keys into the lock before the warning signs emerged. She talked up the "partial view," which was Realtor-speak for a sliver of sky beyond a brick wall. "Old, established building" meant outdated, snooty, or both. And the kiss of death was "such charming potential," which was like describing a person as having a "good personality."

As Laurie walked through the apartment with Alex, she tried once again to visualize their new life together. Timmy had become an enthusiastic trumpeter, so the walls needed to be solid enough to protect the neighbors. Both she and Alex would occasionally work from home, so at least one home office was a must. And, of course, Ramon needed his living space and a kitchen worthy of his skills.

Within moments, they were talking about the need to move walls and replace bathrooms and kitchens. The thought of it was exhausting. This apartment wasn't going to work.

"Is your father's situation a deal breaker?" Rhoda asked.

Laurie blinked, not understanding the question.

"The location," Rhoda explained. "You're very selective about it now. Between your son's school and your father's apartment, I'm working with a six-block radius. If I could broaden the geography, I'm sure I could find something perfect for you."

"We have some wiggle room, but my son has school. My dad has his life. That's not changing," Laurie said.

"I know. But I was thinking about it. You have Ramon, who seems capable of anything, including driving your son. So if your father lived near you—or even *with* you—you could buy just about anywhere in Manhattan, and Timmy would still have a way to and from school."

Laurie pictured her son riding in the back of a Mercedes instead of tagging along at her father's side, backpack in tow. It wasn't how she imagined his future.

"I can't ask my father to move," she said. "Besides, he and Ramon would end up arm wrestling for the role of boss of the household. Too many strong personalities for one apartment."

Alex laughed, picturing the scene.

Rhoda held up both palms, giving up the fight. "Very well then. We'll find you the perfect spot. Another thing to be mindful of are the demands of the various co-op boards. Some of them might have concerns about you."

"We're not exactly a couple of hardened criminals." Laurie knew she sounded defensive, but how couldn't she?

"I know, I know," Rhoda said quickly. "I shouldn't have worded it that way. But I wouldn't be surprised if some of the buildings had concerns about the nature of your work, Laurie. After all, it has put you in danger previously, so just be prepared for them to ask you about it."

"They'll have nothing to worry about," Alex assured her. "As I mentioned, the U.S. Marshals Service is going to insist on adding a top-notch security system to any place we decide to move."

Rhoda let out a dramatic sigh. "Well, that's going to present a different issue for some buildings. I'm sure they'll be worried about the inconvenience to other residents of that kind of work, no different than any other renovation."

"So either I'm a walking target for danger," Laurie said, "or Alex comes with too much security. Any other causes for rejection we should be aware of?"

Rhoda winced, and Laurie knew that more criticism was coming. "I wouldn't be surprised if some of the buildings inquired about Alex's previous work as a defense attorney. Some of his more notorious clients?"

Here we go again, Laurie thought. Alex had been worried about some of his previous cases coming back to haunt him during the Senate confirmation process. "Alex just passed a rigorous FBI background check and got bipartisan support from the Senate. I would think that would be good enough for a co-op board."

"I'm sure I'm being overly cautious," Rhoda agreed. "I just didn't want you to be caught off guard. Not to worry. We're going to find you the perfect spot. I just know it."

After they thanked Rhoda for her time, they climbed into the backseat of Alex's car.

"Did you buy a new apartment?" Ramon asked from the driver's seat.

"Not yet," Alex said.

Laurie closed her hand over Alex's. "I'm sorry I came with so many requirements. Your life would be so uncomplicated without me."

He wrapped an arm around her shoulders. "Are you kidding? I'm the one with a security detail and 'notorious' clients. Rhoda obviously was referring to my defending Carl Newman. She's not entirely wrong. A lot of New Yorkers lost money because of that man."

"It's not as though you were the one helping him doctor the books," Laurie said.

Alex shrugged. He had learned long ago that, to some people, criminal defense attorneys were just as bad as their clients. "It's probably for the best if we don't end up neighbors with one of his victims," he said.

Laurie's phone rang inside her purse. She checked the screen. It was Leo. "Hey, Dad."

"I've got bad news, kiddo. Seems your old man's star is starting to fade at the NYPD."

"I don't believe that for one second."

"Maybe not, but I struck out on getting you inside the Bell investigation. The head of the Homicide Squad told me it's still an active case. My impression is it's cold as ice, but they don't dare close it down because of pressure from the family."

Having met Robert and Cynthia Bell, Laurie could imagine the couple exerting influence over the investigation. "Did you tell them that the family's on board with our production?"

"Yes. I even offered to have the parents make phone calls to the top brass if necessary. But it's obvious to me that they're afraid to do anything that might be second-guessed later—like giving you information that's not yet public."

"He didn't give you any leads at all?"

"Not much. He did confirm the rumors I had heard. Kendra was groggy and out of it the night of the murder, and then became irate when they asked for a drug test. She absolutely refused, and they weren't able to get a search warrant to force the issue. He didn't want to give me anything more, but he eventually confirmed that Kendra was frequenting a dive bar."

"And meeting a man there? What was the bar?"

"He wouldn't give up anything else. As I said, they're not going to hand over their investigation to you. I think he did give me one clue, though. When I was pressing him about the mystery man, he said, 'I'm not saying such a man ever existed, but if he had—and if we had found him—it might have stung Kendra.'"

"*Stung* her?"

"Yeah. Weird word choice. I figured it was his version of a clue. Maybe they were thinking of doing a sting operation to prove she hired a hit man. Mull it over and I'll do the same."

"Will do. Hey, Dad," she said, her tone lightening. "Rhoda suggested you might want to move in with us after Alex and I get married."

Alex was smiling beside her, knowing that she had thrown the comment out as bait.

"And have Ramon monitor my every intake of saturated fat? He'd replace my beer with club soda while I was sleeping. I'll stay at home until they carry me out, thank you very much."

"That's what I thought. I love you, Dad."

"Love you, too. Now be careful while you try to solve a murder, okay?"

"Will do."

15

Laurie sat in her favorite overstuffed office chair and looked out at the city. She was still awestruck by her airy office, with floor-to-ceiling windows that sat above the Rockefeller Center skating rink. It was the end of March, which meant that customers were scattered across the rink, looking to take advantage of the last two weeks of ice. From the sixteenth floor, the ice skaters looked miniature as they circled the rink, the city beneath her orderly from this height.

Laurie felt at home in her office, and had picked everything out herself, from the chair she sat in to the long, white leather sofa to the glass coffee table and suspended lighting. Even if she and Alex moved to a place that felt completely new, she'd still have her office—a familiar space of her very own.

She had finished drafting a bullet list of topics to cover during her meeting with Kendra Bell. As she had expected, Kendra did not want to meet at her house. She also did not want to make the trip up to Midtown given her schedule, making Laurie wonder if she was trying to find a way to stall.

When she told Kendra to name any location, she chose Otto, an Italian restaurant Laurie already knew in Greenwich Village. That made it easy.

The notation at the bottom of her list of topics was *bar/East Village/"stung"?* Her father's NYPD contact had confirmed that

Kendra had been spending time at a bar, but he wouldn't give Leo the actual name of the establishment.

She underlined the word "stung," which the detective had specifically used. Leo had suggested it might have been a reference to conducting some kind of a sting operation, but she wanted to believe it was a clue that would lead her to the bar itself.

If she could only figure out the name of the bar, she could ask the people who worked there if they remembered Kendra and the "mystery man" Leo had heard rumors about. It was a long shot given the five years that had passed since the murder, but maybe she could catch a lucky break. Without the name of the bar, she had no chance at all.

She rose from the chair and made her way to her desk. For years, the only picture on her desk had been of Greg, Timmy, and her on the beach in East Hampton. Now, next to it, she had a photo of Alex, Timmy, Leo, and her outside Lincoln Center after a jazz night. *Let's see*, she thought. She woke up her computer and typed, "New York City Bar Stung" in the browser's search window.

The results turned up an article about undercover drug stings at city bars, a new upscale restaurant called Stung on the Upper East Side, and a rock band called Stung.

Nothing helpful to her.

She was starting to try again with different search terms when her phone rang. She heard Grace answer it outside her office door, and then say, "I think she's in a meeting, but let me check." Two seconds later, Grace appeared. "It's Dana."

No last name was necessary in context. Dana Licameli was the secretary for Laurie's boss, Brett Young, which made her the most patient person at Fisher Blake Studios. "She says Brett's on a tear. He says he wants to see you ASAP," Grace warned.

Laurie looked at her watch. She needed to meet Kendra in forty-five minutes. The cab ride would take half an hour in traffic.

"I've got a downtown meeting at three," she explained.

"You know me. I can weave a cover story from whole cloth, but I also know how to read Dana. This didn't sound like the usual Brett temper tantrum."

Laurie looked at her computer, wanting to find the name of the dive bar, but also trusting Grace's judgment.

She was already past Grace's desk when she heard her on the phone again. "Laurie's on her way, Dana. Try to keep him from having a stroke before she gets there."

16

Laurie could tell from one glance at Dana Licameli that Grace's instincts had been correct. Dana always gave her a tip-off about Brett's mood before she entered his office. This time, she simply shook her head apologetically as she waved Laurie into Brett's inner lair.

Brett hadn't become the head of Fisher Blake Studios by compromising. He was tough and stern, and wasted no time with chitchat. His mind worked on fast-forward, and he expected the world to meet him at his pace. More than once, he had snapped at Laurie for not speaking quickly enough, even though Laurie had been told more than once that her rapid-fire chatter was reminiscent of old movie comedies. But Brett's enduring career had granted him the right to run the studio how he pleased, and Laurie suspected that his classic television looks—a full head of iron-gray hair and a strong jaw—didn't hurt, either.

Today, he didn't even bother with a greeting. "Kendra Bell," he said, with no further explanation.

She should have known that Ryan would run to Brett after she scheduled the interview without him. She didn't know how much longer she could put up with him undermining her to the boss.

"I'm actually on my way to meet with her now," Laurie said, feigning a glance at her watch. "Ryan had a scheduling conflict—a personal training appointment, in fact—and it was the only time Kendra was free." Laurie hated having to defend every small decision about her own show, simply because Ryan was always pushing for more authority.

Brett's face contorted in irritated confusion. He cut off her explanation by holding his hands up in the shape of a capital T, putting her on an effective time-out.

"Why are you meeting with her if you turned down the Martin Bell case?"

Laurie realized immediately that her assumption had been wrong. Ryan wasn't the source behind Brett's inquiry about Kendra Bell; Robert and Cynthia, her in-laws, were.

She shook her head. "I never rejected the case, Brett. It's a long story, but the short version is that Kendra has agreed to participate. When I meet with her, I'll find out her side of the story and make sure we have the other parties we need to start working on the case."

"You've got the victim's wife and parents. What else do you need? The guy was practically a celebrity, even before his murder was on the front page." As usual, Brett was quick to remind her that ratings—not journalistic quality—were the currency of their trade.

"I take it you've spoken to Martin Bell's parents," she said.

He folded his arms across his chest and leaned back in his chair. At least he no longer looked ready to pounce. "Not directly. But Robert's accountant is tennis partners with a fraternity brother of mine from Northwestern." The chain of connections was dizzying, but Laurie got the gist. "I said I'd look into the problem."

"Message received," she said, giving him a quick salute. "I would have hoped you'd trust me by now not to say no to a case without a good reason."

"Trust, but verify, as they say." She held his gaze until he added, "But, point taken."

She had turned to leave when he added one more line, "Next time, try to have Ryan informed from the get-go. The kid's got killer instincts."

Laurie carried her frustration with Brett back to her office, determined not to let him get under her skin.

As she passed Grace, Laurie had an idea. "Hey, what's the name of that website you were looking at last week when you and Jerry were searching for a new place for happy hour?"

Grace's eyes brightened, eager to be of assistance. "Tipsy-dot-com," she announced. "We found a great spot for mojitos. Are we planning a get-together?"

"Not quite," Laurie said, "but thanks." Laurie remembered the way Jerry and Grace had used the website to search for bars with certain characteristics near the studio offices.

At her desk, she pulled up the site and searched for bars within a mile of Kendra Bell's apartment. There were pages and pages of results—a sign that downtown was still the favored hot spot.

Laurie clicked on the "filter" menu and selected the choice of "dive bar." Down to only thirty-six results. On the second page of hits, she knew she'd found what she was looking for. She now knew the significance of the word "stung."

She pulled up her father's number on her cell as soon as she was in a taxi. "Dad, can you call your contact at NYPD and ask him if Kendra's hangout was called 'the Beehive'?" It was a hole-in-the-wall about twelve blocks from Kendra's apartment.

Leo called her back a few minutes later. "Remember my lecture last night?"

Of course she did. "About the NYPD remaining silent if they see no need to correct the record?"

"I asked him if the bar was the Beehive. All he said was 'no comment.' Then he told me my daughter probably took after her father. Good job, Laurie."

She pulled out her notes for her meeting with Kendra and made a change to the final item for discussion: *Myotory Man at the Beehive*.

17

The smells of tomato sauce and fresh cheese immediately made Laurie hungry when she walked through the revolving door at Otto. After running out to view that apartment on her midday break, she had never found time to eat lunch.

She was surprised to see Kendra already sitting at the restaurant's bar, next to a man her own age. Kendra was still in her medical scrubs. Her companion wore a white shirt that appeared one size too small, a striped tie, and khakis. It was only three o'clock and the only other customers seated at the bar were a couple on the opposite end. Laurie wondered if perhaps Kendra's habits hadn't changed so much in the past five years after all.

Kendra made eye contact and appeared to sit up a bit straighter on her bar stool as Laurie approached. Once Laurie took the unoccupied seat next to Kendra, her fellow barfly reached across to offer a quick handshake. He had a lean, soft face dominated by piercing hazel eyes, thinning brown hair, and wide dark-rimmed glasses. "Sorry to crash your meeting, but I insisted after Kendra told me where she was going. I'm Steven Carter. I work with Kendra."

"He means he's my boss," Kendra clarified. "And a very protective one at that."

Laurie remembered the name from her last discussion with Kendra. Carter was the medical school friend who had hired Kendra as a physician's assistant. Laurie wondered why Kendra would have mentioned this meeting to him. She had been adamant the previous night about not wanting her current employer identified in the production. Laurie offered only her name by way of introduction, with no mention of her show.

The bartender interrupted to ask if she would like some Prosecco. He was bald with a neatly trimmed salt-and-pepper beard.

"Is that what you two are having?" Laurie asked.

Kendra shook her head. "I'm not much of a drinker, and it's too early anyway. Sorry, that sounded so judgmental. We just ordered coffee and some gelato. They have the *very* best, on both counts. But Dennis here would be happy to get you whatever you'd like."

"You bet," the bartender named Dennis said heartily. His eyes squinted when he smiled. "And Kendra's not kidding about Steven being protective. I'm under strict orders to shuffle away anyone who tries to bother her. Kendra's good people. We like her."

Laurie had a feeling she knew now why Kendra had chosen this place and had brought along her boss. She wanted Laurie to know that there were people who saw her in a different light than her former in-laws.

Laurie ordered a cappuccino and, at Steven's urging, a mix of blood-orange and mocha gelatos.

"You can probably tell I'm a frequent customer," Steven said emphatically.

"So, Kendra, maybe you and I can discuss that private matter once we're done eating," Laurie suggested.

"Kendra already told me who you are," Steven said. "We're very close. If things had worked out differently, we might even have gotten married. At least I'd like to think so."

Kendra gave Laurie an awkward look. "Steven and I were on and off in medical school." She hadn't mentioned that fact when his name came up the previous night. "And then he remained such a good friend to me after everything that happened. So of course I told him that I had agreed to do the show."

"And I need you to know that Kendra's not crazy. It was Martin who was trying to make her seem that way. I saw it with my own eyes."

"You knew Martin well?" Laurie asked.

Steven scoffed. "As if that arrogant, self-involved man would ever deign to fraternize with a riffraff dermatologist who didn't come with a purebred pedigree."

"Martin wasn't always a kind man," Kendra said, "but he did marry me. I'm not exactly a blue blood."

"No, but you're Kendra, which is better by any measure."

Even after the gelato arrived—as delicious as promised—Laurie noticed that Steven could not take his worshiping eyes away from Kendra.

"I take it you weren't a real fan of the departed Miracle Doctor," Laurie said.

"Miracle Doctor, my . . . backside," he said scornfully. "Kendra of all people is always trying to remind me of the good things about Martin Bell, but it burns me up how he walked on water from the afterlife while Kendra got dragged through the mud. Honestly, if he were still alive, he would have been exposed by now."

"Exposed for what?"

"For being a cheat. And a fraud. And an all-around jerk of a human being."

Kendra sighed. "Oh, Steven, please don't make me regret bringing you here."

To Laurie's eye, Kendra seemed authentically distressed, but she knew by now that people were capable of feigning all kinds of emotion. She wondered if this performance by Steven was precisely what Kendra had planned on. Kendra was letting Steven be the one to speak ill of the dead so she didn't have to.

"Kendra used to call me on the phone, absolutely distraught.

People thought she was under the influence? No, she was just completely depressed and stressed out in that marriage. Martin swept her off of her feet like a fairy tale, but once she was locked away in his castle as a wife and mother, he treated her terribly. He was unfaithful. He was belittling. And he wasn't even a good doctor. He was being sued left and right."

Kendra flinched, and a look of surprise washed over her face. "Steven, how did you even know that?"

"You told me," he said.

"I don't even remember that," Kendra said mournfully.

"Because you weren't yourself back then. Anyway," he said, finishing the last bite of his dessert, "I wanted you to know that this isn't a case of Kendra making up accusations about Martin after his death. Everything she's about to tell you? She told me all of it as it was happening. I saw her deteriorate within that marriage. I'll leave you two alone now. You have a lot to talk about."

Laurie couldn't help but notice that when Steven hugged Kendra good-bye, he was in no rush to let go.

18

Kendra began apologizing for her boss the second he left the restaurant. "As you can tell, he's my loyal advocate. Thank God for him. He was the only friend I managed to keep after Martin was gone."

"Pardon the observation, but it seems like maybe he's interested in being more than just a friend and advocate?"

Kendra waved off the comment. "Steven? Oh, nothing of the sort. Even when we were *on* during our med school on-and-offs, we were mostly study buddies."

"He literally said you might've gotten married if not for Martin."

"That's his attempt at humor. Trust me, it's purely platonic. Look, I've been a widow for five years and see him almost every day. If he was nursing an old crush, I think he would've acted on it by now."

Laurie decided to let the subject drop for now, but made a note to find out more about Dr. Carter. "He certainly had a lot to say about Martin. Infidelity? Lawsuits? You didn't recall telling him that?"

"The affair, yes. I told him all about it. No one else believed me, because Martin had them all convinced that he was such a doting husband to his poor incapacitated wife."

"But you said you didn't remember mentioning the lawsuits."

Kendra shrugged and said it was a long time ago, but Laurie could tell that something about the situation was still troubling her.

It was time for them to get down to the most important question at hand. "Kendra, if you didn't kill Martin, who did?" Before Kendra even began to respond, Laurie scribbled the name *Steven Carter* in her notes.

"If I had to guess, the affair started right after Mindy was born. Between his medical practice, networking, and keeping the Bell name on the lips of the social scene, he had always kept a busy schedule. But where most men would have made an effort to be home with their beautiful new baby daughter, Martin was even scarcer around the house. More glaringly, he'd ignore me when I asked where he'd been. He didn't even care enough to lie by then. He'd just stare at me with disdain and then walk away in silence."

Laurie had no way of knowing if the account was true, and Kendra didn't seem to realize that any negative portrayal of Martin as a family man only enhanced her motive to kill him. "I can't imagine how infuriating that would be," Laurie said.

"If I pressed him about my suspicions, he'd tell me I was going crazy. And then he told his parents and all of our friends that I was jealous and paranoid, accusing him of cheating for no reason at all. So by the time I reached out to them for support, he had already turned everyone against me. Did you ever see that old movie *Gaslight*?"

"Sure, with Ingrid Bergman," Laurie said. The film had been a favorite of Laurie's mother, so Laurie knew it was a 1940s-era adaptation of a play written by Patrick Hamilton. It had also been adapted previously in England, but most Americans were referring to the later version with Ingrid Bergman, Charles Boyer, and a young unknown named Angela Lansbury.

The film was about a new bride whose husband slowly manipulated her into believing she was going insane, by hiding her belongings, staging the sound of footsteps in the attic, and arranging for the home's gaslights to dim and brighten for no apparent reason. All the while, he told his wife that these oddities were figments of her imagination.

"That's what being married to Martin Bell was like. He was gas-lighting me, trying to make me sound like a crazy woman to everyone who knew us. But I wasn't making up stories. A woman knows when her husband is being unfaithful. The truth is that Martin wasn't the kind of man who could be on his own. He was always in a serious relationship—two other very successful women before me. In retrospect, I think he married me because I was the one whose career would never match his."

"You were in medical school. You were planning to be a doctor."

A wave of sadness came over Kendra about the future she never got to have. "All I wanted was to be a good pediatrician—not a superstar. My point is that Martin needed a woman in his life. And even after we started having trouble, I was still that person. But then something clicked, and I could tell his affections were somewhere else. I would bet my life on it. And Martin could be very charismatic. There's a reason I married him so quickly. He swept me off my feet."

Laurie remembered seeing him during his various television appearances and thinking to herself that he had the "it factor." Alex had it, too. *And look what ended up happening with us*, she thought.

Kendra continued to build her case. "Everyone suspects me because no one else would want to hurt Martin. But if he was turning on the charm for another man's wife? He wouldn't be the first paramour to be murdered by a jealous husband."

"Do you have any thoughts about who the woman may have been?"

"Thoughts?" Her eyes widened. "I'm absolutely certain it was Leigh Ann Longfellow."

The name hit Laurie sideways. "As in the wife of Senator Longfellow?"

"As I said: I'd bet my life on it."

19

Laurie felt a chill go up her spine. She already knew that the NYPD was being tight-lipped about the case and that Martin's parents were willing to use their influence to skew the investigation. Now Kendra was accusing Daniel Longfellow, New York's junior senator, of murder. There was no way that Brett Young and the studio lawyers would let her whisper that possibility on television without hard, undeniable evidence to back it up.

"I've read all of the news coverage of the case, Kendra, and never once saw any mention of Senator Longfellow or his wife."

Kendra rolled her eyes dramatically. "Of course you didn't. The Longfellows made sure of it. They're both masters at manipulating the entire political system and the mainstream media."

Laurie could see how little effort it would have taken Martin to convince others that Kendra was less than rational.

"You seriously think that a U.S. senator shot your husband in the middle of Greenwich Village? Whoever shot Martin confronted him as he pulled into your driveway. A neighbor easily could have recognized him." Laurie couldn't picture it.

"He wasn't Senator Daniel Longfellow yet. He was State Assemblyman Longfellow, and he didn't even represent our district. Could you pick a state legislator from two districts over out of a lineup?"

Laurie paused to jog her memory about the timing of Longfellow's elevation to the U.S. Senate. After nearly two decades of uninterrupted service from the same two senators from New York, one of them had resigned to join the President's cabinet. With a vacant Senate seat, the governor of New York was empowered to appoint a replacement. He had turned to an up-and-coming star from the state assembly, a handsome former prosecutor named Daniel Longfellow. Longfellow had then been elected to a full six-year term three years ago, but Laurie realized now that his initial appointment had come right around the time of Martin Bell's murder.

"How did your husband even know Mrs. Longfellow?"

"They both went to Hayden and served on its alumni board," Kendra said. Laurie recognized the name of the Hayden School on the Upper East Side, one of the most competitive private schools in New York City. "Leigh Ann was everything I used to be when Martin and I first met: always put together, one step ahead of everyone, the type who was chosen to lead any group she joined. And, like me, she also seems to be completely happy as the quiet woman behind the prominent man. Look at how far her husband, Daniel, has gotten with Leigh Ann at his side. After Mindy was born, Martin was suddenly volunteering to help run the big annual fundraising auction for the Hayden School. Guess who his co-chair was? Leigh Ann, of course. Part of the reason she had so much time to spend with my husband was because hers was in the legislature in Albany. All of a sudden, Martin was spending more time with Leigh Ann than with me and the kids."

"Did you tell the police about your suspicions?"

"Immediately. I told them that if I figured out the two were having an affair, then Daniel probably did, too. I didn't know it at the time, but rumors were already swirling that Longfellow was the governor's heir apparent for the Senate seat, as soon as the previous senator's cabinet appointment had been announced. Losing his wife to a celebrity doctor could have torpedoed Longfellow's political elevation."

Laurie had watched as Alex had worried that one influential politician—or even a viral tweet—might derail his judicial nomination. She supposed it was possible that a different type of person, perhaps a truly evil person, might kill to protect his political stature.

"Do you know what the police did to investigate your suspicions?"

She shook her head. "You'd think they would keep me updated as his widow, but it was clear early on that I was viewed as a suspect, not as a family member. His parents, however, got the red-carpet treatment."

Laurie would raise the issue with the Bells when she spoke to them. She jotted a note in her pad as a reminder. "In what ways did the police treat you as a suspect? You were never arrested or even named as a person of interest."

"They didn't need to do that. I could see the way they were looking at me when the detectives arrived that night. It was obvious they didn't like me."

"Didn't *like* you? A homicide scene isn't a personality contest."

"Exactly. But they stereotyped me immediately. They even asked me to take a drug test. I told them absolutely not—not without a warrant!"

"Forgive me, Kendra, but your husband had just been killed. Why wouldn't you give the police whatever they wanted?"

Kendra looked around the restaurant, making sure that they were still out of earshot. Three additional customers had come in, but Kendra and Laurie still had privacy. Laurie had a feeling that they had Dennis the bartender to thank for that luxury. "Because they were wasting time investigating me when I wanted them to find my husband's murderer," Kendra hissed.

"I have to say, though: by many accounts, your demeanor was flat, and you were reportedly 'out of it,' so to speak, around that time generally and even after you heard about Martin's death."

"Do I seem like I'm on drugs to you?" Kendra asked.

"Now? Of course not. But I didn't know you five years ago."

"Look, I don't want to have to talk about this on prime time television, but in retrospect, I was suffering from very severe postpartum depression. I think it started when Bobby was born. It's why I couldn't handle going back to my residency. But then instead of getting treatment, it was on to the second baby. I'm not proud of this, but I wasn't a good mother then. I could barely get myself out of bed. Martin—especially as a physician—should have recognized the source of the problem and gotten help for me. Instead, he ran around with his Little Miss Perfect Leigh Ann, and then left the kids and me for poor Caroline to deal with. After he died, I saw a therapist and got the treatment I needed. But his parents can't see that I've changed."

Laurie immediately kicked herself for not seeing the possible explanation of postpartum depression on her own. One of her friends had suffered for nearly a year after giving birth to her first child.

"You think your in-laws are still trying to take the children from you?" Laurie asked.

"A hundred percent. And as much as I hope and pray that somehow you manage to make a break in the case, the real reason I'm doing this show is to placate them. They're the reason Martin was the way he was—charming and talented, but ultimately cruel and merciless. I don't want Bobby and Mindy to grow up like that."

Laurie was beginning to see a more sympathetic side to Kendra, but she was still having a hard time understanding why she hadn't been more cooperative with the police. She moved on to the next topic on the list in her notepad. "There were reports that you had taken many cash withdrawals from your savings, but you weren't willing to tell the police where the money went."

"It's not that I wasn't *willing*. I just wasn't *able* to. I wasn't in the best shape at the time given my postpartum. I needed to get out of the house sometimes, and anything you do in New York City costs money. Some days I would just get in a cab and ask the driver to take me out to Staten Island or Jones Beach so I could have solitude. Or I'd go on shopping sprees. One time, I blew eight hundred dollars on a pair of leopard print Louboutin heels that I've still never worn. Size seven if you're interested," she added with a sad smile. "Maybe wasting all that money was my quiet way of getting back at Martin for his affair."

Rebellious spending was a far cry from murder, Laurie thought.

"I understand you need to rehash everything the police put me through, Laurie, but please promise me that you'll look into what I've said about Leigh Ann Longfellow. I don't think the police believed a single word I said."

"That's the whole point of our program," Laurie assured her. "We examine every possible angle, which is why I also want to ask you about the lawsuits that Steven mentioned. Someone was suing Martin?"

Kendra waved a dismissive hand. "It's the lay of the land when you're a doctor. As much as I wanted to be a pediatrician, one of the downsides was the lawsuits that come with the job. And Martin had it even worse. After all, the people that he treated were dealing with chronic pain. They weren't easy cases."

"So what were the lawsuits about?"

"I honestly don't know the details. Martin had stopped talking to me in any meaningful way by then. After he died, the attorneys reached settlements out of the estate."

"Who was Martin's medical malpractice attorney? I can check with him or her."

"I have no idea."

Laurie made another note to herself to research the lawsuits further. She had only one remaining topic on her list and it was a doozie. "You said before you'd leave the house to seek solitude. Did that include going to bars?"

Kendra groaned. "The tabloids made me sound like I was marinated in vodka twenty-four hours a day. I told you: I was suffering from postpartum. Look it up: it can make you fatigued one minute, then restless, panicky, and unfocused the next. I suppose people confused it with being drunk."

"What about just going out on the town for company?"

"Not really. Honestly, there were days I didn't even take a shower, it was that bad."

Laurie had to be careful here. The information about Kendra frequenting the Beehive was never in the papers, and she didn't want Kendra to realize that she knew more than what had been reported in the media. She needed to save that for the cross-examination that would come when the cameras were turned on.

She decided to press one more time. "I noticed you and Steven have a friend behind the bar here in Dennis. You didn't have a favorite hangout back then?"

This time, Kendra snapped her response. "I told you, no!"

Laurie nodded and tucked her pen into the spine of her notepad, signaling that their work for the day was done. "Thanks again for meeting me on your time off," she said. "We'll be in touch when it's time to start scheduling production."

She did her best to make friendly chitchat while she waited for Dennis to bring the check, which she paid with her studio credit card.

Two strikes and the cameras weren't even rolling yet, she thought. First Kendra had lied to her in-laws about her willingness to help with the reinvestigation of Martin's case. And now Laurie was certain she was lying again. The police would have confronted Kendra with their evidence that she'd been meeting a mystery man at the Beehive. She couldn't imagine Kendra forgetting something like that.

There is a good chance that I just enjoyed a cappuccino and gelato with a killer, she thought. *She doesn't want me to know about the Beehive. So that will be my next stop.*

20

It was nearly five o'clock by the time Kendra and Laurie left Otto, but the spring sun was still bright, a welcome contrast from the dark Italian restaurant. Kendra was relieved when Laurie finally said good-bye as they reached Fifth Avenue. Laurie turned south and began walking toward Washington Square Park. As Kendra headed north toward home, she allowed the sunlight to warm her face and tried to calm the thoughts racing in her mind.

At first, everything had been going exactly as she had planned. Steven had tagged along to make sure Laurie knew that she had raised her concerns about Martin's affair when he was still alive. He also made her sound like a good person—something no one else did anymore. Even Dennis had pitched in on the effort.

Even after Laurie started throwing questions at her, Kendra thought she had done a good job holding her own. She had prepared in advance, knowing that Laurie would be asking about the state of both her mind and her marriage, conflicts with the police, and cash withdrawals. If the conversation had ended there, she would have felt confident that she was on sure footing.

But then Laurie had sneaked in one final topic. When she asked Kendra about going to bars in search of company. Maybe it was simply a shot in the dark, a question prompted by Kendra's rumored alcoholism. But she had a horrible sense of foreboding that Laurie was referring to the man Kendra still knew only as "Mike."

She tasted coffee and gelato at the back of her throat from the mere thought of him.

She had sworn on her life—on her *children's* lives—that she would do the television show without a single mention of his existence. *Now what am I going to do?* she thought.

She pulled out her cell phone, pulled up "Mike," and hit enter. He answered after only half a ring. "You're done with your meeting?" he asked.

She could tell he was on speakerphone, and she could hear the sounds of a car engine and horns in the background. He was in a car. She found herself looking up and down the street for signs of him.

"I just left."

"And?"

He had insisted that she apprise him of every development with the television production, and she didn't dare cross him. "It was a rehash of the old news reports. Nothing I couldn't handle. She didn't ask about you," she added. Technically, the statement was true.

"When do you see her next?"

"I don't know. She said they'd call me about the shooting schedule."

"Remember, if you tell them about me, I tell them about you. You'll go to prison for murder. Your children will be sent off with their grandparents, where they'll be told every day that you killed their father. And that's assuming they're still safe and sound by the time you're convicted."

The threat to Bobby and Mindy, once again, was clear. She felt herself starting to shake. "Please, don't hurt them."

"Then don't make me."

She remembered telling Martin one time during a horrible fight that he should have come with a warning label: Cruelest Man Alive. But now she was dealing with someone even more vile than Martin. With a trembling voice, she said, "I won't tell anyone. I swear."

"It's time for another meeting."

The thought of it made her blood run cold. It wasn't even the money at this point. She had become used to him using her as his personal cash machine. The man terrified her at a primal, cellular level. "When?" She heard the quiver in her voice.

"Not how it works. You know that. I'll call you, and you will come. Bring the usual."

The usual was nine thousand in cash. Her best guess was that he didn't want a withdrawal of ten thousand dollars, which banks must report to the government, to trigger an inquiry. She heard the hum of his car engine accelerating, and then he was gone.

She pressed her eyes closed and took three deep breaths, trying to remain calm.

When she was telling Laurie about the disintegration of her marriage, she had used the word *gaslight* to describe Martin's practice of telling people that she had lost her mind. But the point of the movie was that Ingrid Bergman actually began to doubt her own mind. *Martin literally drove me insane*, Kendra thought.

Did she really tell Steven about those malpractice lawsuits against Martin? She didn't remember it. Just as she didn't remember saying the horrible things she'd obviously blurted out at a dive bar, to a stranger who called himself Mike. *What else did I manage to do in my blacked-out state?* she wondered.

Even though Kendra wasn't religious, she walked into the Episcopal church on 10th Street. They had just opened the doors for weeknight services, but Kendra wouldn't be staying long. She went to the back row of the church and knelt in silent prayer, as she had so many times before, asking forgiveness for something she didn't want to believe she might have done.

Will I ever know the truth? she wondered. *Will I ever know if I had my husband killed?*

21

After she said good-bye to Kendra, Laurie left Otto and started down Fifth Avenue in the direction of Washington Square Park. The sun was out on the first warm day of spring, which was license for New Yorkers to treat the park like the city equivalent of a public beach, with young women still in their work clothes reclined on the grass and a few brave, shirtless guys tossing around a Frisbee. Crowds gathered to take in the park's spectacles, from the piano man playing Chopin under the arch to the break-dancers who spun and flipped by the fountain, their massive speakers drowning out the grand piano. Spring in the city felt like a reawakening, and everyone came out from the dark winter to breathe fresh air.

As she made her way into the heart of the East Village, Laurie prepared herself for the Beehive, which, regardless of season, probably didn't see much sun. She had clocked her fair share of time in tomb-like bars with sticky floors and graffitied bathrooms in college, but it had been a while since she'd spent her evenings underground.

She pushed open a heavy door at the bottom of a steep staircase and stepped into the bar. The familiar scent of spilled beer thinly disguised by Lysol washed over her. It was nearing happy hour, but the place was empty. An LED sign that said "The Beehive" in honeycomb lettering flickered above the bar, and alcohol-inspired neon lights decorated the walls, casting colorful shadows throughout the lair. She had a hard time picturing Kendra kicking back with a drink at the bar or lining up for a game of pinball in the back.

"Just a minute," said an unconcerned voice from beneath the bar. A moment later, a young woman with partially shaven hair emerged. As Laurie approached, she noticed the bartender's eyebrow and lip piercings shift slightly as her expression changed from indifference to surprise upon seeing her. Clearly Laurie didn't fit the mold of the usual customer.

Laurie gave her a friendly smile. "I'm hoping to speak to someone who worked here five years ago."

The bartender looked at her blankly. "Five years?" Her tone implied that nothing of import could have happened so long ago. Laurie got the impression she would have still been in high school.

She opened a door with an EMPLOYEES ONLY sign and called out. Turning back toward Laurie, she said, "Deb has been here for, like, forever."

An older woman with deep wrinkles and a messy bun stepped out from behind the door. Her haggard face did seem to reflect a sort of dive bar "forever," which turned out to be eight years. Good enough for Laurie.

"Did you know a woman named Kendra Bell?" Laurie asked, cutting to the chase and placing a fifty-dollar bill on the counter.

Deb smiled, clearly remembering. "Always liked her. Sad what happened, huh?"

"You knew who she was at the time? With her husband Martin being a public figure?"

"Oh, definitely not. She was just a regular by appearance. We'd shoot the breeze, but I didn't even know her name. She was always railing about how horrible her husband was, though. That he was fake, cruel. Cheating on her." Deb motioned to the liquor, but Laurie shook her head. "Suit yourself," she said, grabbing a bottle of Old Crow whiskey off the shelf and pouring herself a glass.

"And you're positive it was Kendra Bell?" Laurie continued.

"Definitely. Even told me once about how she'd gone to medical school but never became a doctor. I didn't even believe her at the time. Didn't exactly strike me as a dedicated student type. I chalked it up to drunk babbling."

Laurie surveyed the establishment again, taking in the shag carpet hanging on the wall by the pool table. The young bartender had gone back to doing something beneath the bar. "Did she always come in alone?" she asked Deb.

"Usually." She gazed at the ceiling and squinted, trying to remember. "But there were a few times when I noticed her hanging around with a rough-looking guy. Shaved head with really mean eyes. It seemed like he was humoring her. Maybe hitting her up to pay his bar bill at the end of the day in exchange for listening to her blow off steam about the husband."

Laurie fished her phone out of her purse and pulled up a picture of Steven Carter, Kendra's former med school boyfriend and current employer. The fact that Kendra, five years a widow, was still merely Steven's friend and employee, not a girlfriend or wife, suggested that she was not involved with him romantically, but she wanted to make sure she wasn't missing anything.

Deb let out a cackle when she saw the photo. "Definitely not him. That guy's like Mister Rogers compared to the dude I'm talking about."

Laurie nodded, getting a better sense of the character she should be envisioning. "Have you seen him since Martin Bell's murder?"

"Never saw Mr. Tough Guy or Kendra again. When the murder first happened and I saw her wedding picture in the paper, I barely recognized her. The lady really went downhill. I was going to give her my sympathies the next time I saw her, but she never came back in. Him neither." She took a swig of whiskey and paused. "You know her or something?"

Laurie explained the *Under Suspicion* series and the reinvestigation of the Martin Bell case. "I'm collecting as much information about Kendra Bell as I can."

"You're not the only one who thinks something was weird with her. I called the police tip line. Told them how she'd complain and complain about the marriage. Mentioned the Tough Guy, too. There was a reward, and I wasn't going to leave money on the table. And justice," she added. "I liked her and all, but if she did it, she should be locked up."

"Any chance you'd be willing to let us film in here? Maybe sit down with my show's host and repeat what you just told me?"

A broad grin settled across her tired face. "That would be pretty cool."

Laurie thanked Deb and the younger bartender, and left the bar. As she climbed the steps back into the sunlight, she was overcome by the eerie feeling of being watched. *Maybe the description of the mystery man with the mean eyes got to me,* she thought.

But as she walked down Bowery toward the Lafayette Street subway station, she could not shake the thought of someone following her. She ducked into a handbag shop to monitor the flow of pedestrians outside. Her heart jumped at the sight of a tall man with a shaved head, waiting at the crosswalk at 3rd Street, heading in her direction on Bowery. He was wearing aviator sunglasses, so she couldn't tell if his eyes were "mean," as Deb had described.

She looked away from the glass store window quickly to smile apologetically to the clerk. She got her cell phone out of her purse, ready to call 911 if necessary, and left the store.

She glanced over her shoulder. The tall man was half a block behind her. They exchanged glances and he quickened his pace.

Laurie darted into another shop a few feet away. Standing inside, she watched to see if the man would follow her into the shop this time. But, again, he did not. Instead he crossed the street, his gait determined. Laurie felt her heart pounding in her chest, even though she'd been walking slowly. *He was tailing me and knows I made him,* Laurie thought. *Where is he heading now?*

Peering through the shop window, she briefly lost sight of him as a white SUV that had been parked behind a large truck pulled onto Broadway. Struggling to see past the SUV, she thought she spotted the tall man bend down and then stand again before vanishing once again from her view. She could feel her cell phone shaking in her hand and forced herself to manipulate the digital keypad—9, 1, 1. Her thumb lingered over the enter button, as she wondered how long it would take the police to respond.

Only after the light changed and the SUV made a left turn onto 2nd Street did she realize why the man had seemed so purposeful in his movements. On the other side of Broadway, the tall man was now holding hands with a young woman who had a giggling baby strapped to her belly. With an unobstructed view, Laurie could even see that the big, scary man who'd had her so shaken was wearing an Angry Birds T-shirt similar to one Timmy had outgrown two years earlier.

Laurie laughed at herself for letting her imagination run wild. Feeling foolish, she nevertheless waited a full minute before thanking the shop clerk and stepping back onto the sidewalk. And when she saw the dome light of an available taxi, she raised her hand on instinct. *Better safe than sorry,* she thought.

Once she was settled into the back of the cab, she processed everything she had learned this afternoon. She wanted to learn more about Steven Carter and the lawsuits against Martin Bell, but her thoughts kept returning to the Beehive. Having spoken to both Deb and Kendra, she was absolutely certain that Kendra was in fact the same woman Deb remembered. Maybe Kendra needed an escape from her house and unhappy marriage, but why would she lie? Laurie was certain that it all came back to the mystery man, and then she felt a chill return to her spine.

She was so busy thinking about the case that she did not notice that the white SUV had circled back onto Broadway to blend into traffic behind her cab.

22

What a strange-looking couple, the man thought to himself as his white SUV approached a red light. The couple in question was on the east side of the street, standing between 2nd and 3rd. The man was at least six and a half feet tall, with a shaved head and aviator glasses. A real tough guy from the neck up. But he was wearing a cartoon-character T-shirt and holding hands with a petite blond woman carrying a baby in one of those body slings.

They looked like a happy family, which the man found incredible.

He could already picture them fifteen years from now. He'd get fat. She'd drink too much. Their simple, sullen children would know that their parents hated each other.

He considered himself a realist about marriage. Sure, things might be all hearts and rose petals for the time being, but how will things look when life throws you a curveball? When that pretty girl starts losing her looks or can't get out of bed, how long will it take for Happy Husband to find a replacement? And if Daddy winds up in the unemployment line? Forget about it. There was no for better or for worse, in good times and in bad—only selfishness and betrayal.

He shifted his gaze to the passenger-side window, trying to lay eyes again on his target. That's how he thought of Laurie Moran: as prey.

A few months ago, when he was in one of his ruts, he had been spending too much time lying around on the sofa watching cable television. He saw a nature program about the chameleon. He had almost flipped the channel as they showed clips of lizards morphing from red to pink to green to yellow and blue. What kind of idiot didn't already know those ugly things could change colors?

But then the narrator started talking about the eyes. Turns out, a chameleon's eyelids are fused except for a narrow opening, like a pinhole. But instead of blinding the lizard, this extraordinary feature turns each eye into a kind of periscope, plus each eye can move independently of the other. As a result, chameleons can scan a full 360-degree perimeter. They can search for predators and prey simultaneously. A chameleon sees everything at once.

Imagine what that would be like, the man thought. To be one step ahead at all times. No one could fool you or cheat you, that was for sure.

Now, behind the wheel of his white SUV, that was how he felt—all powerful. For the moment, from his viewpoint, there were no predators, only prey. *They don't see me*, he thought, *but I see everything*.

Except wait! Where is she? He had followed her from the dive bar. She had turned on Broadway, and he had done the same, but now there was no sight of her. She couldn't have walked that far. As soon as the light changed, he hung a left on 2nd Street, hoping that he could circle the block and find her again.

Once he reached the intersection of Broadway and 3rd, he pulled over to the curb in front of a hydrant and ducked low in his seat, scanning the street. He felt his power slipping away. It made him want to drive onto the sidewalk and mow down anyone who happened to be there.

His foot was lingering over the gas pedal when she suddenly

emerged from a shop across the street. She took only a few steps before holding up her hand to hail a cab. He counted to three and then pulled into traffic behind her.

Where to now, Laurie Moran? And how much longer should I wait before life starts throwing you a few curveballs?

23

Laurie felt the safety that comes with tagging home base as she entered the lobby of her apartment building. She waited while Ron the doorman transferred a tower of neatly stacked packages from the storage closet to a young woman whom Laurie recognized from the building.

"Do you need a hand with that?" Laurie offered.

"That's okay," the woman said. "This is my punishment for a hardcore online shopping addiction."

Laurie watched in awe as the woman cautiously began her trek toward the elevator, the tower of boxes teetering with each step.

Ron gave Laurie a knowing smile once they were alone. "She's not kidding about an addiction. That girl will be down here tomorrow sending all that stuff back for a refund. The UPS guy is threatening to drop our building if she doesn't rein it in."

Once again, Laurie realized how much she was going to miss this place if she and Alex ever managed to find an apartment. "Hey, Primo. Weird question, but has anyone been around the building asking for me?"

A concerned look crossed his face. "Not that I know of. Are you expecting someone?"

Laurie shook her head, but she could feel the worry lines furrowing her brow. "No, just wanted to make sure."

"We've always got your back down here. You know that, right?"

"Always, but, really, no need to sound an alarm." *But I still have a feeling of being followed*, Laurie thought. *Obviously it wasn't the tall guy who met that woman. But something is warning me to be careful.*

"Primo, do me a favor. If you notice anybody that appears to be watching the building, please let me know."

"We always look out for you, Miss Laurie, but we'll pay extra attention."

When Laurie stepped from the elevator, she was greeted by the smell of garlic and rosemary. She found herself wishing she had ordered dinner to go from the Italian restaurant where she'd met with Kendra. She was surprised when the smell became stronger as she opened the front door of her apartment. She could barely make out the soothing sound of the "Almost Blue" song by Chet Baker beneath a cacophony of voices. *How lucky I am*, she thought, *that my ten-year-old son loves jazz instead of the noise I hear on the radio.*

She hooked her shoulder bag on the coat rack and was immediately greeted by Timmy calling out "Hi, Mom!" She found him in the kitchen, expertly wielding a wooden spoon in her largest saucepan, under Ramon's watchful eye. "What are you doing here?" she asked, giving Ramon a quick squeeze around his shoulders.

"The boss's idea," he said with a smile, hitching a thumb toward the living room.

Alex was already on his feet enfolding her tightly in his arms. He was still dressed for work, but had loosened his tie and taken off his suit jacket.

"Well, this is a nice surprise," she said.

Leo was positioned in his favorite chair. His daily ESPN program, *Pardon the Interruption*, was on. The format involved the hosts debating the sports topics of the day, and Laurie found herself grateful that the sound was muted.

"I could tell you were discouraged by the apartment walk-through today," Alex said, leading her to the spot next to him on the sofa. "I thought we could use a family night at home even if hot-shot Rhoda hasn't found us our perfect home yet."

Leo made a disapproving face at the mention of Rhoda's name. "Alex filled me in. I can't believe she suggested that any co-op in the city wouldn't jump at the opportunity to welcome the two of you and my grandson into their fold. She's only saying that to make you antsy. She wants you to lower your sights so she can swoop in for a fast sale. You tell her that any building that even inquires about Alex's old cases can pound salt."

Leo's invocation of the old police phrase was a sign that he was agitated. She was used to Leo rising to her defense, but she suspected that Leo had a specific reason for being critical of Rhoda. He didn't want Laurie and Timmy to move too far away from his own apartment.

"Nothing to worry about, Dad. We made it very clear that we have no interest in living in a building that takes issue with either of our professions—or a former profession, in Alex's case. She also knows that we need enough room for an office and for Ramon, and that we need to be close to both Timmy's school and your apartment," she added.

Leo's eyes brightened. "And a nursery," he suggested with a wry smile.

"Shhh," Laurie said, with a dismissive wave. "If Timmy hears that, it will be all around his school the next day."

Leo laughed. "I don't hear a denial in there."

"Maybe we should change the subject to Chief Judge Maureen Russell," Laurie suggested.

"Oh, I saw her today," Alex said. "Leo, she said how much she enjoyed speaking to you at the reception."

Laurie was delighted to see her father blush. "Leo and Maureen, I think it has a nice ring to it."

Leo rolled his eyes, but was still smiling. "You win. I tap out. I cry uncle. No more nursery talk. You buy as many rooms as you want, no questions asked."

Laurie and Alex exchanged knowing glances. They had, in fact, told the Realtor they wanted room to grow . . . just in case, someday.

24

Later that evening, Laurie walked through her apartment, turning off all the lights as her final step before going to bed.

Alex had told her he had an early morning breakfast scheduled with the judge for whom he had clerked after law school. His judicial mentor was eager to pass on words of wisdom from his years on the bench.

As she flipped the switch in the kitchen, she marveled at the cleanliness of the room. The granite countertops gleamed, and not a single crumb was visible on the tile floor. She couldn't remember a time when she'd ever cooked a meal in this apartment without dreading the aftermath. She was going to very much enjoy sharing a roof with Ramon.

She had just climbed into bed to enjoy the ending of the latest Karin Slaughter novel when her cell phone buzzed on her nightstand. It was Ryan. He never called her this late. In fact, he never called at all.

"Hey," she said, already feeling a headache coming on from whatever it was he was about to say.

"I wasn't sure you'd still be up."

"I just got into bed. What's going on?"

"Sorry, but I have to ask. Do you know my uncle Jed?"

Laurie definitely did not know Ryan's uncle. She was, however, aware that Uncle Jed had been Brett Young's college roommate at Northwestern, which most likely played a role in nephew Ryan landing a plum job at Fisher Blake Studios. "Yes, I know who he is. What about him?" she asked.

"Well, it turns out his publisher's husband sits on the board of a children's literacy organization with Martin Bell's father."

"Uh-huh," she said flatly, trying to recall the chain of connections that Martin's father had already traced to her boss, Brett. "I think another one of Brett's college friends is tennis partners with Dr. Bell's accountant. Apparently Robert has quite the Rolodex. I take it he called you?" she asked, bracing herself for yet another attempt by Ryan to take over the production of her show.

"He did—just now, on my cell phone, despite the late hour. To be honest, I'm pretty uncomfortable with the pressure he was trying to exert. It's obvious they think Kendra is guilty and want us to railroad her on television."

"Is that right?" she asked, surprised at his disapproving response.

"I was respectful, but said I'd need to get back to them. Have you made a decision yet about whether to go forward with the case?"

Laurie was tempted to ask him to repeat what he'd said. He rarely deferred to her when it came to work. "I think it would be a great case for us," she said, "but we need to make sure that the parents understand that we are going to investigate objectively. We're not their pawns."

"Absolutely," he agreed. "So what if we go speak with them in person tomorrow? We can present a united front, so they know they can't push either of us around."

"That sounds . . . perfect." It was the first time she could remember feeling like Ryan was on her side.

As she hung up the phone, she felt absolutely content.

She had no idea that less than two miles away, a man was Googling her on his computer, learning more about her life and wondering when to make his next move.

25

The following morning, Dr. Steven Carter struggled to turn the locks of his Fifth Avenue dermatology practice while managing to hold on to his briefcase, morning coffee, and the bundle of flowers he'd picked up at the corner deli. As was often the case, he was the first to arrive at the office. He had always been a morning person.

Not that anyone would know by looking at him, but he liked to start the day with a trip to the gym. A few months ago, he had even started working out with a personal trainer to try to maximize the effects of his exercises. According to the trainer, he had increased his muscle mass by 8 percent, but no one seemed to notice, especially the woman whose affection he'd been trying to win over for more than a decade.

Steven knew he wasn't a looker. He was a realist, after all. In college, his writing teachers told him his prose was "stilted." His philosophy professor said he was "unimaginative." After two years of Spanish, he couldn't even manage to order dinner at a Mexican restaurant without earning sympathetic chuckles from the waitstaff. The only classes where he didn't feel like a loser were the sciences. By his junior year, he realized he already had all his medical school prerequisites down, so he figured, *Why not be a doctor?*

And because he was a realist, he knew that his grades were probably only good enough to go to a foreign medical school. Five years in the Caribbean sounded pretty nice after growing up in Iowa. But much to his surprise, he had gotten accepted to SUNY Stony Brook. It wasn't the Caribbean, but it was on an island — Long Island — and it would mean better job prospects once he was finished.

But medical school was much harder than those undergraduate science classes. If it hadn't been for Kendra, he might not have finished. She always made it look so easy and had a way of explaining things more clearly than even the professors could. And she was so beautiful, especially back then.

He remembered the first time she kissed him. It was the night before the final exam in Neuroscience. He was nearly shaking, convinced that he was going to fail.

"Steven, why are you like this?" she had asked.

"Like what?"

"Like . . . you. What did someone do to you to make you so incapable of seeing your own worth?" And then she had kissed him. It wasn't passionate, but it was soft and it lingered. Steven was stunned, but Kendra just looked at him with a smile in her eyes. "You deserve to expect more from the world," she said. Then she went right back to studying.

The next morning, he managed to get a B on the exam, and he knew to this day it was because he walked into the classroom thinking of himself as someone who was good enough to be kissed by Kendra.

He started thinking of her as his girlfriend after that, but between classes and studying, there really wasn't much time for the traditional "dating" activities. In retrospect, it seemed that maybe she just showed him affection now and then to break up the monotony.

In any event, it became pretty darn clear that they weren't anything approaching a real couple once she met Martin Bell their last year of medical school. Martin was everything Steven wasn't. He was a brilliant doctor from a well-known New York City family. He was tall, slender, and handsome. As it turned out, enough to sweep Kendra off her feet.

She started to miss their nightly study sessions to go into the city to see Martin. By the end of the year, the only times she'd call him would be to ask for help running errands to plan for the wedding.

And of course Steven had done it. He would do anything for her.

Steven might not be tall and thin, on television, or a brilliant doctor. In fact, he barely got into medical school, and barely passed once he was there. Nevertheless, it had worked out fine. Only ten years out, he already owned a thriving medical practice. He had chosen to become a dermatologist. He wanted to make patients not only look better, but *feel* better about themselves.

He flipped on the sound system that piped into the reception area and treatment rooms. The radio station on the streaming service he used was called "lounge chill." He filled the aromatherapy burners with eucalyptus oil. He was proud of the number of five-star reviews he had online for making his offices feel more like a luxury spa than a doctor's office.

He dropped his briefcase on his office chair and his coffee on his desk, and then carried the flowers he had purchased to the small desk that sat just outside his office—the one with Kendra's computer terminal on it. He placed the flowers next to the keyboard and then jotted a message on the pad of Post-it notes beside it: *K, Hope your meeting last night went well and that you are OK. —S*

Steven was a realist. Kendra may have married Martin, but Steven never stopped loving her. He knew how grateful Kendra was. He had given her a job when no one else would. Now he got to spend five days each week with her. And she had begun to invite him to Bobby and Mindy's sports games and school recitals. *Does she realize I would do anything for her?* he wondered.

It's all coming together, he thought to himself with a feeling of deep satisfaction.

26

As Dr. Steven Carter was opening his medical office, Laurie and Ryan were in the Bells' penthouse on Fifth Avenue, a few doors up from the Metropolitan Museum. After the doorman phoned for permission for them to go up, a housekeeper let them in. While they waited in the living room, Laurie became distracted by the breathtaking view past the museum to the treetops of the West Side skyline.

When the Bells came in, they settled on the couch close to each other. They did not seem like the same angry couple that had confronted her at her office two days ago. They seemed polite, even friendly, and Laurie knew that was because they believed Ryan was on their side.

Dr. Bell immediately invited them to sit down. Ryan had done his homework and was ready with icebreaker conversation. He had learned that the Bells were friends with one of his law school professors. The law school professor's brother had operated on Dr. Bell's sister three years earlier. Cynthia interrupted the exchange by offering them coffee, which they both politely declined.

"So, Laurie," Robert said, "Ryan told us last night that you've changed your mind about Martin's case, but wanted to speak to us before moving forward."

Laurie saw no reason to tell them that Kendra, not Laurie, had been the one with a change of heart. "Yes, I wanted to make sure we were on the same page about the nature of our program." She gave them the usual introduction she provided when she initially approached family members about cooperating with the show. She emphasized the studio's desire to unearth new or overlooked evidence and the potential for the show to provide some kind of closure if not final answers for the victim's family members. "At the same time," she added, "we are a news program, and we approach each case with the same journalistic standards that any reporter would use. That means we'll be sensitive to your feelings as Martin's parents, but ultimately must remain objective. We'll report the full story, no matter where that leads us."

"Of course," Cynthia said quickly, nodding in agreement.

Dr. Bell was less convinced. A worried look crossed his face. "You don't think Kendra did it, do you?"

Laurie chose her words carefully. "We don't form those kinds of conclusions until we have the evidence to back them up."

"So go find the evidence," he snapped.

Ryan leaned forward in his chair to get a word in. "Trust me, Dr. Bell. I have seen Laurie in action. Her ability to put together a case rivals the very best FBI agents I worked with at the U.S. Attorney's Office. If there's evidence to be found, she'll get it."

"My point," Laurie clarified, "is that we don't decide on the conclusion first and then tailor our investigation to suit that narrative. We go in with an open mind, which means exploring all potential theories and suspects. And of course that will include Kendra. But being objective means that we can't let the victim's family members—even parents—run the show."

Cynthia watched as her husband's gaze moved between Ryan and Laurie.

Finally he said, "We understand."

Laurie was surprised when Ryan pulled two participation agreements from his briefcase, already filled out for their signatures. As Dr. Bell signed on the dotted line, he made yet another pitch of his theory that Kendra was guilty. "I'm sure she still has the ability to be very charming," he warned. "We were quite fond of her when they first got together. But you didn't see her back then. She obviously has a very ill mind. She got her hooks into our son, and the minute she had him locked into the marriage, she turned into an entirely different person."

"Did you ever consider the possibility that she might have had postpartum depression?" Laurie asked, recalling Kendra's explanation for her deterioration after her children were born.

"Psssh," Cynthia said, brushing off the theory. "Why would anyone be depressed about having such beautiful children? I was at my utter happiest when Martin was a little boy."

"Surely, Dr. Bell, you are aware that many women don't have the same experience," Laurie persisted.

"Please. A little depression is one thing. Kendra was completely out of her mind. Poor Martin was absolutely miserable. He knew he'd made a terrible mistake marrying her."

"What makes you say she was out of her mind?" Laurie asked. She remembered Kendra saying that Martin had been "gaslighting" her by telling others that she was crazy.

Cynthia was eager to answer. "Martin confided in us that Kendra had had a 'mental breakdown' and was growing more and more paranoid. She even accused him of cheating on her and trying to alienate her from Bobby and Mindy by hiring Caroline. For heaven's sake, the only reason Martin hired that nanny was because he didn't trust Kendra with the children alone. He was afraid she might just burn the house down—whether an accident or not! Thank God we insisted on an ironclad prenuptial agreement before the marriage."

"If the agreement was so solid, why didn't Martin just get divorced?"

"He was trapped because of the children," Dr. Bell said wearily. "His primary concern was for Bobby and Mindy. He stayed for their sake. He had even conferred with a divorce lawyer to assess the likelihood that he would be able to retain full custody of the children if he were to leave Kendra. But you know how it is: he's the man, and she's the stay-at-home mom. There were no guarantees, and he wasn't willing to risk it, and neither were we. Martin was our only child, and so Bobby and Mindy are the last of the Bell bloodline. They must remain within the family."

"And you think Kendra was aware that your son had met with a divorce lawyer?"

"I'm certain she must have known," he said. "That's why she killed him."

"And you still don't think she's capable of raising your grandchildren?" Laurie asked.

"Capability is no longer the issue," Cynthia said adamantly. "First of all, she's never even with them. She's off working again, even though she gets more than enough money from the trust under the will to live quite comfortably for the rest of her life. We think she only keeps the nanny around so she doesn't blab whatever she knows to the police. And more importantly, how would you feel if the person who killed your son was raising your grandchildren? It's a matter of justice."

Laurie could tell that she would never get the Bells to see even a sliver of a possibility that Kendra might be innocent.

"What did you mean about Caroline blabbing to the police?" she asked. "You think she knows more than she lets on?" From all reports, Caroline called 911 immediately after finding Martin's body. She not only vouched for Kendra's presence inside of the home at the time of the shooting, she was also the one who told police that it had taken several minutes for her to rouse Kendra from sleep, even though she was telling her that her husband had just been murdered.

"I'm absolutely certain that Caroline was covering for Kendra," Cynthia insisted. "She's jittery and nervous whenever she's in our presence. I'm sure the guilt is eating away at her. She's holding something back. Even if Kendra is guilty, Caroline cares about our grandchildren deeply and is convinced we'd fire her if we ever got custody. We have tried to let her know that we would want her to stay on."

"We'll be speaking further to Caroline, I promise," Laurie assured them. "But before we go, I'm afraid we also need to raise two subjects that might make you uncomfortable. I'd rather be direct with you."

"Fair enough," Dr. Bell said, shifting in his seat. "What do you need to know?"

Laurie sensed she was still walking on eggshells as far as the Bells were concerned, so she decided to start with what she thought would be the less explosive of her two questions. "Your son's estate settled a few lawsuits that were pending against his medical practice. We were hoping to know the details."

"Absolutely not," Robert said, not even considering the request. "We only settled to protect Martin's good name. After he died, those money-grubbing lawyers had the nerve to up their financial demands, because he was no longer around to defend himself. It was sickening. We personally added money to the settlements offered by the insurance company to get the plaintiffs to sign nondisclosure agreements. We are bound by the contracts as well, so I'm afraid we can't give you information about them, even if we wanted to. Trust me, though: there's no reason to believe the lawsuits are at all relevant to our son's death."

Laurie would feel much better if she were in a position to make that call herself, but she couldn't see a basis for persuading them to violate a legal agreement. She'd have to find another way to get at the details of the lawsuits. She made a mental note to ask Alex about the nuances of nondisclosure agreements.

"Very well then," she said, conceding the point for now. "The other issue is one you alluded to earlier. Martin told you that Kendra had accused him of being unfaithful."

They both frowned at the memory. "It was absolutely untrue," Cynthia snapped. "Frankly, Kendra was lucky that the Longfellows didn't sue her for slander based on the allegation. He was right on the verge of being named to the vacant Senate seat."

"So you knew that Kendra was suspicious of your son's relationship with Leigh Ann Longfellow?" Ryan asked.

"Of course," Cynthia said. "You have to understand: we've known Leigh Ann since she was a little girl. Her mother, Eleanor, and I are still dear friends, part of the same bridge group that gets together for cards when schedules permit."

Robert interrupted. "Her father, Charles, was one of the wizards of Wall Street before his passing a few years ago. An excellent family by any measure."

"In any event," Cynthia continued, "when the friends would get together, the older kids would keep an eye out for the younger ones—that kind of thing. So to Martin, Leigh Ann was a kid-sister type. Then they were working together on the alumni board. They were several years apart, but both went to the same prep school," she explained. "So Martin immediately told us when Kendra first leveled the ridiculous accusation. He was afraid that Kendra's rantings would become public. He didn't want Leigh Ann or her parents to hear about the whispers from someone else. He was deeply embarrassed. We handled it the only way we knew how."

"Which was?" Laurie asked.

"I called Eleanor," Cynthia said. "I told her that Kendra was going through a difficult time. That she was . . . ill. And that it was manifesting itself in the form of a bizarre obsession with Leigh Ann, and that we were doing everything we could to contain the problem. But no matter how much Martin tried to reassure Kendra, her paranoia only seemed to grow. She even called us at one point, begging us to make him stop the affair—which of course was a figment of her imagination."

"But how can you be absolutely certain of that?" Ryan asked. "My apologies for raising the possibility, but I know I haven't told my mother and father everything I've done that I wasn't proud of."

Laurie realized that Ryan was in a better position to press this particular point than she was.

"We knew our son," Cynthia said firmly. "He was not the type of man to cheat. And we know Leigh Ann, as well as her husband, the senator. It's true love, and a true partnership. He's an extremely talented politician, but Leigh Ann is the one with all the contacts. She was the one who pushed him to run for the state assembly and then managed his campaign behind the scenes. And she's whip smart; if you ask me, she's the brains behind the whole operation. They each think the sun rises and sets on the other. The whole notion of her and Martin as a couple is crazy."

"And you don't even need to take our word for it," Robert added. "We happen to know that the police looked into Kendra's claims after Martin was killed, and we were assured there was nothing to it. There was no affair. Martin and Leigh Ann went to the same prep school and were organizing the auction dinner together; that's all there was to it. And to the extent Kendra was trying to insinuate that Leigh Ann's husband—now our senator, for God's sake—was involved in the murder, it makes no sense. Both he and Leigh Ann were in Washington, D.C., the night Martin was killed."

"It's still so embarrassing that they were dragged into this at all," Cynthia said, shaking her head. "Please don't let Kendra repeat this nonsense on air. We don't want to see our son dragged through the mud."

Cynthia brushed away a tear, and Laurie reminded herself that the reason these people had been pulling every string they could was out of love for the son they had lost. They were now trusting her to handle his case responsibly. "Thank you, both of you, for letting us look into your son's case. I promise I'll do my very best."

27

"Good job," Ryan whispered as they walked onto the elevator. "I think they understand now that you can't be pushed around."

"Thanks," she said. "You were a huge help. I mean it. Hey, do you have a way to find out more about those lawsuits against Martin? I don't want to check those off the list without doing some due diligence."

"Absolutely. Even with a nondisclosure agreement about the settlements, I should still be able to get the original complaints. We'll know the allegations, but won't know whether or not they could have been proven in court."

"I'll take anything you can get," she said. "Thanks."

"Unfortunately, I don't know how I can help you with the Longfellows. The Bells said that the police cleared them, but how are we going to nail that down? I can ask around my golf club. I'm sure we have mutual friends."

"Actually, I think I've got an in with the senator himself," Laurie said, crossing her fingers that she was right.

When she got back to her office, she found Jerry lingering over Grace's shoulder, looking at her computer screen. They both looked startled when they caught sight of her.

"Will the two of you stop acting as if I'm the boss from hell like Brett Young? Why the guilty looks every time I turn a corner?" she asked.

She noticed Grace clicking her mouse, closing windows on her screen.

"What are you two up to?"

"We're not hiding anything," Jerry said, his voice innocent. That only made her more suspicious.

"Sure you're not," she said drily.

As soon as she was at her desk, she called Alex.

"Hey there," he said. "I was just about to text you. Did you see Rhoda's email? She wants us to look at a place on Eighty-eighth and Lex after work. Can you do six o'clock?"

"Of course. At least she's looking in the right neighborhood. In the meantime, I've got a huge favor to ask. Can you get me a meeting with Senator Longfellow? I need to talk to him and his wife about the Bell murder case."

Alex had worked closely with the offices of both senators from New York during his judicial confirmation process. With Timmy around during last night's dinner, she hadn't had a chance to tell Alex about Kendra's suspicions regarding her husband and Senator Longfellow's wife.

"Oh boy." She could picture Alex wincing on the other end of the line. "I can't imagine that phone call will make him happy."

"I know. But the other option is to have his and his wife's name bandied about on TV. I assume he'll want a chance to comment."

"I remember that move," he said. When Alex was on the show, they often used it to get people to cooperate, by helping them to imagine the alternative that would occur in their absence. "Feels like old times."

"Except better. Hopefully you don't know all my moves already."

"Don't worry. You never cease to amaze me. Let me call Longfellow's office and see what I can do."

Laurie's next phone call was to Caroline Radcliffe. It wasn't even lunchtime. Kendra would be at work, the kids would be at school, and Laurie was eager to speak to Caroline alone.

Caroline picked up the phone after two rings. Laurie could hear the apprehension in her voice when Laurie explained that she wanted to speak to her about the night of Martin's murder.

"Everything I know was already printed in the papers," she said.

"I'm sure Kendra told you about the nature of our show. She agreed to participate. Although that doesn't bind you, she's aware that our expectation is that you'd also cooperate."

Laurie expected Caroline to say she wanted to speak to Kendra first, but instead she asked Laurie if she was willing to come to the house. "I still need to shop for groceries and need to pick up the kids at three."

"I can be there in half an hour," Laurie said.

28

Caroline Radcliffe answered the carriage house door wearing dark jeans and a loose, flowing yellow blouse. She still wore her graying brown hair in tight, old-fashioned curls, but the overall effect was more modern than the housedress she'd been wearing during Laurie's previous visit.

"To be completely frank," she said to Laurie once they were seated at the kitchen table with two iced teas, "Kendra already told me that you'd probably ask to speak with me. It's important to me that you know she told me to be completely forthcoming with you. I feel like you and Martin's parents pushed her to do this, but now that she has agreed, I think she hopes something good will finally come out of it. I can't imagine what it's like to lose the father of your children that way and have no answers for them."

I can, Laurie thought.

She listened carefully as Caroline narrated the events of the night Martin Bell was killed. The sound of the garage door opening, followed by three loud pops. Running outside to find Martin mortally wounded. Calling 911 and then struggling to rouse Kendra from what Caroline politely called a "nap."

"And where were the children during all of this?"

"I told them the sounds were firecrackers and had them go up to their rooms. But as soon as Kendra was awake and finally able to process what was happening, I took them over to one of the neighbors' apartments on the next block for an impromptu slumber party. They were thrilled at the surprise. I figured they deserved one more night of normalcy before their lives got turned upside down."

"You were the one to make that decision?" Laurie asked. "Not their mother?"

Caroline's mouth was set in a straight line, and her gaze shifted to the table. "As I mentioned to the police, she wasn't completely focused at the time."

"Was she frequently in that state?"

"She was going through a very hard time. I believe she told you that it was postpartum depression."

"I remember what Kendra told me. I'd like to know what you observed directly."

Caroline shrugged. "When Dr. Bell hired me, he told me that his wife 'wasn't well' since the children were born, especially after Mindy. I assumed it was depression. I've seen it before in new mothers."

Laurie could tell that Caroline was about to say more but then stopped herself. "But Kendra's case was different?" she prompted.

Caroline nodded slowly. "She almost seemed . . . zombie-like. She was often in what appeared to be a dreamlike state. It's possible it was simply a very severe case of postpartum, but . . ."

She didn't need to complete the rest of the sentence. It was clear that Caroline had her doubts.

"Martin's parents think it's possible you've been holding back information that might help them get custody of the children. They said you care very deeply for Bobby and Mindy—"

"Of course I do. Almost as if they were my own."

Laurie saw the desperation in Caroline's eyes and knew that the Bells' suspicions were correct. Caroline was holding something back. "I'm asking you this in complete confidence, Caroline: If you had to guess, are you a hundred percent certain that Kendra is innocent?"

The color drained from her face and she began to shake her head, tears beginning to form in her eyes.

"You have doubts." Laurie said aloud what she knew Caroline could not.

The nanny hesitated then nodded her head in agreement, wiping away the tears with the sleeve of her blouse.

Laurie placed a hand gently on Caroline's free hand. "If you have doubts, eventually they will, too," she said, holding Caroline's gaze. "They're little now, and you're trying to protect the normalcy of their lives—just as you did on that horrible night. But when they get older, they're going to ask the same questions the public has been wondering about for five years. They'll look at their mother and wonder if the woman who raised them killed the father they barely remember. That's no way to live, Caroline. Secrets have a way of spiraling over the course of years. It's better for the truth to come out now."

Caroline sniffed and pulled her hand away from Laurie's. "I saw the money," she said, her voice now low. "The withdrawals the police were asking about. I used to find wads of money—fifties, hundreds, maybe thousands of dollars in total—stashed in her sock drawer and behind her shoes in the closet. And then one day, it would all be gone."

The information was noteworthy, but Kendra had already admitted that she used to go on excessive shopping sprees. "Maybe wasting all that money was my quiet way of getting back at Martin for his affair," she had said.

Caroline's expression hardened. "Kendra has suffered enough," she burst out. "She's finally getting what amounts to a normal life. She has a job she likes. It's pretty clear that the doctor she works for is crazy about her."

"But," Laurie asked, her voice quiet, "Caroline, I know there is something you haven't told me. And if it somehow comes out while we're shooting, it will be a lot worse than if we know it now."

Caroline folded her arms, and her gaze drifted as if she were look-ing directly through Laurie into another dimension. "That night," she said dreamily, "I was shaking Kendra so hard I was worried I might hurt her. I was yelling over and over again that Martin had been mur-dered. And then suddenly the words seemed to get through to her. She stood up and—I'll never forget it—she said, 'Am I finally free of him?' She sounded at once both terrified and—dare I say it—happy. She was finally free."

It felt as if someone had lit a fire beneath Laurie's chair. No matter how bad the marriage, she couldn't imagine a woman being happy about the murder of her children's father.

Caroline was focused on Laurie again, trying to explain away the relevance of Kendra's hazy utterance. "I don't think she did it," Caro-line said. "I think it was just her initial reaction to the news. She was that miserable. It's not like it was a confession or anything."

"Fair enough," Laurie said. "It's important for us to know that. Is there anything else?"

She left the question in the air, sure that the nanny was still hold-ing something back.

Then Caroline added, "There's one more thing. The money hoarding I mentioned? She still does it. And if anything, the dollar amounts have gone up."

29

The maître d' at Daniel led them to a quiet table in the back of the restaurant. Alex immediately ordered martinis for both of them.

Laurie smiled. "If I had known that the reward for seeing yet another horrible apartment was an impromptu dinner at Daniel with you, I would have asked Rhoda to stack our schedule with dumpy apartments weeks ago."

It was Friday evening, and Timmy was spending the night at a friend's slumber party. The four-bedroom apartment Rhoda had just shown them had a lot of potential—the right square footage, layout, and neighborhood. It was a good thing they had looked at it after work, though, because they were halfway through the viewing when the couple upstairs came home. Through the air vents, Laurie, Alex, and Rhoda had heard Trina accusing Mark of lying, that he had not been at a conference in Denver, but in Atlantic City with his secretary. They were treated to Mark's multiple protests to the contrary and Trina's response: "It was my hard luck to have married you."

"With the way sound travels in this building, can you imagine the reaction we'd get if Timmy were to practice his trumpet?" Laurie had asked Rhoda.

She flicked away a lock of hair that had fallen on Alex's forehead. "Please tell me we'll never be like Mark and Trina," Laurie said.

"Don't worry. I can't stand Atlantic City!" Alex said, laughing.

Laurie pretended to ball up her napkin and throw it at him.

The waiter arrived with martinis and menus. Once they were alone again, they clinked glasses. "To never being those people," Laurie said firmly before taking a quick sip of her cocktail. "And now let's forget them."

"Amen," Alex agreed. "And of much greater importance, I heard back from Senator Longfellow's assistant. After I made clear that the show would go on with or without him, he said you can have half an hour with him and Leigh Ann this Tuesday afternoon. He insisted that you interview them together, until I pointed out that any journalist would be skeptical of information given under those conditions. He hemmed and hawed but finally agreed that they will speak to you separately."

"Good job, Your Honor."

"No cameras, though, and he wants you to come to their apartment so no one happens to spot you at his office and starts asking questions. He was adamant that you bring no more than one other member of your staff so it doesn't turn into a circus."

"I can live with that," Laurie said.

"He should only know that if you give Laurie Moran thirty minutes, she'll hook you in until you've spilled your guts."

"We'll see." She lowered her voice to be sure no one around them could overhear. "Even if Martin Bell and Leigh Ann were having an affair, it's hard to picture Senator Daniel Longfellow as a murderer. After all, if the affair had been discovered, he would have been the aggrieved partner in the marriage. If anything, voters would have sympathized with him. And he'd be one more available bachelor in Washington."

"Not to mention, they have no children," Alex noted. "He could simply have gotten divorced and moved on."

Laurie shook her head. "No motive, no warning signs of violence. I just don't see it. What I can see, however, is a jealous and resentful Kendra Bell hiring a hit man over drinks at a dive bar in the East

Village, then slipping him fifties and hundreds that had been tucked away in sock drawers. I can picture her paying him—even now—to remain silent, ever conscious of her in-laws' desire to put her in prison and take her children from her."

She tried to put away the image. She felt as though she'd been working nonstop all week, and she didn't want to think about Martin and Kendra Bell anymore tonight. She took two more quick sips from her glass while she pondered the menu options. Before she knew it, she was thinking aloud about something entirely different. "Maybe Timmy and I should just move in with you. You have plenty of room."

Alex set down his menu, clearly surprised by her comment. "Except it's too far from your father's apartment and from Timmy's school. And besides, it would feel like my space, not ours. You were the one who felt strongly about that."

"I also feel strongly that I'm already exhausted from looking at real estate. None of these places could ever feel like home."

"We'll know the right spot when we see it," he said.

"And we still need to set a date and book a space and make all the arrangements for the wedding. Alex, I'm worried that I might have been selfish when I've said I prefer a small wedding. I'm not sure I ever asked what you want. Would you like a big wedding?"

"Good God no."

"What do you really want?"

"I want the shortest distance between two points."

"What's that supposed to mean?"

"I want whichever plan has us married and living under the same roof the fastest. That will make me happy."

He paused then added, "Laurie, I've been giving this a lot of thought and I know what I want. A quiet church ceremony with our families and close friends in attendance, followed by a festive dinner. Let's target mid to late August. The courts are in recess. It will give you time to adjust your work schedule. If we can work it out, a honeymoon right after."

Laurie smiled. "Wow! You have given this a lot of thought!"

Returning her smile, Alex said, "I've told you what I want. How does that sound to you?"

"That sounds absolutely perfect." And it would be perfect. She knew it. For so long she had been sure that after Greg there would be no one. That had been true until she met Alex nearly two years ago. Now in a mere five months she would marry her second and last great love.

30

L aurie felt underdressed as she emerged from the Fisher Blake elevator wearing jeans and an NYPD T-shirt, but it was Sunday afternoon. Leo had picked up Timmy and taken him to Alex's apartment to watch the Yankees–Red Sox game. She smiled at the thought of the three *men* in her life spending family time together. This freed her up for an unexpected work session.

Ryan was waiting for her at her office door with a manila folder. "I hope I'm not ruining your whole day," he said. "In retrospect, it could have waited until tomorrow."

Ryan had called her cell thirty minutes earlier, excited about something he had discovered while looking into the malpractice claims that had been filed against Martin Bell. Laurie was often annoyed by Ryan's tendency to insist that she drop everything to listen to whatever was on his mind, but this time was different. She had specifically asked him to get a better grasp on the lawsuits that were pending at the time of Martin's death, and she had never known Ryan to work on a weekend.

She motioned for him to sit down. Ryan interpreted the gesture as an invitation for him to plop into her favorite armchair.

"There were three lawsuits," Ryan began. "All claimed that Martin overprescribed pain medication to patients who died. Not a great narrative considering his reputation as a miracle worker. I always suspected that book was a little too good to be true."

Laurie recalled the headline in the *New York Times* the morning after Martin's death: THE DOCTOR WHO CURED PAIN IS KILLED. The article went on to solidify his legacy as the man who revolutionized pain management, trading prescription drugs and surgical intervention for more holistic approaches like meditation and stress reduction.

When Martin published his best-selling book, *The New Pain Doctrine*, his career began to sprint. He left NYU's Neurology Department, started his own practice, and committed himself to advocating for homeopathic remedies, physical therapy, and psychological approaches to physical pain. He was a frequent guest on television talk shows, freely condemning the culture of scalpel-happy surgeons and prescription-pushing physicians. If those lawsuits had become public, he could have gone from celebrity guru to sham doctor in the length of a single news cycle.

Laurie immediately wondered if there might be a connection between the lawsuits and his murder.

"I asked one of my old buddies to look into the plaintiffs to see if any of them had criminal histories." Ryan flipped through the pages inside one of the folders and pulled out a stapled packet. Laurie, surprised by Ryan's initiative, accepted the papers he set in front of her. "One woman, Allison Taylor, claims she got addicted to OxyContin after seeing Dr. Bell to manage bone cancer pain. Turns out she had a serious record of traffic violations."

"Not much of a connection between being a bad driver and being a murderer," Laurie reminded him as she leaned back in her chair, folding her arms across her chest.

"True, which is why I'm more interested in another guy, George Naughten. His sixty-seven-year-old mother had chronic pain after a fender bender on the Long Island Expressway. She was rear-ended by a texting teenager. I thought at first maybe it was that Allison Taylor lady." Ryan chuckled to himself.

Laurie nodded, hoping to move the story along.

"So Mom is seeing doctor after doctor with no relief," Ryan continued, diving into story mode. "After two years, she hears about Dr. Bell on *Good Morning America*, and decides she has to see him. He didn't accept Medicaid, so she had to pay out of pocket to make it happen. She even took out a line of credit on her house to pay for it. Nothing worked at first, but Bell eventually came up with a drug cocktail that kept her pain free. According to the lawsuit, the drugs turned her into a zombie, but at least she wasn't in physical agony. Then George finds Mom unresponsive. The medical examiner says it was an overdose. George swore that, in addition to the drugs Bell prescribed through the pharmacy, he was also dispensing pills directly to her in the office."

Laurie stretched in her chair as she mulled over the lawsuit's allegations. "And you said George has a criminal record of some kind?" Laurie asked.

"Just wait," Ryan said, putting up a hand. He was milking the story's unfolding. "That's where things really get interesting. A year before Dr. Bell was murdered, George had a restraining order issued against him by a twenty-year-old kid named Connor Bigsby, which he violated." He pointed to the police report he had laid out in front of her.

Laurie did the quick math in her head. "I was picturing George as older, given his mother's age."

"Thirty-five at the time, forty-one today. So, yes, I was a little curious about what brought him into contact with a twenty-year-old. I requested the transcripts from his trial for violating the criminal court order." Ryan excitedly pushed a new set of papers in front of her. "Want to take a guess at the connection?" he asked.

Laurie smiled, impressed. She rarely saw Ryan's strengths, but now it was clear that he would have been talented in the courtroom. "Was Connor Bigsby the driver of the other car involved in his mother's accident?"

Ryan raised a knowing eyebrow. "Ah, good theory, right? But it's twistier than that. The driver of the car was actually a young woman who moved to Texas to start college shortly after the accident. Connor Bigsby was the friend who was texting her while she was behind the wheel."

"That's crazy," Laurie said, staring into the transcripts from George's trial. "That was enough for George to blame him for his mother's accident? Seems like he missed a step in the logic there."

Ryan pointed to a section of text that he had highlighted. "Check this out. The protective order was issued after George showed up repeatedly at Connor's job at a sporting goods store. He would berate him, call him reprehensible, say he should be in jail for assault—it was full-fledged harassment. And then one day, George waited in his car outside the store and sped past Connor, apparently just missing him. Connor said George would have run him over if he hadn't leapt out of the way. Hence the court order."

"Why wouldn't he have been charged with attempted murder?" Laurie asked.

"The DA probably didn't think they could prove he had intent to hurt the kid, let alone kill him. But they used all the other harassment as evidence to get a court order requiring him to stay at least a hundred feet away from the kid. He couldn't even manage to do that. Connor's mother caught him parked across the street, watching their house. She called the cops and he was nabbed for violating the court order. But get this." Ryan flipped to another page of the transcript, this one marked with a yellow Post-it. "George called a psychiatrist in his defense. The shrink testified that George goes through obsessive phases. Apparently it's par for the course for stalkers to transfer their obsession onto others. The judge sentenced him to lengthy probation and warned him that if he violated, he would go to prison."

"I just can't believe he connected his mother's injury to a kid sitting at home texting his friend," Laurie said, thinking aloud. "If he's willing to make that kind of leap, I can only imagine how he felt about the doctor who prescribed his mother the pills she OD'd on."

"We should talk to him, right?"

Usually Laurie hated it when Ryan proposed that "we" do something, but he had earned the right to be involved in the research this time. "You want to set it up?" she asked.

"I'm on it," Ryan said enthusiastically. "But wait, there's one more thing I have to tell you. As of four years before Martin's murder, George Naughten was the registered owner of a Smith and Wesson nine-millimeter pistol, the kind used to kill Dr. Bell."

"Wow. I wonder if we can ask him to make the gun available. We could get the police to test the ballistics."

Ryan rose from the armchair. "That's extremely unlikely. The DA's office insisted he turn the gun over as part of his sentence for violating the protective order, but his lawyer came to court claiming it was stolen in a burglary two months earlier. So instead of handing over the gun, they presented a police report that said it was stolen along with some of his mother's jewelry. There's no way to be sure though. For all we know, George made up the fact that the gun was stolen so he'd be free to use it later."

Laurie thanked Ryan for all the hard work as he left her office. Once she was alone, she began reading the pages of police reports and trial transcripts, paying extra attention to the passages Ryan had marked.

Had the police been so focused on Kendra that they had failed to consider George?

Her thoughts drifted back to the fact that Kendra Bell had been meeting a mystery man at the Beehive bar in the days leading up to her husband's murder. She flipped through the pages Ryan had given her, searching for a booking photo, but found none. Was it possible she had conspired with a man who had his own grievances against her husband?

She didn't know if George Naughten was a murderer, the Beehive man, or just a creep with some psychological hang-ups, but she knew she had a new name to add to their list of potential suspects.

She got up from her desk, walked to the whiteboard at the other end of her office, and picked up a red dry-erase marker. By the time she was done, the entire board was filled with ink, documenting the possible links between all the parties. Kendra. The unidentified stranger she met at a dive bar. Her dermatologist boss who might still be carrying a torch. The disgruntled son of a deceased patient. Even the junior senator from New York, whom Laurie was scheduled to interview the following afternoon.

Her cell phone pinged. There was a text from Ryan. *George will meet with us. I'm on phone with him now. Tomorrow at 10 work for you?*

It would be a busy day, but she could handle it. She confirmed with a yes and added the appointment to her calendar.

I still have so much to do, she thought, her attention returning to the whiteboard. *But the killer's right here, on this board. I feel it. And whoever you are, I'm going to find you.*

31

The following morning, Laurie and Ryan parked down the block from George Naughten's house in Rosedale, Queens. He lived in a tan townhouse on a block lined with other tan townhouses. As they crossed the street, a low-flying plane roared above them on its approach to neighboring JFK. Ryan opened the rusty, wrought iron gate for Laurie. Together, they stood under the faded gray awning and knocked on a wooden door that needed a fresh coat of paint.

Naughten undid two locks and a slide chain and cracked the door just wide enough to get a look at his visitors. "You're the TV detectives?" he asked, squinting, his voice an octave higher than Laurie expected.

"Laurie Moran," Laurie said, extending her hand. "Thank you for agreeing to speak with us."

Naughten opened the door fully. "Come in, come in." He ushered them past the threshold and into a dark living room. The ceilings were low, and heavy Marie Antoinette–style curtains were drawn. The red UV light from a reptile tank made the room feel like a brothel, and Laurie noticed that inside the tank, a bearded dragon was toying with a cricket that was probably not long for this world. Above the tank the wall was covered by framed photos. Every picture was of George at different ages with his mother.

"Please, make yourselves at home," Naughten said as he sat in a worn La-Z-Boy in the center of the room. He swiveled it away from the box-style TV set on the floor and faced two wicker rocking chairs in the corner. Whatever money he had gotten from the lawsuit against Martin Bell had probably gone to paying off bills and subsidizing living expenses, not remodeling.

Once seated, Laurie got a proper look at George Naughten. He was wearing crimson sweatpants a few sizes too small and a baggy brown T-shirt a few sizes too big. He looked older than forty-one, his hairline creeping away from a forehead that already bore deep wrinkles.

She recalled the bartender's description of Kendra's mystery friend from the Beehive bar. Rough-looking with a shaved head and mean eyes. That was definitely not the sad-looking man sitting across from her.

"We appreciate you inviting us into your home, Mr. Naughten," Ryan said.

"Please call me George. My mama used to call me Georgie boy. My father left us when I was a baby. She said it was just the two of us against the world. I know the place isn't much, but it has everything I need. There's the Green Acres Mall just over there. And the Walmart. Kohl's. And it's nice to wake up every morning knowing that Mom was happy here once."

As far as Laurie could tell from her research, George had lived with his mother from the day he was born until the day she died. Laurie began to feel pity settling in her stomach, but she knew she couldn't let it overshadow the investigation. She pushed through it. "George, we'd like to know more about your relationship with Connor Bigsby."

"Oh, that whole thing was a misunderstanding," he said, shaking his head. "I would never have hurt the kid. I just wanted him to know how dangerous the texting was."

"But he wasn't even driving the car that hit your mother," Ryan said.

"But he knew. The police read the texts. The girl who was driving had told him she was stuck in traffic. He knew, but he distracted her anyway!"

Ryan frowned, but let it drop. They weren't there to unpack the logic behind George Naughten's past offenses. "What about Dr. Martin Bell? What was your contact with the late doctor? We know you were suing him when he was murdered."

"That I can't discuss. Sorry. I signed a nondisclosure agreement about the lawsuit."

Ryan leaned forward in his rocking chair, assuming a prosecutor's attack. "The NDA is in regard to the wrongful death lawsuit you filed. It doesn't cover your personal contact with Dr. Bell."

George dug his toes into the shag carpet, and Laurie thought she saw a flicker of fear in his deep-set brown eyes.

"We know what your own psychiatrist said about your obsessive tendencies," Ryan said. "If you were willing to go after a kid barely involved in your mom's accident, I bet you didn't hesitate when it came to the doctor you blame for her death."

"I swear I only had direct contact with Dr. Bell that one time. And he didn't even file a police report. The cop told me to stay away, and after the problems I'd had with that kid, I listened. I never went back to his office again."

Laurie and Ryan exchanged a quick glance. Apparently there had been some kind of run-in with the police at Dr. Bell's office, and George had assumed they already knew about it.

They took the new information in stride. "Why do you suppose he even called the police in the first place, George, unless he was frightened of you?" Ryan asked.

"I didn't mean to scare him, and I swear, I never meant to scare that kid either. I'm not such a scary guy," he said, shrugging and looking down at his own soft frame. "I just wanted him to know the harm he was doing, just like I wanted that Connor Bigsby kid to know he shouldn't text a friend who's behind the wheel. I needed Martin Bell to know that he wasn't saving people. He wasn't a miracle worker. His drugs took the life out of Ma. I called him and called him, but he never picked up or called me back. So I showed up in person. What other choice did I have?"

George stared into the lizard tank as he spoke. "I told the lady at the front desk I wouldn't be leaving until he came out to talk to me, man-to-man. I was never going to hurt him, and I told that to the police when they came. They said Dr. Bell would file charges for trespassing if I came back, so I never did."

Ryan tried a new angle. "What about the gun, George? A Smith and Wesson nine-millimeter pistol was registered under your name. The same model used to kill Dr. Bell outside his home that night."

"I bought that thing years ago for Ma's safety. There were some break-ins in the neighborhood and I wanted to be prepared. I had fun with it at first, going to the range to practice. But after Ma's accident, I sort of forgot about it. I didn't have time anymore, seeing as I was looking after her so much, so it sat in a closet. Sort of ironic it got stolen. Serves me right for trying to be such a tough guy. Not in my nature."

"Did you buy another one?" Laurie asked. "Didn't the burglary confirm your fears about the need for protection?"

"Nah. I had the thing to protect Ma. There's nothing of value here anymore."

Laurie asked him the name of the range he used to frequent, and scribbled it down in her notebook. "And after Dr. Bell was murdered, did the police interview you?"

George shook his head. "I kind of expected them to, but that mis-understanding in his office was more than a month before his mur-der, and there was no police report. So . . ."

He didn't finish the thought, but Laurie knew he meant that it had fallen through the cracks. Whatever police officer responded to a quick call about a man who wouldn't leave a doctor's office had probably never connected the dots to Dr. Bell's murder over a month later. And Laurie was certain that the police hadn't unearthed the details of George's prior interactions with law enforcement, let alone the fact of his supposedly stolen gun. After all, they had been too busy investigating Kendra.

"And the night of Dr. Bell's death," Ryan started, "where were you that evening?"

"I was here," George said, motioning to the space around him. "Alone."

The three of them sat quietly for a moment. The windows rattled as another plane flew overhead. "Will you go on camera to clear your name?" Ryan asked.

George winced. "I'd like to speak with my psychiatrist first."

"Well, make sure he knows this reinvestigation isn't going away," Ryan said. He looked to Laurie to see if she had more to ask, but Laurie thanked George for his time and stood to leave.

As they stepped into the bright sunlight and made their way back to the car, Laurie turned to Ryan. "What's your gut?" she asked.

"I wouldn't fix him up with my sister, but so far I'm not feeling him as a murderer."

She nodded, wishing that gut instincts were enough for her to scratch a suspect's name from her board. Personally she wasn't sure. It was obvious that George Naughten was obsessed in his belief that Dr. Martin Bell had caused his mother's death.

"Thanks for all your good work," she said. "You were great in there."

"Thank you, Laurie. That means a lot coming from you. I know I wasn't exactly a team player straight out of the gate."

"Don't take this the wrong way, but what's changed?"

Ryan hesitated, and Laurie noticed his brow furrow. "A woman I was seeing dumped me."

"Oh, I'm so sorry to hear—"

He shook his head. "It was never serious. But, man, she really called me out when she broke it off. She said I was selfish—and entitled. Said I was born on third base and go through life thinking I hit a triple." He shrugged sadly, then opened the back door of the car for Laurie, beating the driver to the task.

Once he was settled into the seat next to her, he said, "Anyway, I realized she might just have a point. So consider me humbled."

Laurie wasn't sure how to respond to this unprecedented moment of vulnerability from Ryan, so she opted for humor. "Humbled, perhaps, but not quite humble."

"Never," he said, breaking out into a broad grin. "Ryan Nichols doesn't do humble."

32

Laurie and her assistant producer, Jerry, arrived at the Longfellows' Upper West Side apartment on West End Avenue at 3:30 on the dot, precisely as scheduled.

"These ceilings!" Jerry marveled as the elevators opened on the nineteenth floor. "They must be thirteen feet high. And I love the finishes. So classically art deco."

"Maybe you should be my Realtor," Laurie quipped. She had decided that she needed to bring someone else with her in case she learned important information from the Longfellows and needed a witness to back up her version of events. As much as she and Ryan had been getting along lately, she thought that bringing the show's host and a former prosecutor might set the wrong tone. After all, Alex had asked the senator a personal favor by arranging the meeting. Unlike Ryan, Jerry was impossible not to like.

The chime of the Longfellows' doorbell was immediately followed by a crescendo of high-pitched dog yips. "Ike! Lincoln!" A woman on the other side of the door was making shushing sounds. The barks decreased in volume and eventually settled into the whining noise Laurie associated with attempts to get treats. "How many times do I have to tell you? Be nice when people come to visit."

As the door opened, two small dogs greeted them, running in circles around them and smelling their shoes. The woman following them extended her hand and said, "Hello, I'm Leigh Ann Longfellow." She was wearing a classic navy sheath dress and nude pumps. She wore her dark brown hair in a neat, shoulder-length bob, much like Laurie's own style. Her alabaster skin was as creamy as milk. "Sorry about these two scoundrels. You'd never know they're actually quite well trained. Unfortunately, they seem to decide for themselves when to turn it on and off. Right now, I think they're excited to have Mommy and Daddy home so early in the afternoon."

"No problem," Laurie said, returning the introduction. "I love dogs. They're—Pomeranians?"

"So close. Papillons. They're eight years old, but they still act like little puppies when they meet someone new."

Jerry was already crouched on the floor, allowing the dogs to crawl up on him and lick his face. He grinned upward between their kisses. "Hi, I'm Jerry," he said with a quick wave. "Laurie's production assistant."

His official title was assistant producer, but Laurie knew he was trying to keep the tone friendly and informal.

Leigh Ann led them into a spacious living room with tasteful, modern furnishings layered in neutral tones. The only hint at clutter was a large dog bed near the fireplace with an array of stuffed toys around it. From the looks of a decapitated fleece lamb surrounded by white cotton stuffing, Ike and Lincoln had recently finished a fierce round of tug-of-war.

Laurie and Jerry were just about to sit when Senator Longfellow walked into the room. He was as striking as he appeared in his campaign ads and press conferences.

Laurie was familiar with the background that had catapulted Daniel Longfellow to several national short lists of "young politicians to watch." The only son of a doorman and a housekeeper, he had attended West Point and earned a Bronze Star with Valor for his service in Afghanistan after 9/11. Laurie remembered the campaign video highlighting his personal biography. He said he had returned to New York from the military determined to help the city he loved to be a safe and prosperous place for all.

He was tall, probably around six-foot-three, with dark blond hair and bright blue eyes. When he stood next to Leigh Ann and placed an arm around her, it seemed completely natural.

"I see you met the kids already," he told Laurie and Jerry, gesturing at the two dogs panting at his feet.

"They made sure of it, Senator Longfellow," Laurie said, then introduced herself.

"Ike and Lincoln. I call them the Papillon Presidents. And, please, call me Dan. Sorry, but the majority leader pushed back a conference call. Don't tell anyone, but I just hit mute to come out and say hi. Why don't you talk to Leigh Ann first and I'll be right around the corner."

"Sounds good," Laurie agreed, watching as he gave his wife a quick kiss on the lips before leaving the room. Laurie tried not to stare, but she could feel the energy between Dan and Leigh Ann. She remembered what Cynthia Bell had said about the two of them: they each think the sun rises and sets on the other.

Laurie hadn't asked a single question yet, but she was already certain of one thing: this was a couple that loved each other dearly.

33

L eigh Ann gestured for Laurie and Jerry to sit, and then positioned herself across from them on a matching light gray sofa. She seemed unfazed as the two Papillons leapt up and sat on either side of her.

"I should start by congratulating you, Laurie. Dan told me that in addition to your own successful career, you're engaged to our newest federal judge. That's very exciting. Quite the power couple."

Laurie wasn't sure how to respond. It had been a long time since she'd thought of herself as half of a couple at all, let alone a so-called power couple. "Thanks," she said. "There's still so much to do."

"Well, not that you asked, but my advice is to just enjoy it. Let it be about the two of you instead of all the wedding plans and whatnot. My parents talked Dan and me into the whole hullabaloo at the Central Park Boathouse. I had to have my cousin follow Dan around the whole night reminding him who everyone was."

Laurie smiled to herself. She and Alex still hadn't told anyone else that they were planning a late summer wedding, precisely because they wanted a little more time before sharing the details.

"Anyway," Leigh Ann said, "you're not here for wedding consulting. Dan told me you're reinvestigating Martin's case." Her voice took a more somber tone. "I still can't believe someone would do that to him."

"How did you hear about his death?" Laurie asked.

"My mom called me. The police had gone to the Bells' apartment to break the news to them in person. As it happened, my parents were with the Bells at the apartment having cocktails before going out to dinner with them. You can only imagine the reaction when they were told about the tragedy."

"Cynthia said you'd known Martin for a long time."

She nodded sadly. "Since I was a kid. He was six years older than I, so we weren't exactly friends. But our parents were close, so we'd be at the kids' table together, or the older kids would play hide-and-seek with the young ones. That sort of thing. And then when I joined the alumni board at the Hayden School, it turned out he was on it, too."

"Did you know Kendra?"

"Not at all. Dan and I were invited to the wedding, but it conflicted with a campaign event Dan had already scheduled."

"He was already in the state assembly by then?" Laurie asked.

Leigh Ann looked up at the ceiling, doing the math. "Running for his second term, so that must have been . . . a little more than ten years ago? Mom and Dad went, and they said Kendra seemed nice, but they didn't really get to spend any time with her. And then Mom mentioned a few times over the years that Cynthia thought Martin had made a terrible mistake, but, as I said, I didn't know Kendra at all, and only reconnected with Martin through the alumni board."

"Sorry to be blunt, but I'm sure you know why we wanted to speak with you. Kendra was convinced there was more to your relationship."

She laughed and shook her head. "I'm sorry to laugh. I feel horrible for her, but it really is absurd. We'd see each other once a month at best, in a conference room with twenty-two other alumni. Then we wound up serving as co-chairs of the auction committee, which is a ton of work between planning the event, drumming up attendance, and locking down donations. These days, I'd never have the time for something like that, but back then, Dan was in Albany more often than not"—her face made it clear that she was not a fan of the state capital—"and I wanted to continue to have a purpose in the city. So when the previous chair of the auction couldn't handle it that year, I figured, *What the heck. I'll do it as long as I have someone to help me.* And Martin was practically a celebrity by then, and we'd known each other since we were kids, so I twisted his arm until he relented. The only thing I can think of is that Kendra saw how many phone calls we had between us and jumped to conclusions. But I promise you: the sexiest thing Martin Bell and I ever talked about was where to place the ice sculpture."

"But the police interviewed you when Martin died?"

"Yes. I was absolutely flabbergasted. My mother told me later that Martin's parents had warned her that Kendra had this crazy notion in her head, but no one had ever mentioned it to me while Martin was still alive. At first when they contacted me, the police simply told me that my number turned up frequently in Martin's call records, so of course I explained the work we'd been doing on the auction. But then they told me that Kendra believed I was having an affair with Martin, and they wanted to know where Danny had been the night of the murder, in case he shared the same suspicions as Kendra."

"And?" Laurie asked.

"He was in D.C. With me, in fact. The Senate seat had just become vacant, and we knew the governor was on the verge of naming Danny to the empty seat. In preparation, Danny drove down to D.C. to meet with several party leaders in the capital. I didn't hold his hand through the meetings, of course, but I decided to take the trip down with him for moral support. And, well, to be honest, I much prefer accompanying him to D.C. than Albany. We stayed overnight so he could have breakfast in the morning with the Senate majority leader. We had just gotten back to the city when my mother called with the terrible news about Martin's death."

If Leigh Ann was telling the truth, it would have been easy for the police to confirm Dan's alibi for the night of the murder. Once again,

Laurie wished that she could convince the police department to be more open with her about their investigation.

"Having spoken to Kendra," Laurie said, "I think part of the reason she suspected Martin of having an affair was that they were having serious problems within their own marriage. They were still living together, but it sounds almost as if they were estranged within the same home. I hate to be so personal, but how was the state of your marriage around that time?"

Leigh Ann smiled, but Laurie could tell that her patience was being tested. "You're right. That is quite personal. What can I say? Danny and I are one of those lucky couples that found each other early on and decided to build a life together. I was finishing law school at Columbia, and he was completing his master's degree in International and Public Affairs after leaving the military as a junior officer. I dropped my international law book in the line at Starbucks while I was trying to get my wallet out of my backpack. He picked it up for me, and we just started talking about foreign policy and then everything else under the sun. We had an immediate bond. We must have sat in that coffee shop for three hours. I went home that night and told my roommate that I had just met the man I was going to marry. When he proposed, he presented the engagement ring inside the paper coffee cup he had kept from that night. He said he immediately knew, too, that we were going to end up together."

Effortless, Laurie thought—the way it was supposed to be.

"With your husband's Senate appointment so imminent, you must have been concerned about your names surfacing in the media coverage of Martin's murder. It was the top of the local crime news for a couple of weeks."

"Honestly, it never dawned on me to worry about us. I was just rattled that someone I knew was murdered. And I was sorry to hear that Kendra, on top of losing her husband and being left with two young children, had any doubts about my connection to Martin. But it was obviously only in her imagination. Besides, by the time Martin was killed, the governor had already told Dan that the Senate seat was his. The trip to D.C. was pro forma—to kiss the rings and whatnot. In fact, if I recall correctly, the governor had made the announcement by the time the police detective interviewed us."

Laurie had Googled the Longfellows to prepare for this interview. The outgoing senator had accepted a cabinet position ten days before Martin Bell was killed, and the governor appointed Longfellow—a forty-year-old, fourth-term assemblyman and war hero—to the vacant spot exactly two weeks after the senator announced his decision. If Leigh Ann's recollection was correct, the police had taken at least five days to get around to interviewing the Longfellows. Laurie was raised by a cop. She knew exactly what that kind of delay meant: the police had not viewed the Longfellows as an investigative priority. It was yet another sign that the police had not found Kendra's accusations credible.

"Did Martin ever talk to you about Kendra or the state of their marriage?"

"Not really."

Laurie smiled. "*Not really* isn't the same as *no*."

"Look, I've got to be honest—I'm biased. My mother has told me that Cynthia and Robert feel quite strongly that Kendra was responsible for Martin's death, but I have no firsthand knowledge of that."

"But Martin did say something to you about Kendra?"

She nodded. "Not in a personal way. We weren't close enough for that. But when we were initially scouting out potential venues for the auction, he couldn't make the time I suggested because he had a meeting with a lawyer. I didn't think anything of it and started proposing other dates, but he kept going. He let out kind of a sarcastic laugh"—she mimicked the sound—"and said, 'Hey, tell me if you and Dan know any really good divorce lawyers. Apparently, I'm going to need a shark if I have any hope of keeping my children.' Honestly, it was more than a bit awkward. I told him I was sorry to hear that and went on with finding another date on the calendar."

It was yet another indication that Martin had been determined to divorce Kendra if only he could maintain custody of Bobby and Mindy.

Laurie did not have anything else to ask Leigh Ann, and the senator hadn't returned yet from his conference call. "So did the auction go forward without Martin?" she asked, making small talk.

Leigh Ann smiled, appreciative of the question. "We sent out the invitations in his honor, in fact. His graduating class had a hundred-percent donation rate for the first time ever. Robert and Cynthia attended and even brought Bobby and Mindy. I thought all of us were going to break down in tears, those poor children. What hope do they have for a normal childhood after losing their father to such a ghastly crime?"

Plenty of hope, Laurie wanted to say. *Maybe they will be strong and resilient and full of love and light like my amazing Timothy.*

Leigh Ann looked up at the sound of her husband entering the room, and Ike and Lincoln immediately jumped down from the sofa to welcome the new arrival.

"Wow," Jerry remarked. "They may be the Papillon Presidents, but they surely are excited to greet the senator from New York."

"They do love their daddy, don't they?" Leigh Ann cooed in baby talk as Dan bent over to give the dogs a few scratches behind their ears.

"You have to forgive us," the senator said. "You may have noticed we dote on these little fellas. If it hadn't finally warmed up over the last few days, you would have had the pleasure of seeing them in their turtleneck sweaters. Before too long, they'll be in Gucci booties and designer sunglasses."

"Stop it," Leigh Ann teased. "They love their little outfits, don't you, sweeties? You know how happy they make your mommy."

Daniel and Leigh Ann had had a blitz of positive media coverage when he was first named to the vacant Senate seat. He may have been the darling of the New York State Assembly, but he was suddenly a national name after his elevation to the United States Senate. Political reporters loved the entire package of his personal background, centrist policy views, and picture-perfect marriage to a dynamic and intelligent commercial litigator. If there was any misstep during the rollout of his introduction to a national audience, it had belonged to Leigh Ann.

One of the cohosts of a daytime talk show, Dawn Harper, had asked Leigh Ann whether the couple ever planned to have children. Another one of the cohosts reprimanded Dawn for the question, and Dawn replied, "What? I'm just asking. Dan's forty. She's thirty-six. How about it, Leigh Ann? Is the biological clock ticking?"

Some members of the live audience groaned at the intrusiveness of the question, but it was Leigh Ann's response that drew the true fire. "With all due respect, I graduated at the top of my class from Columbia Law School, am about to make partner at one of the largest law firms in the country, and am an equal partner to my husband in every way. The last thing I need to make me feel whole as a woman is a child."

While some defended Leigh Ann's comment as a rebuttal to Dawn's assumption that all women were desperate for children by their mid thirties, many interpreted it as an attack against stay-at-home mothers. After a bruising twenty-four-hour news cycle, Dan and Leigh Ann made clear in a joint interview that they admired and respected all hardworking parents—both mothers and fathers, working inside or outside the home—but that they had made a personal decision not to have children. Laurie had been impressed at the time with their frankness about an intensely intimate topic. The pictures they had brought of their two "spoiled babies," Ike and Lincoln, had helped soften Leigh Ann's image.

Laurie could see now that they weren't kidding when they said they treated their pets like their children.

"I expect you're ready for me?" Senator Longfellow asked, rubbing his palms together.

Leigh Ann rose from the sofa and gave him a kiss on the lips before he took her place. "Make sure they read you your Miranda rights," she called out as she walked away. "You've got a lawyer in the next room if you think you're about to confess to anything, Senator."

34

Laurie began by thanking the senator once again for agreeing to speak with them.

"It was my pleasure. I gained a great respect for your fiancé during the confirmation process. He was honorable and unflappable, even when some of my more partisan Senate colleagues were threatening to raise hay about his defense of a certain swindler."

Laurie wondered if the barely veiled reference to the Carl Newman case was intended as a reminder that Longfellow had been instrumental in making certain that Alex was confirmed to the federal bench. She was determined not to let that sway her opinion.

"I understand that the police interviewed you as part of the original investigation," she said.

The light, joking tone he had shared with his wife moments earlier was immediately replaced by a somber demeanor. She could picture him as a leader in the military. "It was surreal," he said. "I never actually met Martin, but I used to joke with Leigh Ann that he was replacing me as her city husband while I was at the capital. Then we had just gotten back from D.C., suddenly on the verge of me getting appointed to the U.S. Senate, and she gets the phone call about his murder. It was all over the news the next day. I guarantee that if you look at the local papers from that week, two of the biggest stories were his murder and my Senate appointment. The phones in my Senate office were barely hooked up before I got a message that the NYPD wanted to speak to me and Leigh Ann. At first, I thought it might be about grant funding or something official, but then they said it was about Martin."

"At the time, what was your understanding of the reason your name would have come up in their investigation?"

"Of course we assumed it was because of the work Leigh Ann had been doing with him for the Hayden School. A routine check of everyone in his phone records and whatnot. They met us here and then asked to speak to Leigh Ann alone, which didn't strike me as unusual. In fact, your fiancé insisted on the same today," he said. His smile was polite rather than warm.

Laurie nodded, indicating for him to continue.

"Then they spoke with me separately and asked if I could tell them where I was the night he was murdered. I almost started laughing, thinking they were hazing the new senator or something. But then I realized they were serious. I told them they could find photographs in the *New York Times* and *Washington Post* of me in D.C. that day. I gave them the name of the hotel where we stayed overnight and even offered to put them in touch with the Senate majority leader if they needed to confirm that I was still there for breakfast the next day. They looked quite chagrined, to be honest. Much respect for the NYPD, but it became immediately obvious they should have realized on their own that we weren't even in the city that day. With that out of the way, I asked them why in the world they were even inquiring. That's when they told me that Kendra believed that Martin and Leigh Ann were— Well, I can't even say it, but surely you know the allegation."

"And what was your reaction, Senator?"

"I was stupefied! It was . . . nonsense. And by then the news reports had made it pretty clear who the number one suspect was. Innocent until proven guilty, of course, but I've always felt that the strongest sign of Kendra's guilt was her baseless attempt to try to lay the blame at my door." There was a momentary hint of anger in his voice, but he quickly gained control over it. "I wanted to make it a hundred percent certain that the police had absolutely no doubts about my involvement. I sent them my hotel receipt, including proof of overnight parking, my E-ZPass toll records, and the articles about my visit to D.C. And I had read the insinuations in the media that Kendra might have been hoarding large cash withdrawals to pay someone to carry out the attack on her behalf. To prevent anyone from saying the same about me, I even, without being asked, gave the police my bank records."

"That does seem like full disclosure."

"I had nothing to hide then or now," he said firmly. "We have this beautiful apartment thanks to my brilliant and hardworking wife, but I insist on covering my half on a politician's salary. Trust me, there's no room left for a hit man slush fund. I figured the quicker they could check me off their list, the more time they'd have to find the real killer."

"I imagine you had other considerations in addition to helping the police. Despite the massive media interest in the case, it would appear that no outlet ever reported that the police interviewed you and your wife as part of the investigation."

"Can you imagine the circus that could have been? Newest U.S. senator wrapped up in a homicide case?"

"There's a reason you didn't want to meet today at either my studio or your office."

He nodded. "Of course. In fact, I'm not ashamed to admit that I even made a call to the commissioner's office. I wanted the police to know at the very highest level that I would cooperate in every imaginable way, but I didn't want us swept into a media frenzy just because I happened to be having my own fifteen minutes of fame. He assured me I had provided more than sufficient evidence to establish my innocence. I got the impression they had even spoken to other members of the Hayden School Alumni Board, who had confirmed that it was simply impossible to imagine Martin and Leigh Ann together. But now here we are again," he said, smiling but holding Laurie's gaze sternly.

She could hear his unasked question, so she gave him the closest thing she had to an answer. "We don't air theories about alternative suspects unless we believe there's a good-faith factual basis for doing so."

"That's comforting to hear, Laurie. I've seen every episode of your show, by the way, and I admire the work you do. But just between us? I think this time the one person under suspicion — Kendra Bell — deserves every bit of it. I hope you're able to prove it once and for all."

35

As soon as Laurie and Jerry were settled into the back of the black SUV that had been waiting for them outside Senator Longfellow's apartment, Jerry clapped his hands together in a tiny round of applause. "That was a first for me," he said. "I'd never met a senator and his wife before. And they were every bit as charming as everyone says. They're both stunningly gorgeous, and so . . . real. I totally get the hype now. We may have just met a future president and first lady, Laurie!"

"Before you're ready to put them in the White House, maybe we can talk about their connection to Martin Bell?"

"Sorry." Jerry nodded. "You know how crazy I get around celebrities, and they felt like movie stars—only smarter! But yes, you're right. No more fawning. Look, we knew going in that the only reason to question the Longfellows at all was because Kendra insists that he had something going on with Leigh Ann, right?"

"Correct."

"And it was at best a hunch of hers, right? No hotel receipts. No reports of hand-holding or stolen kisses outside the Hayden School Alumni Board meetings?"

"Nothing but time spent together and phone calls, combined with a wife's instinct that he was seeing another woman."

Jerry shrugged. "Well, we have a perfectly good explanation for the contact between them, and absolutely nothing to back up Kendra's suspicions."

Laurie continued the thought. "And Kendra isn't exactly the most credible person. She claims that Martin was—quote, unquote—'gaslighting' her, but, by her own account, she wasn't in the best condition at the time."

"Besides," Jerry added, "do you really think Leigh Ann would step out on her husband for Martin Bell?" The way he said Martin's name made it clear that he believed Leigh Ann was too good for the deceased physician.

"They do seem like polar opposites," Laurie said. "Martin may have been looking to get out of his marriage, but, by all accounts, he was determined to maintain custody of his children. No matter what, that was his first priority. Leigh Ann, on the other hand—"

"Go ahead and say it," Jerry said. "The woman obviously hates kids."

Laurie smiled. "Well, let's just say she prefers the company of pets. I certainly can't see her playing stepmom to little Bobby and Mindy."

"And it's not just a matter of the kids," Jerry said. "Don't forget that Martin and his parents pushed Kendra to stay home after the children were born. Martin wanted a stay-at-home wife and mother, not a power-broker law partner. You saw those two together: Leigh Ann's clearly the senator's right-hand woman. Do you think Martin Bell wanted that?"

"Oil and water," Laurie said.

"Exactly. Any motive Daniel Longfellow would have to kill Martin depends on an affair between Martin and his wife, which seems unimaginable. Not to mention, he has an ironclad alibi. It's not just Leigh Ann's word regarding his whereabouts that night. He had receipts, photographs, witnesses—the works."

Jerry was right. Laurie owed it to Kendra to pursue every possible lead, and had lived up to her responsibilities as far as the Longfellows were concerned. She was ready to check the senator off her list of possible suspects.

Jerry held up an index finger as if an idea had suddenly come to him. "Sorry, driver, we may have a change in plans," he said. "Laurie, I was thinking of including some background shots from the church where Martin and Kendra were married. It's pretty much on the way back to the office. Do you mind if we swing by so we can scout it out?"

She looked at her watch. It was approaching five o'clock. Knowing that Alex was out of town at a conference, Charlotte had invited her for a quick drink after work, but she figured this would be a brief stop. "Sounds good."

Jerry gave the driver an address in the West Forties. Laurie tried to think of a church in the theater district that would be up to the Bells' standards, but nothing came to mind.

"Pretty soon, we won't need to use a car service for trips like this," Jerry said. "The dealer thinks they'll have my car in stock this week."

Jerry had been talking for weeks about the plug-in hybrid BMW he had decided to purchase. Laurie thought it was crazy for a young person to own a car in the city, but she knew how much Jerry enjoyed going to Fire Island on weekends in the summer. Instead of cramming himself like a sardine onto the crowded Long Island Railroad, Jerry's approved "clean" car would entitle him to a comfortable spot in the express lane. Laurie could already picture him cruising down the Long Island Expressway with a carefully curated playlist of his favorite tunes.

When the driver pulled to the curb on West 46th Street and they stepped out of the car, Jerry told the driver that he didn't need to wait for them. "Jerry," Laurie said, "I assumed this would be a few minutes. I've got to be back at Rock Center by six." She was meeting Charlotte at Brasserie Ruhlmann near the studio offices.

"We'll just get a cab," Jerry said. Laurie opened her mouth to speak, but the driver had already pulled away.

"I don't know why you did that—"

Jerry gently placed a hand on her back and began guiding them to their destination. She did not see a church anywhere on the block.

They had taken only a few steps when he suddenly halted. He looked at her and grinned, gesturing toward the sign at the establishment next to them.

"Fancy's," in hot pink neon letters. Broadway's hottest male dancers.

No, she thought, *this is not happening.*

The tinted glass door opened, and Charlotte and Grace appeared, wearing matching purple boas. They both screamed out a high-pitched "whoooo!" sounding like the young bachelorettes competing for a single man on one of Fisher Blake's most successful reality shows.

"You have got to be kidding me," Laurie said drily.

"Come on," Charlotte said. "You and Alex have been so low-key with your engagement. We've been plotting for weeks and decided you needed a lowbrow night of celebration."

"By acting like an idiot swooning over scantily clad men? Not in a million years." Laurie now understood why Grace and Jerry had been so skittish around her recently while they were huddled over their computer screens. They had been planning this absurd event with Charlotte.

"But I already paid a guy named Chip for your first dance with him," Grace said, pouting her lower lip in disappointment.

Laurie glanced at their three eager faces and decided this was her punishment for always being the serious one. They were determined to force her to have brainless "fun."

She had taken two steps toward the door, accepting her fate, when Charlotte and Grace jumped outside and gave her a big hug. "We had you going!" Charlotte said, adding "good job" as she handed out high fives to both Jerry and Grace.

Jerry was smiling sheepishly. "We were just messing with you, Boss. Please forgive us." He pressed his palms together into prayer hands.

Laurie felt a wave of relief wash over her, grateful she did not actually have to go inside. "Wait, does this mean we're not going out?" she asked.

"Oh, we're definitely having drinks," Charlotte said. "Just not here."

Jerry and Grace pointed to a spot across the street. Don't Tell Mama, it was called. Laurie had been there once before with Grace and Jerry and had told them she enjoyed it. It was a dimly lit piano bar in the theater district, relatively quiet compared to Fancy's with the male dancers. Broadway actors would sometimes pop in to sing a tune, and customers were free to do the same.

A table nestled close to the stage was marked with a reserved sign. A bouquet of heart-shaped balloons was tied to the back of one of the chairs, and a purple boa was awaiting Laurie on the tabletop, but otherwise it was a perfectly respectable scene. As soon as the waitress took their drink order, Jerry and Grace took to the stage and serenaded Laurie with a rendition of "Chapel of Love."

"Goin' to the chapel, and we're . . . gonna get married."

Laurie could not stop smiling. She didn't notice the man who walked through the front door, took a seat at the bar, and began to watch her.

36

The man flicked the edge of the parking lot claim ticket with the edge of his finger, reading the small print he hadn't had time to review when he hastily decided to leave his white SUV with the attendant. Ten bucks per half hour; twenty-eight bucks would get you from two up to twenty-four hours.

He wondered to himself whether anyone had ever been stupid enough to pay thirty bucks for an hour and a half. Probably. He of all people knew how gullible other people could be. There had been a time when he never would have stopped to worry about the price of a parking spot in Manhattan, but those days were gone now, along with everything—and everyone—else.

The bartender finally made his way to the man's end of the bar—he was near the front door, but not so close that Laurie Moran might spot him if she were watching for another friend to join what appeared to be a party.

"What can I get you?" The bartender was a mangy-bearded hipster in a checkered shirt and suspenders. He probably paid his entire salary to share a trendy apartment in Williamsburg, but looked like he was one washboard shy of playing in the band on that old TV show, *Hee Haw*. *People are so silly*, the man thought.

He ordered a Johnnie Walker Black. Even though he knew he should remain clearheaded, he also knew that he didn't have the will-power to walk into a bar and not have a drink. It was one of her main complaints back when he still had a woman in his life. *You're mean when you drink*, she used to say.

One Scotch became two and then three as he watched Laurie Moran, so happy with her friends. Two of them—the younger woman and a skinny guy—had sung a song for her about going to the chapel and getting married and being in love until the end of time and never being lonely again. What a bunch of nonsense.

They were opening presents now. The first couple of gifts must have been gag gifts in light of the laughter that erupted at the table when she unwrapped them. The third present was big, wrapped in a messy bundle of paper. It was a large leather duffel bag. He heard Laurie's friend—the woman around her same age—say something about it being for the honeymoon.

Then they handed her a notebook-shaped box. It was robin's egg blue, tied with white glossy ribbon. It had to be from Tiffany. Back when he was part of a happy couple, she used to love seeing one of those blue boxes. *Good going*, she would whisper, usually with a kiss.

From his spot on the bar stool, he was able to make out the gleam of a crystal picture frame when Laurie opened the box. The way she beamed over it told him the frame must contain a photograph of her with her fiancé.

The happy couple. They don't deserve to be so happy. It isn't fair.

The Laurie-aged friend gave the bride-to-be a hug and asked for the check, and then Laurie began to stack all of her presents as well as her briefcase inside the new duffel bag. It was efficient. Sensible. One bag to carry everything home.

She was going to be missed, he was certain of it.

37

A little more than a mile away from Laurie's engagement party, in the offices of Dr. Steven Carter on Fifth Avenue in the Flatiron District, Kendra Bell took the cotton-wrapped ice pack from Mrs. Meadows and placed it on a metal tray. The light blue cotton was speckled with tiny spots of blood from the Botox injections that Steven was now inspecting.

"Looks great," Steven said as he approved his work. "You'll have those little bumps like bug bites for just a couple days, but then you'll be good as new. Remember to keep your head upright for the next four hours, preferably six. Don't apply any pressure, so no baseball caps, helmets, or turbans."

Mrs. Meadows let out a giggle at that one, as most of the patients did. "But what will I do without my favorite turban?" she joked.

"And this is the part everyone likes best: no workouts for the next twenty-four hours. You want the product to stay inside the muscle, not get sweated out."

"Oh, not to worry, Dr. Carter. I haven't seen the inside of a gym for the last twenty-four years, let alone hours. It's one of my finest accomplishments."

Steven snapped off his latex gloves and tossed them next to the ice pack. All of it would go into a medical-waste disposal bucket.

Mrs. Meadows gave a quick wave as she hopped out of the treatment chair, adding a blown kiss for Kendra. "See you next time!"

Once she was gone and on her way to the reception desk to pay, Steven pulled the treatment room door closed. Their final appointment of the day was finished, and they were officially off the clock. "So what was the gossip this time?"

Mrs. Meadows was one of their favorite patients, full of personality and moxie. Some of the patients were wary of Kendra, and two of them had even insisted on being seen by a different assistant. But, if anything, the whiff of scandal on Kendra only made her a more attractive gossip buddy for Mrs. Meadows, the name she absolutely insisted on.

"She has a new man," Kendra announced. "This one's only thirty-two years old." That made him less than half the age of his seductress.

Steven shook his head. "Poor boy has no idea what's coming his way."

Some might worry about a younger man taking advantage of an older, wealthy widow, but Mrs. Meadows was no victim. She had left a long trail of ex-boyfriends in her wake. "I already had my one great love," she liked to say. "Now I prefer a frequent change of faces."

Steven's tone suddenly grew more serious. "I haven't wanted to raise the subject, but is everything all right with that television production? I could see how concerned you were about the way they might present the story."

Kendra's first instinct was to clam up. The last thing she needed was another person prying into her secrets. But Steven had been such a good friend to her, and she sure did need a trusted confidant right now.

She quickly decided which bits of information to share and which to keep to herself.

"It turns out that Caroline disclosed some information that doesn't present me in the best light," she said.

Steven's expression twisted into a disapproving scowl. "But she's practically family at this point. Where's the loyalty?"

Kendra waved her palms, trying to set aside his outrage. "She's so devoted. That's why she told me every word she said to the producer."

"Such as?"

"It doesn't matter, because I know I'm innocent. In the end, there's only so much damage they can do to me." Even as she spoke the words that were meant to comfort both him and her, she remembered her promise to the Beehive man—the horrible man she knew only as Mike. She had sworn on her children's lives that the producers would never know about him. But now Caroline admitted that she had told Laurie about her habit of stashing away piles of cash that continued to this day. It was only a matter of time before they grilled her about the reason.

And that terrible quote that Caroline had provided: *Am I finally free of him?* She had been so unhappy in that marriage. Broken, desperate. A shadow of her former self. Even so, it was shameful to say that.

She had been so miserable that she had wished her own husband—the father of her children—dead. It was hard to imagine, and yet she had unmistakably heard the words in her own voice. That outburst, plus the unaccounted-for cash, combined with whatever negative testimony the police could patch together, would be enough to put her in prison for life. Bobby and Mindy would be raised by their ice-cold grandparents, groomed to be miniature versions of them.

She couldn't allow it. She'd pay Beehive Mike whatever amount he wanted to keep his mouth shut until the end of time.

She was pulled from her thoughts by the sight of Steven, staring at her with nothing but adoration.

"I can't thank you enough for all that you've done for me and the kids, Steven."

"I'd do anything for you, Kendra. I love you." She could see that he was surprised by his own words. "Like family," he added, giving her a quick hug before opening the door to leave.

She knew his feelings ran deeper than that, but—as ridiculous as it seemed—the only man she had ever loved was Martin Bell. But that was before she truly knew him, before he had acted as if he owned her. Was it possible that with Steven she might have another chance at trust and love?

38

Laurie was opening gifts at her surprise party by the time Senator Daniel Longfellow poured himself a glass of Cabernet in the kitchen. His wife was preparing dinner for the dogs. Because of Lincoln's food allergies, he required a mix of prescription canned food and kibble made from rabbit and squash. And because Leigh Ann was convinced the dogs would notice if they received differential treatment, that meant Ike received the identical recipe.

The senator noticed Leigh Ann glance at his glass, but she didn't comment. It was rare for either of them to drink wine on weekdays. It was a rule they'd both adopted not long after they met, when they realized they were imbibing a bit too frequently given the demands of their studies at Columbia. "Dry weekdays" then became part of their routine—one of many they had adopted to maximize both their health and their productivity.

But the visit from the *Under Suspicion* producers had him in the mood for a glass of wine. "I think it went okay," he said to Leigh Ann. "How about you?"

"I can only speak for my part of the conversation. They seemed quite reasonable. I got the impression, though, that she didn't know much about the original police investigation. That surprised me."

Daniel took a sip of his wine. "Then you underestimate the number of chips I had to cash in to make sure that the police left our name out of the entire case. Apparently the commissioner meant what he said when he assured me that the investigating detectives saw no reason to involve us any further."

He had worked so hard—no, *they* had worked so hard—to get to this place. When he was first elected to the state assembly, he was certain he'd go to Albany and accomplish all of the sweeping changes he had called for during that first, energizing campaign. But he was only one of one hundred fifty members of the assembly, and the entire place was mired with gridlock, patronage, and cronyism. He had barely learned his way around the capital before it was time to start hustling for campaign donations and locking down ad buys again. The political pundits kept calling him a rising star, but there was nowhere for him to rise to. The state senator and governor weren't going anywhere. He was stuck in place in what was supposed to be his "starter job" in politics.

Not to mention, the place where he was stuck was a place Leigh Ann hated. Behind very closed doors, she called Albany "All-Boring" and reminded Daniel on a daily basis how much smarter they both were than his elected colleagues. Because of the commute between the capital and the city, for all practical purposes they had a long-distance marriage for large parts of the year.

And then suddenly, thanks to a cabinet appointment for one of New York's two U.S. senators, the sky opened up, and rising Daniel Longfellow had a place to go. After completing the remaining two years of the previous senator's uncompleted term, he had been handily elected in his own right three years ago. He enjoyed a nearly 80 percent approval rating statewide, which was unheard of in these divided times. And most importantly, at least to him, he believed he was actually making a difference. He tried to ignore all the chatter about pursuing an even higher office. Every day, he tried to use the power of the office he currently occupied to improve the lives of ordinary Americans, just as he had promised.

But sometimes he felt as if he might never be able to put the dark phase of their past behind him. When Alex Buckley had called last week asking him to meet with his fiancée about the Martin Bell case, he felt the reemergence of a panic he hadn't known for the last five years. *Maybe I should have told the police the full story when they first asked about Martin Bell*, he thought. *After surviving a war, I should have been tough enough to let the chips fall as they may. I've tried to live my entire life honorably. I made one mistake, and sometimes I think this guilt might just put me in the grave.*

Trying to calm his nerves, he told himself that Leigh Ann was probably right, as she almost always was. Their answers had seemed to satisfy Laurie Moran, just as they had satisfied the police after Bell was murdered.

"Do you think I should have someone from the office call to follow up?" he asked. "We could mention the possibility of a defamation suit if they were to repeat Kendra's suspicions on air."

She looked at him as if he had suggested flying to the moon on a bicycle. He knew that Leigh Ann loved him—almost as much as he loved her—but he also knew (and adored the fact) that his wife didn't suffer fools.

"And give them a story about a senator trying to silence a widowed mother?" She placed the dogs' meals into their personalized feeders. "Don't give them fire when there's no smoke. Our statements made it all well and clear: Martin Bell was just a man on the board with me, an old childhood acquaintance."

They both knew that wasn't exactly true.

39

Laurie glanced at her watch. It was already nine o'clock. They had been having such a fun time at the piano bar that she had completely lost track of time.

She started to signal for the check, but Charlotte quickly grabbed her hand and pulled it down beside her. "First of all, brides-to-be do not pay for their own parties. And second, you can't go yet. I heard that couple over there ask the pianist to play 'Schadenfreude' from *Avenue Q*. From the gleam in their eyes, I think they have something hilarious planned."

"I wish I could stay. This has been such a blast, but I've got to get back home for Timmy."

"I assumed your dad was with him tonight when we made drink plans," Charlotte said.

"Nope. He had a dinner thing to go to, but Timmy was over at a friend's working on a science project and was eating over there. The plan is for the parents to walk him back to the apartment at nine-thirty, so I really have to scoot."

"Such a good mom," Charlotte said, giving her a hug before signaling for the check.

As Charlotte fought off Jerry's and Grace's attempts to kick in for the bill, Laurie began to stack the gifts they'd brought inside the duffel bag Charlotte had given her. It was a new addition to the Ladyform line, and the leather was thick and buttery. Charlotte had made a point to say it was for the honeymoon, but tonight, it was perfect to transport all of these presents. As much as Laurie loved the bag, her very favorite gift was the framed photograph of her and Alex. It was from the set of the first episode they had filmed together. Even though their relationship was strictly professional at the time, the camera had managed to catch the obvious feelings between them.

As a final step, she tucked her briefcase into a gap at the side of the bag. "This thing is ginormous!" she said, showing off her accomplishment of fitting everything neatly inside.

They had just risen from the table when the pianist announced the next number. It was the funny song from *Avenue Q* that Charlotte had anticipated. An enthusiastic couple two tables down jumped up. Their friends cheered as they made their way to the stage. Charlotte looked at Laurie with pleading eyes.

"Seriously, I've got to go. You guys stay, though. I can tell you want to." She hoisted the duffel bag over her right shoulder, making clear that she was fully capable of lugging it to a cab on her own.

Charlotte sat and signaled for Jerry and Grace to do the same. She gave a quick final wave to Laurie and mouthed "good night" as the piano began to play.

As Laurie walked toward the exit, she felt the thud of her bag bump someone at the bar and yelled out an apology over the music.

Outside, she had her back to the door as she monitored 46th Street for an available taxi. She was cutting it close to get home before Timmy, and it could be tough finding a cab this time of night in the theater district. She thought about ordering an Uber, but her phone was in her briefcase, which was zipped inside the giant bag over her shoulder. The last thing she wanted to do to her beautiful new duffel was drop it on a city sidewalk.

Her mind eased as she spotted the lit medallion number of an approaching cab. She took two steps out from the curb and raised her left hand enthusiastically. *Please*, she thought, *do not let this be the night some jerk appears out of nowhere to steal my ride home.*

She sensed motion behind her and, on instinct, waved her hailing hand even higher as the cab began to slow. *My cab. This is my cab.*

The impact was fast. And hard. It felt like she had been head butted by a professional football player. Before she knew it, she was falling onto the street, the skin on her left calf scraping against the rough concrete. She screamed as she saw headlights approaching at eye level. The cab's tires made a skidding sound as the car came to a sudden halt, stopping just in time not to hit her.

She scrambled to her feet, losing one of her sling-backed heels in the process. Her bag was gone. She spotted a man dressed in dark pants and a hoodie running toward Eighth Avenue, her bag in his right hand, and began to yell.

"Stop! Someone stop him! He mugged me! That's my bag!"

The taxi driver was out of his car, asking if she was okay. A woman stopped to pick up her shoe from the street and return it to her. Other pedestrians simply continued on their way, pretending not to have noticed a scene that was none of their business. No one had tried to stop the man from running away from the lady wearing a ridiculous purple boa.

"Please, can we go follow him?" Laurie asked the driver.

He held up both palms and waved them. "That is a job for the police, ma'am," he said in a lilting accent. "I have a wife and five children. I can't go playing hero."

She nodded her understanding and then watched as a man in a well-tailored suit got into the backseat of what was supposed to be her cab.

40

Laurie refused help from several passersby. Without her briefcase and purse, she stumbled back into the piano bar. Before she was able to tell Charlotte and the others what had happened, several members of the police came in. Someone must have called 911.

Laurie was never comfortable as the center of attention and now had a piano bar full of people watching her as she spoke from a bar stool to an ever-growing number of police officers.

"You've got injuries," one of the officers noted. "Are you sure you don't want an EMT to check that out?" He gestured toward the ice pack she was holding awkwardly against her scraped calf.

"Really, I'm fine. Just . . . rattled. That cabbie could have run right over me. Thank God he had quick reflexes."

Another officer—this one the oldest so far—arrived on the scene. She could see from the insignia on his shoulder that he was a lieutenant. Her suspicions were now confirmed. Someone had connected the familial dots between the complainant and former First Deputy Commissioner Leo Farley.

The new arrival introduced himself as Lieutenant Patrick Flannigan. "I'm sorry this happened to you in our precinct."

"No apology necessary . . . unless you're living a double life as a mugger," she added with a smile. "And trust me, I'll tell my father that the NYPD was here within two minutes."

"Unfortunately, my officers are telling me the response time wasn't quick enough to find the man who did this. We found one woman who says a guy pushed past her with a large bag, but she didn't get a good look at him. Seems he managed to blend into the theater district crowd and disappear. We'll be pulling surveillance camera footage, though."

She shook her head. "He was wearing a hoodie. I'm not sure what you'll find."

Flannigan waved the bartender over. "You have any customers here tonight who left the same time she did?"

The bartender squinted, searching his memory. "Maybe? There was one guy—same seat you're in now, in fact," he said to Laurie. "Johnnie Walker Black—a few of them. Don't remember much more about him, though."

"Do you have his credit card payment?" Flannigan asked.

"Paid cash. And I already told the other officer we don't have cameras or anything like that. I feel terrible. This never happens around here. People just come here to have fun."

Laurie heard Grace a few feet away crack a joke to Charlotte and Jerry about the male dancer establishment across the street, even as she was making phone calls to have Laurie's credit card accounts frozen. A few of the police officers seemed to disapprove of the laughter, but it made Laurie feel safe. She wanted to believe that everything was normal, but she couldn't help but wonder if the mugging was related to the Martin Bell investigation.

"Can I ask you, Lieutenant, whether it's common to have a random mugging around here?"

He sighed. "I wish I could say it never happened, but this is New York City. Anything could go down at any time. But statistically? This area is pretty calm, especially this time of night. Two, three in the morning? That's another story. But the bartender wasn't lying when he said this was a rare occurrence. Why do I get the feeling you're asking for a reason?"

"I'm a television producer. My show, *Under Suspicion*, reinvestigates—"

"I know your show well, Ms. Moran. You do good work."

"Thank you, and please call me Laurie. We're in the middle of a production right now. It's the Martin Bell case," she said, lowering her voice.

He let out a puff of air. "That's a biggie. I don't know the inside story, but seems like the case went stone cold."

"Well, it did. And to be honest, we haven't made as much progress as I'd like. But we have poked some bears and ruffled some feathers. And my briefcase with my laptop and notes was in that bag he just stole."

"Any candidates come specifically to mind?"

She ran through all the possibilities. It definitely wasn't Kendra. Even though she didn't get a look at her assailant's face, she could tell from his build and the way he moved that it was a man. Senator Longfellow was probably four inches taller than the man she saw running away, and was in the clear as a suspect anyway. George Naughten, on the other hand, was shorter and pudgier, but she didn't believe he was physically fit enough to knock her down and sprint so quickly from the scene.

She briefly entertained the thought that Kendra's boss, Steven Carter, might fit the bill. It was certainly possible, but how could he have known where she would be tonight? If this was something other than a random robbery, then her attacker must have been following her for hours.

No, of all the names waiting for her back on her office whiteboard, only one made sense—and it wasn't even a name: Kendra's mysterious drinking partner from the Beehive. She remembered how the woman at the dive bar had described him: rough-looking, with a shaved head and mean eyes.

She had never even seen the man's face, yet somehow she could imagine those eyes—cold and steely—as he pushed her into the street.

41

She had just started to explain her theory to the lieutenant when the bar door opened again. It was her father, and he immediately ran to her and gave her a hug. When he finally let go, she could tell he was inspecting her for injuries.

"Dad, I'm fine. What are you doing here?"

After speaking to the police, Laurie had used Charlotte's phone to ask Leo if he could meet Timmy back at the apartment. She had hated to interrupt whatever dinner obligation he had, but she didn't want Timmy left to wait at a friend's house with no explanation.

"Don't worry. Timmy's in excellent hands. His babysitter just texted that she made it to the apartment minutes before him and they're now becoming fast friends."

"Fast friends? Dad, I'm sorry I dragged you out of your dinner, but you can't just hire a stranger on a second's notice to watch Timmy."

"It's not a stranger," he said, suddenly flustered. She had never seen her father be so clumsy about making a point. "She's very trustworthy. In fact," he said, lowering his voice to a whisper only she could hear, "she's the chief judge of the federal district court."

Laurie didn't think anything could make her smile, but that did the trick. She pictured her father at dinner—on a date—with Chief Judge Russell. He must have called her after they met at Alex's induction last week. Then, forced to leave early, he would have explained the urgent circumstances. Now he was here, and she was keeping his grandson company.

"Well, if it all works out, you'll certainly have an interesting first date story," she teased.

"Sorry to have to make an executive decision on the fly, but Alex called me in a panic as Maureen and I were leaving the restaurant. He was going to miss the rest of his conference to fly back here tonight until I assured him I was on my way to the scene of the crime."

After calling Leo, Laurie had phoned Alex in D.C. She had tried to mitigate the severity of the incident, but she should have known how worried he would be.

Lieutenant Flannigan interrupted to introduce himself. "It's an honor to meet you, Commissioner."

"Call me Leo. I thought you all might have moved to the station house to talk to detectives by the time I got here."

"I figured we'd send the detective to the witness tonight, under the circumstances. Laurie was just telling me about the man who might have been following her last week."

"What man?" he asked, clearly alarmed. "Someone was following you?"

"I thought I was imagining things at the time," she said, explaining her decision not to mention her fears earlier. "Now? I'm not so sure. It's a stretch, but if Kendra hired someone to kill her husband, she certainly could have hired him to find out how close we're getting to the truth. My notes and my laptop were in my bag, and now they're gone." In truth, her notes contained nothing but conjecture. If anything, the man from the Beehive would be comforted by the fact that she'd gotten no further than the police in determining his identity.

Leo shook his head. "It's not just your notes, Laurie. Charlotte told me what happened. You were pushed in front of a car. You could've been killed."

"That would certainly be one way of halting your investigation," Flannigan said drily. She had been terrified when she saw that taxi headed toward her, but she hadn't let herself think about the possibility that someone had actually been trying to kill her. "Or," Flannigan added, "it was just a random mugging. No way to know unless we find him."

She could tell that he was not optimistic.

42

Fifteen blocks from the piano bar, in a bathroom at a Starbucks, Laurie's assailant was replaying the night's events in his head.

I knew I shouldn't have started with the Scotch, the man thought. *It makes me mean, just like everyone always told me, back when I had people in my life who tried to make me better.* Tonight, he'd been stupid and impulsive when he'd wanted to be smart and methodical. He acted without thinking; now here he was with a bag full of her belongings.

He had already rifled through what most people would call the "gag gifts" from the evening: an "I Do" workout shirt, an "I'm getting meow-ied" coffee mug (complete with a cartoon of a cat in a bridal veil), and a few barely R-rated stickers about marriage.

Her cell phone was useless, at least to him, since it asked for a password he didn't have. The first thing he had done once he blended into the crowd in Times Square was to duck into a restroom stall in a McDonald's. A quick search of the duffel bag revealed the phone. He had turned it off and dropped it in a trash bin. Rookie mistake to get caught with a trackable phone.

Fortunately, her computer wasn't similarly protected.

He had gone through her calendar and recent emails, searching for information that might be relevant. Her inbox had several recent messages from a Realtor named Rhoda Carmichael, complete with photographs of luxury apartments and lavish descriptions of amenities in five-star co-ops. He remembered a time when he was able to afford a home not unlike those. He got the impression from the messages that Ms. Carmichael was eager for Laurie and her accomplished fiancé to select a property quickly.

He knew that once they moved in together, it would be even harder to get to Laurie. After all, she was marrying a federal judge. The Honorable Judge Buckley had enhanced security not only at work but also at home. For now, though, Laurie had a separate apartment, without all the bells and whistles.

He had moved on to reading the scribbles in her spiral binder. The most recent handwritten notes on paper were about Daniel and Leigh Ann Longfellow. He wondered briefly how much money he could make by selling these pages to a tabloid, but then realized he could be jeopardizing his anonymity by cutting that kind of deal. Instead, he took a small amount of satisfaction reading information to which only a few people would be privy.

From what he could tell, Laurie had plenty of theories about who might be guilty in her latest case, but could not yet prove who had murdered Dr. Martin Bell.

He closed both the laptop and the notebook and returned his attention to the crystal frame in the robin's-egg-blue cardboard box. He yanked the frame from the box, flipped it upside down, and pulled the photograph from the crystal, tearing it up in pieces and throwing the scraps in the toilet. He watched the tatters of glossy paper swirl with the flush, just like his own fairy-tale romance— down the drain.

He stuffed the contents of the duffel bag into the garbage, covering up the top with wads of paper towels. The garbage bag might seem a bit heavy to whatever employee carried it out later tonight, but the man had schlepped fifteen blocks from the piano bar for a reason. He was well beyond any feasible radius for a police search.

And no chain store coffee-shop employee was going to wade through the contents of a New York City trash can out of curiosity.

This leather duffel bag, however, was a problem. It was simply too large to fit into a garbage container. He flopped it over his shoulder, tucked his chin to his chest, and made his way to the street outside. When he passed a homeless man sleeping next to a cardboard box that appeared to contain his belongings, he slipped the bag from his shoulder and left it as a gift, checking all directions to make sure no one noticed his good deed.

Now what? he thought. He considered going back to 46th Street to pick up his SUV, but it was too risky. The police might be watching the block. He'd take the subway home tonight and come back for his car tomorrow morning. The police wouldn't be scoping out the area by then.

As he took the stairs down to the Q train, he thought again about all those meandering notes Laurie had made about her latest investigation. She would be gone before she could solve the case; he was certain of that. He just needed to find the right opportunity. Next time, he wouldn't make a stupid mistake.

43

The following afternoon, Laurie felt the fabric of her newest spring pants chafe against her scuffed leg. The saleswoman at Bloomingdale's had described the cotton-nylon blend as "the closest thing you can get to jammies for your work wardrobe," but right now the black trousers felt like sandpaper against an open wound. She could still feel the concrete of 46th Street scraping her skin. In retrospect, she should have worn a dress today, but she didn't want Timmy to notice she was hurt. She had decided to downplay the incident by telling him that someone had stolen her briefcase while she was out with Charlotte. She believed in being honest with her son, but he had already lost one parent to violence. There was no point in scaring him unnecessarily.

She had spent the morning at the Apple store with Grace, replacing both her cell phone and laptop. Fortunately, Grace had kept everything backed up in the cloud, so the wizards at the store's Genius Bar had gotten her up and running again before lunch. She wouldn't have her replacement credit cards and driver's license for a few days, but in the big scheme of things, she felt back to normal. The one thing she was still really missing was that beautiful crystal frame with the photograph of Alex and her.

She heard a light tap on her door, and then Jerry and Grace peeked in. She had scheduled a meeting to storyboard the production of their Martin Bell special. To her surprise, Ryan had suggested that she take the lead and call him only if he could be helpful.

"Ready for us?" Grace asked.

"Of course."

They walked in side by side. With her four-inch heels, Grace was the exact height of Jerry. Each of them carried a single, familiar item. Jerry had a leather duffel bag from Ladyform, and Grace held a robin's-egg-blue box, wrapped with a silky ribbon.

"You guys," Laurie said. "This is too much."

Taking the box from Grace, she slipped off the ribbon to find another crystal frame with the identical photograph that had been stolen from her the night before. "Really, I can't accept these gifts again."

Jerry set the duffel bag on one of her guest chairs and took a seat at her conference table. "You shouldn't feel the least amount of guilt. The manager at Tiffany insisted we accept a replacement frame when I told her everything you went through last night," Jerry said.

"And that bag?" Grace said. "I adore Charlotte's company, Laurie, but do you know the markup on that stuff? Trust me: Girlfriend can spare a tote bag."

Laurie gazed down at the photograph in her hands and smiled. The thought of some thief—or worse—looking at it last night after the robbery made her stomach feel sick. She imagined a rough-looking man with mean eyes cavalierly tossing it aside, rifling through the duffel bag for something more valuable.

This—more than her wallet or her phone or her laptop—was the item she had missed the most. She propped it beside her computer, between the photograph of the two of them with Timmy and Leo, and the one of her with Timmy and Greg. Somehow the three pictures felt right together.

• • •

Forty minutes later, they had mapped out their plan for the next entry in the *Under Suspicion* series. Ryan would narrate the early phases of Martin and Kendra's relationship over B-roll footage of the medical school where they had met, the church where they had married, and the carriage house outside of which he was eventually murdered.

They had already obtained signed participation agreements from Kendra and from Martin's parents. Predictably, the Bells would point the finger at Kendra, while Kendra would portray herself as a misunderstood wife and mother. But they had new information to reveal on camera. As host, Ryan would cross-examine Kendra, confronting her with evidence that Martin had been planning to divorce her and gain custody of the children.

"Don't forget the information from the nanny," Jerry noted.

Grace nearly leapt up from her seat at the mention of Caroline Radcliffe. "Where is Kendra spending all that cash, and what kind of woman says, 'Am I finally free?' when her husband is shot? Sorry, but it seems obvious to me. That lady hired a hit man to kill Martin Bell and now she's still paying him to keep his mouth shut. Case solved."

Jerry's face made it clear that he agreed with her assessment.

Laurie tried to focus on each scene of the planned production, but she kept thinking about the previous night's assault. *Kendra might have paid the hit man to kill me, too,* she thought. She shook away the thought, reminding herself it might have been a random robbery.

The sound of her office phone broke through the noise in her head. Grace rose from the conference table to answer on her behalf. "Laurie Moran's office." A few seconds later, she hit the hold button and announced that the caller was George Naughten. Laurie got up to take the call.

Jerry and Grace watched her expectantly as she listened to what George had to say. He had spoken to his psychiatrist since they'd visited his home the previous morning. The psychiatrist thought it would be good for him to help the show with its investigation. "It will be a chance for me to talk about Ma—on television to a huge audience. About the car accident and about what Dr. Bell did to her with his so-called treatment."

"That would be great," Laurie said, feigning enthusiasm. George had initially seemed like a prime suspect, a man with a grudge to harbor and a history of gun ownership. After meeting him yesterday, although she did not feel as strongly about it, she still had lingering doubt. Now here he was, wanting to appear on their show. If she had to guess, she'd say he planned to use the airtime to vent his grievances about the people he blamed for his mother's death. "So this will basically be what you told us yesterday?" she asked.

"No," he said adamantly. "There's something else—something I've never told anyone."

She sat up straighter in her chair, and Grace and Jerry looked at her, sensing that something had changed on the other end of the line. "Can you give me a hint now?"

"No. I can only tell you if you get me out of the nondisclosure agreement I signed."

"As I said, George, we don't need to know the specifics of your lawsuit against Dr. Bell."

"Take it or leave it," he said, suddenly insistent. "Those are my conditions. I have something you want to know—trust me—but not with the NDA."

She pressed her eyes closed. She was pretty sure George wanted to drag them into grudges he had harbored for years, and none of it would have anything to do with Martin Bell's murder. But Laurie's motto was to leave no stone unturned. He wanted to be released from the nondisclosure agreement, and Martin Bell's parents had the power to make that happen. They also wanted to solve their son's murder.

"I think we can manage that," she said.

Once she was alone in her office, she called Martin Bell's parents and left a message asking them to call her.

Looking at the photographs on her desk, she realized that she wanted to be home, surrounded by family. Last night had left her more rattled than she wanted to admit. But Alex was in D.C., Timmy was at school, and her father had an all-day meeting with the anti-terrorism task force up near Randall's Island.

I'll put in one more hour of work, she thought. *Then I'll leave early, pay cash for groceries like the old days, and still have enough time to walk my son home from school. Tonight, it will be just the two of us, while we still have the chance.*

44

The following night, Laurie caught sight of Alex through the front windows of Marea. He looked relaxed and confident standing next to the hostess desk. It had only been four days since she'd seen him, but somehow she had forgotten how handsome he was.

His blue-green eyes lit up behind his black-rimmed glasses when she walked into the restaurant. "There she is!" He pulled her into a tight embrace, and she realized how much she had missed him.

Once she and Alex were settled in at their favorite table, she asked him if the new judge orientation had gone well. Almost all of their phone time while he was in D.C. had been spent mulling over the assault at the piano bar. She had made him promise that there would be no mention of it tonight.

"I learned more than I expected. I know a criminal case backwards and forwards, but there was some helpful material about handling large-scale civil suits and class actions. Now I just have the rest of the week to get my chambers in order before the chief judge starts giving me case assignments next week."

He sounded surprisingly anxious about the prospect, but she knew he was more than competent to handle the work. His nervousness was a sign that he was humbled by his new responsibilities.

"You probably never thought your chief judge would pull a babysitting stint for your future stepson before she even assigned you a case."

He smiled at the thought of Judge Russell on a date with Leo. "I noticed a spark between them at the induction. She's normally quite the social butterfly at those types of events, but it seemed as if she only wanted to talk to your father."

"Just think," Laurie said, "if things ever get serious between Dad and Judge Russell, she could end up as my stepmother, which would make her your . . . stepmother-in-law? Is that a conflict of interest?"

He seemed to entertain the question and then shook his head in confusion. "I have absolutely no idea. You think it could actually get that serious?"

"Who knows, but after all his nudging about my relationship with you, it's going to be so much fun with the tables turned."

His tone grew more somber. "Seriously, are you okay if he does get involved with someone else?"

"Of course." Laurie's mother, Eileen, had passed away before Timmy was born. She always liked to tell people that she had married the first boy she ever kissed. Laurie's mother and father were the kind of couple that held hands whenever they were beside each other, without even thinking about it. "I know he's happy being Dad and Granddaddy, but it's time. I don't want him to be alone forever. He's seeing her again on Friday night, so . . . we'll see. For now, it's just a couple of dinner dates. I'm glad he's having fun."

"Speaking of dinner dates, guess who invited me to dinner to celebrate my confirmation to the bench?"

"Should I be jealous?" she said, arching her brow.

"Definitely not. It's Carl Newman," he said, lowering his voice.

She had no idea what rules governed a judge's communications with former clients, but that particular client was so despised in New York City his acquittal had threatened to derail Alex's appointment to the bench. "You're not going, are you?"

"Oh no, not in a million years. It wouldn't be appropriate. And, to be honest, he is one of the very few clients I actually wish had been convicted."

"Except he had too good of a lawyer," she said.

"Don't blame me. Blame the investigators and maybe the jury."

"You know what I think?" she asked.

"What?"

"They were distracted by your good looks and infectious charm."

He laughed and shook his head. "I need to leave town more often." He reached for her hand without even thinking about it.

45

From across the street on Central Park South, the man watched Laurie enter a restaurant called Marea. Her fiancé had gone in only moments earlier. Perfectly in sync, weren't they? Completely nauseating.

He was still kicking himself for the incident outside the piano bar two nights ago. What a failure that had been. He blamed the Scotch he had drunk at the bar. Was he still the impulsive idiot he used to be, unable to deny himself a drink when presented with a wall of liquor?

That sort of recklessness was exactly what had led him to this point. Next time, he wouldn't mess up. He would keep watching and be ready to act when she was alone and isolated, when the moment was right.

He heard a startling thump and whipped his head around, expecting to see someone rapping on the window of his white SUV. No one. He peered out the passenger window and realized the source of the banging: two kids were drumming on upside-down buckets on the sidewalk. A few people were getting up to dance on the grass. *Maybe if I sat among these happy people, their lives would rub off on mine*, he thought. Then he scoffed. That was not how happiness worked. Happiness was when every man got what he deserved.

A couple, arm in arm, crossed the street in front of his car, heading toward the restaurant where Laurie and Alex were having dinner. The man was wearing a fitted suit, the woman a little black dress. Marea was understated from the outside, but he knew it was the kind of place that had three-fork place settings and investment banker prices. He used to stroll into places like that without thinking twice, sidle up to the bar, and drink martinis till he lost count. He missed the sleek bars, the mood lighting, and the service that recognized your importance. When he craved a drink these days, he found himself in a sticky dive bar, usually underground, throwing back Four Roses straight up.

He saw Laurie emerge from the restaurant more than two hours later, just as he was fighting off a drowsy spell. She was with her fiancé this time. They were holding hands. Even with the sidewalks overflowing with people, he could taste that guy's arrogance.

He won't walk with that kind of pride for long, he thought. *Maybe when she's gone, he'll be just like me.*

46

The following day, in late morning traffic, Jerry looked absolutely content behind the wheel of the generic sedan they had rented for the ride out to Rosedale, Queens. He had suggested the rental car so they could discuss the case without worrying about an eavesdropping driver, but Laurie realized he was also anticipating his upcoming car purchase. He had mentioned as they got into the car that the dealer would have his new car ready for him to pick up after work.

Adele's latest hit single was playing on the radio. As Jerry sang along, Grace indulged him with some harmonies from the backseat. *So much for discussing the case*, Laurie thought.

George Naughten's block was nearly vacant. They were here to gather whatever information he swore he had for them about his lawsuit against Martin Bell. Laurie had convinced Martin's parents to waive the nondisclosure agreement that George had signed as part of his settlement with Martin's estate. They were eager to protect their son's professional reputation, but she had persuaded them that this was the only way to learn whatever secret George was harboring.

Jerry pulled to the curb in front of George's house, and the production truck followed behind them. A third vehicle stopped at the curb across from them, on the left side of the street. Leo hopped out and tossed his police parking permit on the dash. After the incident on Monday night, he was not about to let Laurie meet with a convicted stalker without an additional level of protection. He had promised to maintain a "low profile," going so far as to drive separately, but she knew he had his gun in a shoulder holster beneath his sports coat.

Laurie turned down the radio and looked at Ryan.

"You all set?" she asked.

He flashed her a thumbs-up. They had spent the morning trying to anticipate all the possibilities of what might unfold here today.

"Living in this neighborhood is one way to cut down on the commute to JFK," Jerry said as he stepped out of the car, noticing a plane taking off overhead.

"So is living in Lakeview," Grace said. "Before my parents moved, I was over this way all the time."

"Hope they never had a neighborhood run-in with Mama Naughten. You know how angry George would get if you crossed her," Jerry joked.

"Or know someone who knows someone who crossed her."

Laurie waved her fingertips across her throat, signaling for them to knock off the banter as they approached George's house.

As he had for their last visit, George poked his head out the barely cracked front door and squinted suspiciously at the small crowd gathered on his stoop.

"Hi, George. Laurie Moran from *Under Suspicion*?" she offered, even though she was certain he knew her identity.

"Oh, yes, okay," he said, motioning for them to enter. "I just didn't expect all these people."

"Well, if we want this on camera, these are the people who make that happen."

Laurie introduced the crew as they began to set up in the living room. They had brought extra lighting to compensate for the room's darkness, and the space soon transformed into a proper studio. George, wearing the same T-shirt and sweatpants as the last time, watched the operation with wide eyes.

"No reason to be nervous, George," Ryan said cordially.

Ryan extended a copy of their standard participation agreement to George for his signature, along with a pen. George glanced at the provisions only briefly before signing. The document gave Fisher Blake Studios exclusive control over both the use and editing of the footage. They fully expected George to air his grievances against Martin Bell, but they weren't required to use the footage.

"I'd like to sit in my chair for this," George said, heading toward the La-Z-Boy.

Leo immediately rushed to the chair and conducted what Laurie recognized as a quick pat-down for any hidden weapons. "Just want to make sure there's nothing there that could interfere with the equipment," he muttered by way of explanation.

Seemingly satisfied, George got comfortable while a production assistant mic'ed up his T-shirt.

Once the cameras were in place, they began rolling.

"Let's start with the events that inspired the lawsuit," Ryan said. "How did you find your mother's treatment under Dr. Martin Bell?"

"Oh, Ma, she used to be so spunky," he said longingly. He paused, and then a smile broke out across his face, the first Laurie had seen. "You know she was going to bike across the country? From New York to California! She got the crazy idea when she turned sixty-three. She was following a whole training program, doing her speed-walking around the neighborhood on Mondays and Wednesdays, swimming over at the community center on Tuesdays and Thursdays. I promised her I'd buy her a good bike, something reliable that wouldn't break down on her in Tennessee or Kansas.

"But then the accident happened and everything changed. At first, the doctors all said, 'Oh, it's just a fender bender, let's not blow it out of proportion.' But that 'fender bender' was the beginning of the end. Sure, there were still days when she was okay. Her old self. But for two years, I'd wake up to Ma crying out in pain from her bed.

Once she started to see Dr. Bell, the crying stopped, and the pain went away. But the meds left her totally out of it—emptied her so she was just a shell of herself. Like a zombie. Then I found her there on the floor." George pointed toward the kitchen.

Laurie had already known the basic allegations of the lawsuit, but had never heard George describe his mother's impairment in his own words. *Like a zombie.* That phrase had been in his lawsuit, and it was precisely how Caroline Radcliffe had described Kendra Bell toward the end of her time with Martin. *Out of it. A shell of herself.* George could have been talking about Kendra.

Why hadn't she seen it before? She told herself that she could confirm her suspicions later. Right now, she needed to focus on what George had to say.

"You blamed Dr. Bell for your mother's death, didn't you?" Ryan asked.

"Of course I did."

As Ryan walked George through the confrontation at Martin's office, Laurie watched George's face on the screen in front of her, wondering what new information he was about to drop on them.

Ryan continued pressing George on the details of his encounter with Martin. "The police warned you about returning to his office."

"And I took it to heart," George said. "I never went back to his office again."

Laurie saw a glimmer flash across Ryan's eyes, and she immediately understood why. George had insisted that he had never gone back to Dr. Bell's office. He had used the same phrasing the last time they interviewed him: *I never went back to his office again.*

"But you didn't exactly leave Dr. Bell alone either, did you?" Ryan asked pointedly.

"I never approached him. Or spoke to him. Or anything like that."

"But you watched him, didn't you?"

George put his head in his hands. "I couldn't help it. He was all

I could think about, and seeing him in person somehow helped me. He couldn't hurt other people under my watch."

"Were you watching him the night he was killed?" Ryan asked. The entire set fell silent, as if they were holding their collective breath, waiting for George's answer.

"No," he finally said. "I was home."

"By yourself," Ryan added.

George nodded.

"So no one can vouch for you. You have no alibi."

George looked at his feet.

"Here are the facts, George," Ryan started. "You have no alibi. You have a history of obsessing over the people you blame for your mother's demise. You were stalking Dr. Bell. And you owned the very model of gun used to kill—"

"I was trying to do the right thing," George blurted out, interrupting Ryan's cross-examination. "Yes, I blame Dr. Bell for Ma's death, but I'm no killer. I know it all looks bad. That's why I never mentioned what I saw."

"What did you see, George?"

"It was a night about a week before the murder, around lower Manhattan, in the Greenwich Village area. I was following Dr. Bell when he got into a cab. A woman was waiting for him in the backseat, and he kissed her. I know I should have come forward, but I was scared I might become a suspect. I feel so guilty."

"Who was the woman?" Ryan asked, ignoring George's plea for sympathy.

"It was too dark to make out her face. I couldn't tell." George's high voice shook with fear. "I just assumed it was his wife, but then after the murder, everyone said they weren't getting along. So, you know, maybe it was some different lady."

Of all the scenarios Laurie and Ryan had gamed out, this wasn't among them. Ryan followed up with the obvious questions—Hair length? Hair color? Age?—but George had no other details to offer.

"Why should we believe you after all these years?" Ryan asked skeptically.

"Because if I was lying, I'd make up some answers to all these questions you're asking me. Look, I can't even swear it was a woman in the cab. I just saw a kiss. To be honest, it made me mad he had someone who'd let him do that." He looked away sadly. "And I know how pathetic this makes me sound, and that's another reason everyone should believe me. I swear to you . . . I'm telling the truth."

Ryan glanced in Laurie's direction, and she nodded her confirmation. It was a good place to end the interview.

47

As the crew reloaded the production equipment into the truck, Ryan pulled Laurie aside. "Do you mind if we sit in the car for a minute?" he asked, glancing toward George's house to indicate that he wanted to talk discreetly.

"I actually believe the guy," Ryan said as he settled into the passenger's seat.

Laurie thought for a moment. "There's no way he could have known Kendra was accusing Martin of cheating. It was never in the papers. He was going on what he saw in the back of a cab."

"Could it have been Kendra who he was kissing?" Ryan asked.

"I doubt it," Laurie said. "By all accounts, they were both miserable with each other. Maybe Kendra's hunch about an affair was right after all, but she just suspected the wrong woman."

"So now we're looking for some other woman, potentially with a jealous husband? How are we going to follow up on this?"

Ryan was right. It would be a fishing expedition. In addition to having a mystery man from the Beehive bar, they now had a mystery woman from a taxi on their hands.

Laurie analyzed the consequences of the new information. On the one hand, if Martin had been involved with another woman, it added to Kendra's motive to kill her husband. Not only had he been planning to leave her, but he already had a replacement waiting in the wings. On the other hand, an affair also created the possibility of alternative suspects—the unidentified mistress, and potentially a jealous husband as well.

Laurie had to remind herself that they wouldn't always be able to solve a case. They moved the needle even if they unearthed new information, which they had now done.

At least she had yet another piece of the puzzle to lock in. "I was thinking about George's description of his mother before she passed," she said. "I'm pretty sure I know why Kendra was so out of it the night of the murder."

After she spelled out her theory, Ryan said he would supplement the cross-examination he had prepared for when Kendra finally went before the cameras.

Laurie shook her head. "I don't feel right about ambushing her on television with something like that."

"Isn't that kind of what we do?" Ryan said, wrinkling his nose. "No kid gloves, plus she's still our number one suspect."

"This is a private health issue," she said. "It's different. I'll talk to her one-on-one."

She expected him to argue, but he held up his hands, acquiescing.

There was the rap of knuckles against the glass of the car window, and she looked up to see her father. She cracked open the door. "Dad, thanks so much for being here. If you keep helping out at my job, I'm going to have to add a line item to the budget to put you on payroll."

"And have you as my boss? Or Brett Young?" He feigned a shudder. "Consider me free labor."

She looked at her watch. It was four o'clock. "Can I hit you up for more work?" She explained that Timmy had trumpet practice until five, and that she might be running late tonight.

"Consider it done," he said.

If she was lucky, she could catch Kendra at home.

48

Ryan's comment about Laurie using "kid gloves" with Kendra must have struck a chord, because she decided to go to Kendra's house unannounced.

She was about to confront a woman about a highly personal health-related issue. On the other hand, that woman was the most likely suspect in Martin Bell's murder. A pop-in without cameras seemed like a fair compromise.

From the sidewalk outside of Kendra's carriage house, through the living room window, Laurie saw Kendra playing with her children. To someone else, their awkward, staccato movements might resemble a bizarre avant-garde dance routine, but Laurie recognized the familiar arm waves and pirouettes of a Wii video-bowling tournament. She had lost more than her fair share of virtual lanes to Timmy.

She suddenly questioned her decision to interrupt what was obviously a family night. Her conversation with Kendra could wait until tomorrow. After five years, it wasn't as if Kendra was going to flee the jurisdiction.

She turned to head toward Sixth Avenue to hail a cab, but then heard voices behind her. Kendra was now on her front porch, saying good-bye to her children. "I'll be back to kiss you good night," she called out. Laurie saw Caroline lingering in the doorway behind a young boy and girl.

Even in the dark, as Kendra took her front steps down to the driveway, Laurie could make out the silhouette of some kind of bag cross-slung against Kendra's hip. She wondered for a moment if it might be the leather duffel that had been stolen from her on Monday night.

Laurie put her head down, pretending to check her phone like so many other pedestrians. She slowly tilted her gaze toward Kendra, who was walking quickly in the opposite direction, heading toward Fifth Avenue.

Laurie decided to follow.

49

On either side of the book bag cross-slung over her shoulders, Kendra Bell sank her hands deep into the pockets of her charcoal-gray cardigan sweater. It was cashmere, from Escada, with a shawl collar and a sash belt. Oversized, almost to her knees. It was the first Christmas present Martin had ever bought for her, back when she was still in medical school. To this day, it was her favorite piece of clothing, like home in a sweater. It felt cozy and safe, but she knew that nothing—let alone an article of clothing—could protect her from the man she was supposed to meet tonight.

It had been more than a week since she first told him about the television show. She had promised him—under threat against her children—that she would not breathe a word about him to the producers. But of course that hadn't been enough for him. Of course he had demanded more, because he knew that he could.

She'd had the cash set aside for days, ready for delivery. She'd been so anxious over the weekend that she'd broken the rules to call him and arrange for a drop-off, but the number he had last given her had been disconnected. She wondered how many burner phones the man went through in a year.

Then today, while she was on lunch break, her cell phone rang. The call was from a blocked number. She immediately felt a rock in her stomach, knowing it was him. "Meet me at Greene and Houston," he ordered. "Northeast corner, under the scaffolding. Bring the usual."

In other words, bring the cash.

As she approached the intersection, she understood why he'd chosen this location. Developers had torn down an entire city block to make room for a new building that had not yet broken ground. The site was surrounded by chain-link fence, and scaffolding covered what had once been the sidewalk. No ordinary pedestrian would choose to walk into such dark, abandoned territory. But she had no choice.

He was waiting there for her, with a hoodie pulled up over what she assumed was still a shaved head. She couldn't believe this was the same man who had briefly been her drinking buddy at the Beehive — back when he was "Mike" with the sympathetic ear.

"The show," he said. "What's happening with it?"

"They don't know anything more than the police did five years ago," she said. "Less, in fact, from what I can tell."

"Remember what I said to you. About what's at stake. I'm not afraid to hurt Bobby and Mindy if that's what it takes."

She felt herself trembling inside her warm, cozy sweater. "Please," she gasped. "I promise, you don't need to do that." Her shoulders started to heave.

"Get yourself together," he hissed, grabbing the bag violently from her as she struggled to extract herself from the cross-slung strap.

Once she was free, he handed her a torn edge of notebook paper with a ten-digit number scrawled on it. "The new burner number. Call me when that show's done . . . and if they throw you any surprises along the way. Don't hold anything back from me."

"I won't, I swear."

She felt completely helpless as he walked away. She would never be free of him. He owned her.

50

Laurie was waiting in Kendra's driveway when she returned to the carriage house. She had watched the bag handoff from the west side of Greene Street, so she'd had a block-long head start on Kendra.

Kendra flinched when she saw her, clearly startled. "What are you doing here?"

"Something came up today during an interview with one of our other witnesses. I wanted to ask you about it in person."

"You couldn't call first?" Kendra asked.

"Honestly, I didn't want to give you time to come up with a lie. There was some talk of showing up with cameras, but that seemed unnecessary."

Kendra raised a hand to her mouth. "What is it?"

"Your state of mind after your children were born—it wasn't just postpartum, was it? You were taking drugs. Drugs that Martin gave to you." Laurie had put the pieces together when George Naughten had described his mother's condition prior to her overdose. "You said he had moved on without you. He was drugging you, wasn't he?"

Kendra nodded her head, pressing her lips together for composure.

"But then he stopped giving you the pills," Laurie said. "The lawsuits were filed, and he knew he'd have lawyers scrutinizing his drug-dispensing habits. He couldn't just hand the stuff out like candy anymore."

Kendra's gaze drifted to her front door, but the house was silent. They were alone. "I did have postpartum depression, just as I told you. But Martin had no sympathy. He just kept telling me to get my act together. He said it wasn't natural for me to be so helpless when I had children to care for. Instead of helping me get proper treatment, he told me he could take care of me himself— and that meant pills. I didn't know what they were. I just trusted him. After all, he was the Miracle Doctor. Days would go by, and I wouldn't even know what happened until Caroline helped me fill in the blanks. Then, all of a sudden, it was cold turkey. When I found out about the lawsuits after he died, I made the connection. But at the time, he wouldn't even tell me why he couldn't keep giving me the pills. He just yelled at me and called me an addict and a junkie."

"Because that's what you were," Laurie said. "That's what he turned you into."

She nodded again, wincing at the memory. "Please, you can't tell anyone. I'm clean now. If the Bells find out—" Her face went ashen.

I came here thinking I had it all figured out, Laurie thought. "You weren't spending that cash on shoes and spending sprees, but you also weren't hiring a hit man. You were buying drugs on the street to feed your addiction."

"Don't you see why I couldn't tell the police that? I had no way of proving it, and I knew Martin's parents would fight me for my children. I did everything right since Martin died. I got myself clean and sober. I work hard, and I'm a good mother."

"The only thing I couldn't figure out, Kendra, is why you still hoard large amounts of cash."

As Laurie suspected, Caroline must have told Kendra that she had shared that particular piece of information, because the question did not seem to catch Kendra by surprise. "Most of my money comes from a family trust. I keep cash on the side so the executors—including my in-laws—don't monitor every dime I spend."

"So who was the man you just gave a bag to on the corner of Greene and Houston?"

Kendra's entire body lurched as if she had been punched in the stomach. She placed both of her hands on top of her head and began saying, "No, no, no, no, no." For a second, Laurie wondered if she was in a trance.

"Kendra, I believe you're a changed woman, but I also think it's possible you made a horrible mistake in your impaired condition. I can try to help you as much as possible, but I can't keep this to myself." Kendra looked up at her with pleading eyes, but Laurie continued to confront her with the reality of the situation. "If you don't tell me what's going on, I'm going to go on air and tell a national television audience what I saw tonight. I'll inform the police as well. They'll fill in the blanks. You hired a hit man to kill your husband. That will be the entire story."

"Please," she whispered, "please don't make me do this. I can't. You'll get them killed. They're still innocent babies."

Laurie reached out tentatively and placed her hands gently on Kendra's shoulders, trying to calm her down. "Who? Who are you talking about?"

"Bobby and Mindy," she said, tears beginning to stream down her face. "That man. That awful man. He said he'd . . . hurt my children if I told anyone."

Laurie immediately looked around for someone who might be watching them, but saw no one. "Kendra, I'm not going to let that happen. We have resources. I can try to help you, but we should get out of the street."

Kendra's eyes darted around wildly. She pushed past Laurie and headed for the garage door on the ground floor of the carriage house.

She entered six digits into a security keypad, and the door began to rise. There was no car inside, just a few stacks of cardboard boxes. "Follow me."

Once they were inside, she looked Laurie directly in the eye: "You have to believe me. I have no idea who killed Martin."

51

Kendra pressed her palms to her eyes, trying to keep herself from crying again. She could not believe this was happening. She never should have agreed to do this television show. The Bells were going to continue to hate her and fight with her, no matter what she did, so why had she bothered trying to please them?

Now the floodgates had opened to her worst nightmare. She had promised that man she would make no mention of him, but Laurie Moran had now seen them together with her own two eyes. Kendra had no choice now but to appeal to this woman as a fellow single mother. She had to trust her with a truth Kendra had never spoken to anyone.

"You asked me before about whether I had ever made any friends in bars back then," Kendra said. "I knew what you were getting at."

"The Beehive," Laurie said. "I met Deb the bartender. She remembered you fondly."

Kendra smiled wistfully. "She's a tough broad, that one. I started going there as a little escape from the house, and for a while, it became kind of a habit. Not as if they'd yell 'Norm!' when I walked in like on *Cheers* or anything, but—"

Laurie nodded that she understood the point.

"Anyway, I was mixing alcohol and pills, and I'm sure that I was the messy drunk at the end of the bar, and that's saying something at that place. I remember feeling embarrassed when customers would move to a table to get away from me." Kendra rubbed her eyes. Over the years, during meetings with her AA group, she had referred elusively to some of her darker moments, but talking about her former self to a total stranger was harder than she'd expected. "Then one guy seemed to have sympathy for me. Or maybe I just thought he was a fellow drunk willing to tolerate my stories for a night."

"So who is he?" Laurie asked.

Kendra shook her head, hoping Laurie would believe her. She had only a vague recollection of so many of her days from back then. How could she possibly convince anyone of a truth that she herself did not quite understand? "I have no idea. I think he began talking to me one night when I was alone at the bar. Once I started complaining about Martin, I couldn't stop. He'd let me drone on about Martin and how miserable he made me. He'd even egg me on with 'what a jerk' and that kind of thing. In retrospect, he was pretending to act as volunteer counselor. He's a grifter, and I was his mark. Still am, as you saw tonight."

She could tell from the confusion on Laurie's face that she'd lost her.

"You didn't hire him?" Laurie asked.

"No!" Her voice was louder than she'd expected, echoing against the concrete and metal of the empty garage. She had donated Martin's car to charity after he was shot inside of it and never bought another one. "Sorry, it took me a while to understand his plan, too. About a week after Martin died—when the tabloid headlines were really doing a number on me—he was waiting for me outside Bobby's school at pickup time. He pulled a little digital recorder from his pocket and began playing it. I didn't even recognize my own voice at first, but it was definitely me. He had spooled together excerpts of our conversations."

"Which he recorded at the Beehive," Laurie said. "Your complaints about Martin."

Kendra nodded. "They were nothing to be proud of anyway, but given Martin's death? They were . . . horrific. He told me it would be 'such a shame' if the police or my in-laws heard the recordings. He demanded cash for his silence."

She could hear her slurred, slow voice in her head: *I just want out! My father died of a heart attack not much older than he is. Maybe that will happen to him.* And, echoing what she had said to Caroline the night of Martin's murder: *What I wouldn't do to be free of him.*

"He's been blackmailing you all this time?" Laurie asked.

"Not on a schedule. That would make it too easy to set up some kind of trap for him. He disappeared for nearly eleven months once, but he always comes back. He knows I'll keep paying. In fact, he threatened to expose me—or even harm me or my kids—if I agreed to do your show. I managed to convince him that it was in his interest for me to cooperate. I think he's smart enough to realize that if I lose my kids, I lose access to the trust, and then what good would I be to him?" She could hear the bitterness and anger in her own voice. "I swore to him that I would never reveal his existence—not to the police, and not to you. And now here we are."

Kendra searched Laurie's eyes for some clue of how she was going to handle the information that had just been dropped on her.

"Didn't it ever dawn on you that this man—this blackmailer— might have been the one to kill Martin?"

"At first, yes. And I was going to go to the police—even if it meant that I'd be arrested, too. But he told me that he made the recordings with a plan to sell them to Martin. I guess in my haze I had told him that Martin wanted to leave me and take the kids, so he figured Martin would pay good money to make that happen. But then Martin's death ruined his plan, and now I'm the one who has to pay."

"And you believed him?" Laurie asked.

"Yes, absolutely." Her voice was strong and confident, but how many times had Kendra wondered? She had temporarily become a different, darker, more desperate person, steered by a foggy, drug-addled haze. After all, she couldn't even remember the conversations that the man recorded at the Beehive, and living with Martin had driven her to the brink of insanity. Was it possible she had planted the seed in this dangerous stranger's head? Might she have even paid him to pull the trigger? Even now, she couldn't swear to having clean hands.

Laurie was staring off into the distance, as if she were struggling to weave together various threads of information. "It's possible that he's been following me, too," Laurie said. "Someone even stole my case notes on Monday night."

Kendra shook her head. "I mean, I guess it's possible. He's always three steps ahead of me, but he didn't say anything about it tonight. He was, however, very curious about what you knew and has been insistent that I keep him in the loop."

"You really have no idea who this man actually is?" Laurie asked.

This time, Kendra could tell the unvarnished truth. "Not at all. He calls me from blocked numbers and always meets me on foot, so I don't even have a license plate to track down. All I have is a burner number and this."

She pulled her cell phone from the back pocket of her jeans and scrolled to a photograph that she had looked at too many times. It was slightly blurry, and she hadn't been able to use a flash, but she'd used the tricks on her phone to sharpen the edges and add some light. It wasn't exactly magazine-ready, but anyone who knew this man should recognize him from this shot. "I pretended once to be check-ing my messages as I walked to one of our meet-ups. It's blurry be-cause I was shaking with fear that he'd catch me."

Laurie looked at the screen. It was a pretty good image under the circumstances. "Can you send that to me?" she asked.

"I have your email address," Kendra said as she uploaded the picture and hit send.

"So now what?" Kendra asked.

Laurie paused, looking around the garage as if she might spot the answer. "I don't know."

"But you believe me?"

Laurie opened her mouth to speak, but then stopped. "We'll figure something out. In the meantime, be careful."

As Kendra watched Laurie walk west toward Sixth Avenue, she thought it was possible that someone might finally believe she was innocent—not of everything, but at least of Martin's murder.

52

By the time Laurie had gotten home from Kendra's the night before, she barely had enough time to eat takeout with Timmy and her father and then call Alex to say good night. Only a few months ago, she had hesitated to blend her life with his. Now she couldn't wait for them to live together under one roof. She wanted him to be the last person she saw at night and the first person she saw in the morning.

She was working at her desk the next day when her office phone rang. She could see the call was coming from Grace's line and hit the speaker button.

"What's up?"

"I hate to tell you this, but Dana just called. Brett Young's on his way to see you. Oh—I see him now." She hung up, and a few seconds later, Laurie heard a tap on her office door.

"Come in," she called out, trying not to allow her voice to reveal the dread she felt in her stomach. She wondered if Brett had seen the charges yet for her new computer and cell phone. She steeled herself for an argument about whether the replacements were a personal or company expense.

She placed a fake smile on her face as she heard her office door open. She was shocked when Alex walked in. Grace was giggling at her desk behind him.

When Laurie saw him at the door, she jumped up, ran over, and kissed him. His arms went tight around her. "What a wonderful surprise," she said.

"I was nearby and suddenly needed to see you. Ever since that man pushed you, I've been so worried. If anything had happened to you . . ." He didn't finish the thought.

"Stop worrying, Your Honor. I really am okay."

They walked over to the conference table. When she sat in a chair, he began to gently massage her shoulders.

"For someone who says she's okay, you feel really tense," he said as he massaged more deeply.

"Don't worry. I promise I'm all right."

She rolled her neck as the soothing effect of the massage took hold. "It's your last free day before the chief judge starts assigning you cases. Are you doing anything special?"

"Yes, I'm visiting you. By the way, it's my last 'weekday' before cases," he corrected. "My docket assignments begin Monday, and it's only Friday."

"Well, I know tomorrow you're taking your clerks to the Yankees game."

As a federal judge, Alex would employ two recent law school graduates as judicial clerks. Until the fall, he'd be working with the clerks who had been hired by his predecessor, who had decided to retire on his eightieth birthday. Laurie had met both clerks briefly at the induction. Samantha was a Yale grad, and Harvey went to Stanford. They both seemed bright, enthusiastic, and pleasantly surprised to be working for a boss who offered them first-level Yankees seats as a way to kick off their work together. "Get used to them calling you Your Honor."

She could tell he liked the sound of it.

"Are you really holding up okay?" he asked. "I know you were torn last night about how to handle this new information about Kendra. It took every bit of restraint for me not to call the police when you told me. That has to be the same man who attacked you."

"Maybe," she said, turning more toward him. "But we don't even know who he is, so what's the point? This man is obviously critical to the case, but I have no way of identifying him on my own. I could air his photograph and ask for tips, but then he'll know Kendra told me about him, and she swears that he's been threatening both her and her children. I can't have that on my conscience."

"Of course not," Alex agreed. "But you could go to the police with it. That's probably the safest route."

As much as Ryan had turned a corner in his working relationship with her, she missed having Alex as a sounding board for her cases. When they brainstormed together, she always felt better afterward.

"Part of me wants to do that, but what am I supposed to tell them? I don't know who he is, or what he's even done. Kendra says it never dawned on her that the man might be Martin's killer, but that seems hard to believe. On the other hand, I can't prove she hired him, either. I also have no idea if he's the same man who attacked me on Monday. No matter how I game it out, I keep hitting a wall. Something doesn't feel right. I'm missing the bigger picture, I just know it."

The impromptu massage Alex was delivering suddenly stopped. "Please tell me you aren't working with Joe Brenner. Did that slimeball manage to weasel his way into the studio? Was it Brett Young who hired him? I could see him falling for something like that."

She swiveled her chair to face him. "What are you talking about?"

"Him," he said, reaching for a photograph on the conference table and pulling it closer. "Joe Brenner. He's totally low-rent. Did he convince Brett to take him on as an investigator? If so, you must get rid of him. I'll talk to Brett myself if I have to."

It was a printout of the photograph that Kendra had emailed her from her cell phone the previous night. Beehive Man. "Alex, you know this guy? This is the guy from last night—the one Kendra claims is blackmailing her."

Alex leaned forward to get a closer look. "That's definitely him."

He reached for her new laptop, typed a few keystrokes, and then turned the screen to face her. She saw a photo of the same man, but in a black open-collar shirt and black sports coat. He was losing his hair, and had shaved it close to the skin. His eyes were narrow and cold. "Mean," as the bartender at the Beehive had described them.

The text next to the head shot read "Joe Brenner is the owner of New York Capital Investigations, a private investigative firm with a quarter century experience conducting discreet and effective investigations."

Laurie's thoughts were reeling. Why would a private eye shake down Kendra for money? Or did he? For all she knew, Kendra could have been lying. Maybe Kendra had been paying Brenner for stealing Laurie's case notes and laptop.

"How do you know him?" Laurie asked.

"I don't, not anymore. But about fifteen years ago, I was working on a multi-defendant conspiracy case. The attorney for one of the codefendants hired Brenner as an investigator. When he took the stand, I was absolutely convinced that he exaggerated the exculpatory evidence he claimed to have located. At one point, I thought he had even perjured himself. I couldn't prove it, and the defendants were all convicted regardless. But I confronted the attorney who had hired him. He said sometimes clients were—quote—willing to pay extra for an investigator who goes the distance."

"So you think he lied on the stand for an extra fee," Laurie said.

Thoughts were pinging inside Laurie's head so quickly, she was having a hard time keeping track of them. A stranger who started talking to Kendra at a dive bar just happened to be a lowlife private eye who recorded her conversations? That was too much of a coincidence. She thought about Martin Bell's desire to leave Kendra and retain custody of his children. Maybe he had hired Brenner to chat up his wife and gather incriminating evidence. But if the plan had worked and Brenner had damning recordings of an impaired Kendra, why hadn't Martin filed for divorce? And wouldn't he have told his parents about his intentions?

Or maybe the alleged recordings didn't even exist. Kendra could have fabricated the entire story to cover the fact that she had paid Brenner to kill her husband.

Laurie could tell she was close to connecting the dots, but each time she was about to have a breakthrough, she felt the truth fall from her grasp.

Alex was staring at Brenner's photograph, clearly upset that this man had entered Laurie's orbit. "As I said, I can't prove it. But I was certain enough that I spread the word among defense lawyers that they should avoid him, and apparently I wasn't the only one. His work for litigators has completely dried up. No one will touch him because they think it could backfire at trial."

Stretching the truth under oath was one thing; murder for hire was another. Maybe Brenner's detective business had disintegrated to the point that he had crossed the line to working as a paid killer.

"Yet he still has a private eye website," she said, gesturing toward his image on her screen. His face—those dark, mean eyes—gave her a chill. "Apparently someone is still hiring him?"

"Where there's a will, there's a way," Alex said drily. "People think lawyers have no scruples? If Brenner's bankroll is any lesson, then politicians are even worse."

"He has political clients?"

"That's what I've heard. You see, lawyers need to worry about him getting caught on the stand playing loose with the facts. But if you just need a tough guy willing to cut corners to dig up dirt on your political enemies? Brenner's the go-to man in certain circles. My guess is the guy's a regular on the Amtrak back and forth to Albany."

And with one little word, Laurie finally had a breakthrough. Albany.

She reached for her cell phone on the table and pulled up her father's number.

"You figured it out, didn't you?" Alex asked.

"Almost." When her father answered, she spelled out her theory as Alex nodded along beside her. When she was done, she asked Leo if he could make another call to his NYPD source.

"Let me see what I can do."

53

Three hours later, Laurie was alone with Daniel Longfellow in his Upper West Side apartment. After he explained that Leigh Ann was still at work and the dogs were at doggie daycare, she made quick work of thanking him for finding time to meet with her.

"To be honest, Laurie, you didn't give me much of a choice. I think you know how much my wife and I would like to keep our names out of your production. I assumed by now you had confirmed our lack of involvement."

Opting for a blunt introduction, she dropped a photograph of Joe Brenner on the living room coffee table. "I think you know this man," she said.

His face immediately validated her instincts. A less decent man could have hidden his link to whatever was going on between Joe Brenner and Kendra Bell. But Daniel Longfellow wasn't a talented liar. She would be able to extract the truth from him.

"Where did you get that picture?" he asked.

"He's not exactly in hiding," she said. "He's basically the center of our investigation. And we know you have a connection to him."

She allowed the silence to permeate the room. She could tell from the way he bit his lower lip that her instincts had been right. Longfellow knew Joe Brenner, and their relationship had something to do with Martin Bell's death.

Laurie decided to take a stab in the dark. "All these years, Kendra thought she had the worst luck in the world. She vented about her unhappy marriage to a random stranger, and, lo and behold, the man recorded her and then blackmailed her when her husband just happened to be murdered. She never connected the dots. She never even entertained the possibility that this man might be the killer until I suggested it."

Longfellow was struggling to maintain the aloofness of a man with a healthy distance from the subject at hand. "Ms. Moran, I'm a supporter of the work you do for your television program, but I'm afraid I need to call this a day."

"Please," she said, "hear me out, or else I'll have this conversation with my television audience. What are the odds that Kendra Bell happened to pour her heart out to a man who would use that information to blackmail her for years? Or even worse, maybe he even killed her husband in cold blood as just the first step in a blackmail scheme."

Laurie paused to search out Longfellow's expression. Any stranger who had nothing to do with the man in the photograph would have been completely perplexed. Longfellow did not strike her as a man out of step with the conversation.

"This man," she said. "He's a private investigator. Joe Brenner. Brenner was never a random stranger at Kendra's bar, was he?"

Daniel covered his mouth, as if he were suddenly imagining a series of horrible events he had never envisioned before.

"I'm fundamentally a good man," he said, his gaze moving behind her in the distance.

"Then this is your chance to prove it," Laurie said. "Whatever mistakes you made were years ago. I need you to tell me what you know about Joe Brenner."

Senator Longfellow swallowed, and Laurie could tell that he

was weighing the consequences of the decision he was about to make. "Brenner's a well-known quantity in Albany," he muttered. "I hired him—almost six years ago. Somewhere along the way, Leigh Ann and I became almost a long-distance relationship, even though we never planned it that way. I wanted to believe that we were both doing the work that was important to us, but, at some point, I could tell that something was broken. I suspected she was seeing another man."

Laurie sensed that Longfellow was ready to open up to her. "So you hired a private investigator to confirm your suspicions," she said.

It made perfect sense. Kendra had not been the only spouse to worry about the amount of time Martin and Leigh Ann were spending together. Brenner may have been disreputable among New York City lawyers, but he was also willing to use questionable tactics to unearth dirty secrets when necessary. That was the kind of person Longfellow had turned to in a moment of jealousy.

He swallowed before answering. "That's not how I thought of it. At least, not at first. I told myself he would *disprove* my theory. He'd check on Leigh Ann in the city and tell me it was all in my imagination. It was a gamble, but it would have felt so great to have a shark of a private investigator come back and tell me I had nothing to worry about."

"But that's not what happened," Laurie said.

"There's that saying: *Be careful what you wish for.* I had heard such questionable things about Brenner's tactics, but I became consumed with knowing the truth. And then"—he shook his head—"I got what I'd wished for."

"He obtained proof that Leigh Ann was more than friends with Martin Bell," Laurie said. She thought about George Naughten's memory of Martin Bell kissing a woman in a taxi. It was Leigh Ann Longfellow, exactly as Kendra Bell had suspected all along.

Daniel wiped his face with his hands. "His work confirmed my worst suspicions. He even had photographs. I was paralyzed with indecision."

"Why didn't you just leave her?" Laurie asked.

"Because I didn't want to!" He made the answer seem so obvious. It was true love, exactly as she had sensed when she first met them. "Why would I leave Leigh Ann? I'd known she was my perfect partner and my one true love since we first met at Columbia."

Daniel's gaze shifted to the floor as he ran nervous fingers through his full head of hair.

He pressed his eyes closed and shook his head. "At that moment, if I could have taken it all back, I would have. Because I knew that if I confronted her with the evidence I had collected, it would have broken us forever."

"But what about that saying, *the truth will set you free*?" Laurie asked.

Longfellow scoffed. "Total nonsense. Think about it: If I had confronted my wife—my *wife*—with photos of her kissing another man, she would have known that I had spied on her. And, maybe even worse, she would know that I still wanted her, despite the affair. She never would have respected me again. I just wanted the affair to end."

Laurie had come here knowing that the connection between Daniel Longfellow and Joe Brenner was important. Now her instinct was telling her that Longfellow was a flawed but honest man. She tried to put herself in his shoes and ask what he would have done next after learning from a private eye that his wife was seeing another man.

She saw the scene as if it were unfolding before her eyes. "You told Brenner to take the photographs of Leigh Ann and Martin to Kendra."

He pinched the bridge of his nose with his thumb and forefinger. "In some of the photographs Brenner showed me, you couldn't make out Leigh Ann's face, but the man was definitely Martin Bell. I figured Kendra had more power than I did to make the affair stop."

Laurie pictured Kendra five years earlier—suffering from postpartum depression and drug and alcohol abuse.

"Kendra had no power at all," Laurie said.

"Of course she did. She and Martin had young children. I assumed she would demand that her husband end the affair or risk losing his entire family."

Laurie shook her head. "What kind of way is that to salvage your marriage?"

He scoffed, seeing the irony. "Probably a really bad one. But I thought once the affair ended, I could work harder to be a better husband. I'd leave the assembly if necessary, come back to the city, and go into the private sector if I had to. But no matter what—I'd win back Leigh Ann's heart, and everything would return to normal. At least, that's what I assumed."

"So what happened when Brenner told Kendra about the affair?"

The laugh that followed was bitter and completely unexpected. "At first, I thought the plan had worked. Brenner called me, saying he'd met Kendra at a dive bar and—quote, unquote—'had it all taken care of.' And, literally, a few minutes later, I got a phone call from the governor about the Senate appointment. It seemed as if fate had turned a corner. The next night, Leigh Ann surprised me with dinner—at the same table at the same restaurant where we had our first real date after we met. All of a sudden, she was back. I assumed Kendra had confronted Martin about his affair and that Martin had broken things off with Leigh Ann. We'd get to live happily ever after, as if the affair had never happened. But then Martin was killed. Don't you see? Kendra must have been so angry about the affair that she hired a hit man."

"Why didn't you tell the police this?"

222 Mary Higgins Clark & Alafair Burke

He took a deep breath, struggling not to cry. "Because I love my wife, and I don't want to see her humiliated in public. I also don't want to lose her. To this day, she has no idea that I found out about the affair."

"You may think Kendra hired a hit man, but it's just as likely that *you* did. After all, you're the one who initially involved Joe Brenner, and you're the one who was desperate to have your wife back."

"Absolutely not. I would *never* do something like that. And I showed the police our financial records at the time. Everything was in order. I only paid Brenner a few hundred bucks in cash—certainly not enough to order a hit!"

At Laurie's request, Leo had already confirmed this information with the NYPD, but she had wanted to hear it directly from Daniel. The lead detective told Leo that the senator had provided complete financial statements from both his and his wife's accounts, and no large amounts of cash were unaccounted for.

"Well, I don't think it was Kendra, either. Because, here's the thing, Senator: Brenner never did as you instructed. He never gave Kendra proof of an affair."

She waited to see if Daniel would draw the same conclusion she had. His face went pale. "Dear God. You think *Brenner* killed Martin?" She could tell that he had never entertained the idea.

She nodded. "At least, I think so. He entrapped Kendra into saying terrible things about Martin and recorded the conversations. I think he shot Martin, knowing that he could blackmail Kendra for the rest of their lives."

"In which case, I'm the one who set it all in motion," he said, his voice drifting off. "I should have known that lies never go away. They ripple through time. I have to do what's right, even if it means telling Leigh Ann what I know. Even if it ends my career. I'll go on your show. I'll go to the police. I'm willing to drag my secrets into the light."

"That's good to know, Senator. Right now, I'd like to ask you to sit tight. I have an idea that could take Brenner down."

As soon as she was in a cab, she pulled up Kendra's cell phone number and dialed. After four rings, the call went to voice mail. "Kendra, it's Laurie. Give me a call. I know who the Beehive man is. It's time to turn the tables on him."

54

The following afternoon, Laurie and Leo stood in Kendra's garage. The show's lead cameraman, Nick, was waiting outside in the driveway, behind the wheel of their production van, and they were waiting for Grace and Jerry to arrive in Jerry's new car.

Laurie's phone pinged. It was a text from Jerry. *Sorry, bad traffic, but we're out front. Battle stations ready.*

"Okay, everyone's in place," Laurie said.

Kendra stared at her cell phone, her hand visibly shaking.

"You're sure you want to do this?" Laurie asked. "Another alternative is to go to the police."

Kendra's eyes widened. "No. From the sounds of it, this man Brenner has political connections. I saw how the police treated me when Martin was killed. I'm convinced someone in the department pulled strings to gloss over Martin's affair with Leigh Ann. All these years, I was right about the two of them, but they treated me like I was crazy."

Laurie looked at Leo and knew he was biting his tongue. Her father was blue through and through. He had no tolerance for people who did not trust the police, but Laurie understood Kendra's reservations. For all they knew, Brenner had a friend or two in the NYPD. And if Kendra went to the police now, there was no guarantee they would believe that Brenner acted on his own. Brenner could use those tapes to say that he had killed Martin at her request and cut a deal to save himself by testifying against her.

"I can't promise this will work," Laurie said.

"I know," Kendra whispered. "But it's the best chance I've ever had to clear my name." She ran her fingertips along the silver chain of her necklace. The pendant contained a hidden audio recorder that transmitted to the production van outside.

"You ready?" Laurie asked. She texted Kendra a photograph from her phone. It was step one of putting the plan in motion. She already had the telephone number from Joe Brenner's website pulled up on her phone. Step two.

Kendra nodded, looking more certain than she had since Leo and Laurie's arrival. "Let's do this. Let's nail him to the wall."

Laurie hit the dial button.

Three rings in, the call went to voice mail, as Laurie had expected on a Saturday. "Mr. Brenner, this is Laurie Moran." Leo nodded at her, encouraging her to keep her voice confident and level. "I'm a journalist and a producer at Fisher Blake Studios. Your name has come up in the course of our investigation into the murder of Dr. Martin Bell and we'd like to give you a chance to tell your side of the story on camera before we go to air. Please give me a call at your earliest convenience."

Laurie felt her heart racing as she hung up the phone. Both Alex and Leo said that private investigators directed their calls to their cell phones so they could check messages at all hours. If they were right, then Joe Brenner was listening to Laurie's voice right now. They sat in complete silence. There was nothing for them to do but wait.

Less than two minutes later, Kendra's phone rang in her hand. She cringed at the sound as if her hand were burning. She held up the screen to show them that the call was coming from a blocked number.

It was Brenner.

Kendra's voice quivered when she answered. "Hello?"

She leaned toward Laurie, and Laurie was able to make out Brenner's end of the conversation. "You've been a very bad girl, Kendra. Did you forget our rules? What did you tell those producers?"

"Nothing," she said. "I didn't say one word about you, but I just got off the phone with Laurie Moran, the head producer. She somehow knows all about you."

"Why didn't you call me immediately?"

"I literally had my phone in my hand when it rang. I had to go down to my garage so the kids wouldn't hear me. Then you called me."

"So I know where little Bobby and Mindy are now. That was considerate of you."

His voice was icy, and Laurie felt a lump form in her throat. She reached for Kendra's free hand and gave it a squeeze.

"Please, I promise I didn't say anything. But we should talk . . . in person. I'll tell you everything she said, but I'm afraid she may have gotten the police to wiretap my phone."

The call suddenly went dead. Kendra looked at the screen, wondering if she had lost the signal. A text message appeared from a blocked number.

Meet me at Cooper Triangle. Forty minutes.

"Is that a bar or something?" Laurie asked.

Kendra shook her head quickly. "It's that little triangle of grass next to Cooper Union. I've met him there before." Cooper Union was a small arts school in the East Village. Laurie knew the exact spot.

Kendra hit the button to open the garage door, and Laurie and Leo hopped into the van with Nick. She directed the cameraman where to go as she texted the location to Jerry. Cooper Union was only a few blocks away. They'd be in place before Kendra or Brenner arrived. That was the only way their plan would work.

55

Exactly thirty-eight minutes later, Laurie watched from the passenger seat of the production van as Kendra walked east on 8th Street and turned right on Cooper Square. Kendra waited for the light to change and made her way to the small, triangular park made from what used to be a concrete traffic median.

"Almost there," Kendra said. "Hope you can hear me."

At Laurie's direction, Nick called Kendra's cell phone, let it ring one time, and hung up. It was the signal they had agreed on to confirm that the audio was transmitting to the van.

Laurie's phone buzzed. The text was from Jerry. *She's here! I have a good angle. You guys?*

Laurie hopped up and joined Nick and Leo in the back of the van. Jerry was operating a small dash-mounted camera from his vehicle, but Laurie was depending on Nick for the better footage. Nick was capturing Kendra on video with a long-zoom lens. The camera was mounted on the exterior of the van, hidden inside of a roof-mounted rig. She watched on the screen as Kendra arrived at the traffic median as planned.

Good here too, she texted back.

They had never done something this clandestine before. New York required the consent of only one party in order to record a conversation. Thanks to Kendra's cooperation, they might finally be able to prove whatever role Joe Brenner played in Martin Bell's death.

Two minutes after Kendra arrived, a solidly built man in a navy blue hoodie approached from the north, his hands in his pockets. As Kendra and Brenner began to speak, Laurie signaled to Nick and pointed to her ear. They needed more volume. Nick turned a dial, and soon they could hear the conversation clearly.

"We had a deal," Brenner said. "You were the one who decided to do this show. You were supposed to keep me out of it. Now I'm getting a phone call from the producer. You owe me an explanation."

"I swear, it wasn't me. Laurie Moran called me today out of the blue. She told me she knows who killed Martin. And then she texted me this photograph." Kendra held up the screen of her phone and showed Brenner the photograph Laurie had sent moments earlier. The time stamp would line up to the story Kendra was feeding Brenner if he decided to inspect the photograph more closely. Instead, he gave it a cursory glance. It was Brenner's head shot from the home page of his private investigator website.

"She give you my name?" Brenner asked.

Laurie physically crossed her fingers, hoping that Kendra was a competent liar.

"No," Kendra said quickly. "Just a photograph. Like I said, I made an excuse to hang up and was about to call you when you reached me first."

"What else did the TV people say?" Brenner asked.

"They asked me whether I was ever approached by a private investigator about the affair I suspected Martin was having. Of course, I told them no. Everyone had been treating me like a looney tune, even before Martin's death. They were all so convinced that I fabricated the affair from scratch. But then after I called you, I realized the truth. *You're* the private investigator they were talking about. Maybe whoever hired you to befriend me told the producers about you. That show is going to prove that you killed Martin."

He laughed bitterly. "You might be as crazy as you were five years ago if you think I'm the one who killed your husband."

"All these years, I thought you were just a dangerous stranger that I was stupid enough to trust with my problems. But it's no coincidence that you made those tapes of me complaining about my marriage. You were sent there—hired by a client. Who was it? Daniel Longfellow?"

He scoffed. "It's just you and me here, Kendra. After all these years, I'd love to know the truth. You mean to tell me you didn't have anything to do with taking out your husband?"

"Of course not," she insisted. "I think *you* did it!"

"You're barking up the wrong tree with that one, sister. Look, it sounds to me like the producers don't know a thing. Keep your mouth shut like we agreed. I'll let you know when it's time for the next payment." He started to walk away, but Kendra called out after him.

"The producers never told me your name, but I figured it out, Mr. Brenner."

Brenner's lips were moving, but he had stepped too far away from Kendra. They couldn't hear him over the sounds of passing cars.

Kendra spoke again. "After the producer sent me that picture of you, I uploaded it into a Google Images search. Your website came up right away. Your name is Joe Brenner. You have a private eye license that you probably don't want to lose." She took three steps toward him. Even on the screen, Laurie could see the fear in her face, but Kendra must have remembered what they had told her about keeping the recorder close to Brenner. "You have been threatening for years to turn those recordings of me over to the police. But a good cop might suspect that *you're* the one who killed my husband, all so you could drain me of money until I go to my grave."

"Be very careful, Kendra. I don't respond well to threats."

"You're a bully. You've known all along that I was innocent, but you've been blackmailing me for five years. It ends today. Just tell me the truth, and we can go our separate ways. Otherwise, I'm going to the police to tell them everything I know, and let the chips fall where they may."

Brenner smiled and shook his head, but said nothing. He snatched the phone from Kendra's hand and inspected it.

"Just what I was afraid of," Laurie sighed. "He knows she's recording him."

He began to pat down the front of Kendra's dress, but she recoiled from his touch. They heard the sounds of a struggle and a loud "Stop!" come through the audio feed.

Brenner suddenly stood up straight and began turning in a methodical circle. His gaze did a double take when he spotted their van, with the roof mount.

"He made us," Leo said.

Before Laurie knew what she was doing, she was opening the back door of the van.

"Laurie, no!" her father called out.

"Dad, he won't shoot me in front of a rolling camera. Just keep filming!"

An approaching taxi laid on its horn as Laurie sprinted across the street.

56

Brenner turned to leave, but had nowhere to go. Cars were racing by on either side.

"I have an armed ex–police officer in that van, so don't even think about hurting us," Laurie said.

He held up both of his hands. "I don't know what's going on here, but it's a huge misunderstanding. I'm a private investigator. I don't hurt people, let alone kill them."

"I have definitive evidence that you were hired by Daniel Longfellow and gathered proof of an affair between his wife and Martin Bell. Then Longfellow instructed you to disclose that proof to Kendra."

He shrugged. "Even if that's true, so what? That's what private eyes do all the time."

"Except you never told Kendra about the affair, did you? You saw a chance for a payday. After you got her on tape saying she wanted to be free of her husband, you killed him and have been blackmailing Kendra ever since."

"You're crazy. I'm the good guy. I never gave Kendra the pictures of her husband with another woman because she was nuts already. There's no telling what she might have done."

As he offered what sounded like an innocent explanation, Brenner's face softened and his voice sounded less icy. He seemed like a completely different person than when he had been speaking to Kendra alone a few minutes earlier. "Everyone knows Kendra was hanging by a thread."

"So you grabbed the chance to blackmail her!"

"Listen to me, lady. That's not how it happened."

"Why did you record her when she was venting about her marriage?"

He removed a small digital recorder from his jacket pocket and held it up. She saw a red light on the front. "Because I'm a private eye. I record everything. I erase the stuff I don't need. But then when the doc was killed, I figured Kendra did it. She had a husband who wanted to dump her. The doc and his parents wanted to take away her kids. They would have left her high and dry with nothing."

"If you thought Kendra was guilty," Laurie asked, "why didn't you come forward with the tapes?"

"Because I know how trials work. It wouldn't give the police what they needed to make a case. She couldn't have been the one who pulled the trigger. She was inside the house when it happened. That means someone did it for her. They would have pointed the finger at me—just like you are—and I'd have had to explain why I got payments from Kendra. I was only trying to help. Plus it would've meant exposing Leigh Ann Longfellow's affair, and that would have killed me with my clients in Albany. I was looking out for myself, but I'm no murderer."

"No, but you're a blackmailer."

He looked around nervously. "You've got it all backwards, lady."

"We just got you on camera, Brenner. *I'll let you know when it's time for the next payment*? What's that, if not blackmail? And you've been following me, too. Once the police start investigating you, they'll find out where you were on Monday night. You pushed me in front of a taxi and robbed me. That's at least two other felony charges."

When there was a gap in the traffic, he said, "You don't know what you're talking about, lady. I'm done with you." He turned his back to the production van, jogged across Bowery, and began walking south. When he reached the corner, he pulled his cell phone from his pocket and appeared to be making a call.

"He didn't confess," Kendra said.

"We knew it was a long shot," Laurie replied. "Trust me: overall, the footage is going to help you. And we have him dead to rights for blackmail."

"Now what?"

Laurie watched Brenner, still on the phone. She wasn't ready to let him go. She pulled out her own phone and called Jerry, who was parked on 5th Street. "Pull up to Bowery, take a right, and then turn on Sixth. Hang tight."

She still had eyes on Brenner. She called Leo. "He's contacting someone. I want to see where he goes next. We can't follow him in the van, but he didn't spot our second car. I'm going to tail him with Jerry."

"Not without me," Leo said.

They dashed across Bowery and made their way to 6th Street, where Jerry was idling at the curb. A pair of binoculars dangled from a rope around his neck. As she reached to open the back door, she saw that the rear seats were folded forward to make room for all the boxes and bags filling the small hatchback.

"Sorry, Laurie. I was planning to move some stuff out to Fire Island once we were done."

Laurie could feel Brenner slipping away. She had to make a quick decision. Jerry wasn't going to like this, but if she could choose only one person to go with her, she knew it made more sense to bring an armed former police officer than her assistant producer.

"So . . . can we borrow your car? And let me have those," she said, pointing to the binoculars.

57

Joe Brenner felt his feet shuffling down Bowery. For five years, his meetings with Kendra had been easy money. In theory, she could have tried to turn the tables on him, but she never had. Not once. She was too afraid. She had the money and would continue paying. Easy.

But today, Kendra suddenly had surprises up her sleeve. She had played him, and now a television show with millions of viewers had him on tape—probably on camera based on the looks of the roof mount on that van. He replayed the conversation in his head, knowing how bad it was.

He had denied killing Martin Bell—of course he had—but he had told Kendra to keep her mouth shut, an obvious sign that he was hiding something. And he had said something about the next payment. They'd have him locked and loaded for extortion. He'd lose his license and have to go to prison.

That was not going to happen.

He needed someone with power to shut this entire thing down. He knew exactly what to do. He pulled out his burner phone to make the call. The voice that answered was nervous, the usual reaction when he rang.

"It's me," he said. "You're going to do something for me."

"How much this time?"

"Not money," he said. "A favor. And then you'll never hear from me again."

"What kind of favor?" More fear in that quivering voice.

"Not on the phone," he said, paranoid after that stunt Kendra pulled with the television producer. He needed to clear his head. He needed open space, away from the city. "Meet me at Randall's Island, in the parking lot by Field 9." Sometimes Brenner drove there for no reason at all other than to be surrounded by green grass.

There was a long pause, then the voice on the other end of the line said, "I'll leave right now."

58

Laurie could see the familiar exit signs along the FDR Drive ticking by. They had spotted Brenner, still walking south on Bowery, and then watched as he got behind the wheel of a black Dodge Charger. Now they were following him from a safe distance behind, unsure of their destination.

"Still can't believe this thing's electric," Leo said. "Handles like a race car."

"Well, handle it carefully. It's Jerry's baby. Where is Brenner heading? He better not be going to Albany. Jerry said the car can only go one hundred sixty miles before it needs to be charged."

"He's signaling now. We're going on the Triborough Bridge. Maybe he's headed for LaGuardia? He could be making a run for it. Wait, he's got his blinker on again. I think we're headed for Randall's Island." It was an island in the East River between East Harlem, the South Bronx, and Queens. Most of the island was a city park.

"Keep your distance, Dad. Parts of the park can be pretty vacant. There won't be many cars to blend in with."

"You know how many stakeouts your old man has done? It's under control."

Laurie fixed the binoculars on the Charger's license plate. She grabbed a piece of paper and pencil from the glove compartment and wrote it down. "A little insurance in case we lose him."

"Good idea, but I'm not planning to lose him," Leo said. Then, pointing, he added, "He's pulling into the parking lot by the baseball fields."

"Well, don't follow him! He'll see us."

Laurie had taken Timmy here for a few birthday parties and remembered the general layout. The park was home to more than sixty athletic fields. Even on a nice day, not all of them would be in use.

"Trust me," Leo said crisply as he approached the parking area where Brenner had turned. Laurie leaned low in her seat as Leo drove past. "There's a grove of trees beyond this field," he told her. "We can park behind it. He might be able to see the car, but there's no way he'll be able to see us."

After a short drive, she felt the car come to a stop.

"Dad, maybe we should call for backup."

"Not yet. My gut tells me that right after the encounter with you, he called somebody to meet him here. I don't want to scare off whoever that somebody is."

Brenner had gotten out of his car and was smoking a cigarette while leaning against the hood. He checked his watch then glanced around, his gaze lingering on the grove of trees.

"He keeps looking at us, Dad."

"Don't worry. He can't see you from where he is."

Another vehicle, a Volvo wagon, pulled into the lot and parked next to Brenner. As it slowed to a stop, Laurie adjusted the binoculars and was able to see the driver. "It's a woman," she said. "She looks familiar.

"Oh my God, Dad. I can't believe it. It's Leigh Ann Longfellow."

The senator's wife got out of her car, looked in all directions, and walked over to where Brenner was standing. Even though the day was overcast, she had on a pair of dark sunglasses.

Neither Leo nor Laurie took note of a white SUV that entered the park and turned toward an adjacent field.

59

Brenner was used to being in control. As a child, he was the kid who ran the playground, choosing which games to play and terrorizing anyone who dared to challenge him. In college, he knew exactly what he wanted to study—law enforcement. He wanted to enforce rules and have a badge to back up his authority. When the classroom work proved tedious, he took matters into his own hands and joined the army. Military service would make him a shoo-in for the police department.

Even when he was kicked out of the service for assaulting his sergeant—a beating Brenner still believed was long overdue—he had taken control. He managed to get the discharge bumped to "other than honorable," when the army had wanted to court-martial him with a dishonorable discharge. And when his military record made it impossible for him to work as a cop, he found another way to put his skills to use: as a private eye. When lawyers stopped hiring him for work, he became the political crowd's go-to guy for what they called "opposition research."

Time and time again, when circumstances threw Brenner a challenge, he found a way to stay in control and look out for number one.

But now his usual coping skills were eluding him. He couldn't believe that the brilliant plan he had hatched five years ago was coming apart fast. It had all begun with the most routine request: a jealous husband wanted to know if his wife was stepping out on him. But the husband wasn't any old Joe Blow. He was political darling Daniel Longfellow. In all his years delivering the bad news to clients, Brenner had never seen a spouse so crushed by the betrayal. He thought Longfellow was going to start bawling right in front of him.

Any respect he had for the man was destroyed when Longfellow pleaded with him to "make them stop." Brenner offered him the names of some of the best divorce lawyers in town, but all Longfellow wanted was to get his wife back. The senator told him to take the evidence to Kendra Bell. "They have kids," he said. "She'll make him end the affair."

In other words, he wanted her to do his dirty work for him. Well, Brenner was never one to miss an opportunity. He actually started blackmailing Leigh Ann first, right when he heard the rumors that the governor was thinking about Longfellow for the vacant Senate seat. It was a no-brainer. He lied and told her that Martin Bell's wife had hired him to trail her husband but that he was willing to sell her the incriminating photos instead if the price was right. She was the earner in the family, plus it was clear she had big plans about being first lady someday. Future first ladies don't get caught kissing someone else's husband. She paid.

The situation with Kendra had been more complicated. When he first approached her at that bar, he wasn't sure how to play her. But he knew her husband was loaded, and he had a chance to collect. What were the chances she would spill her guts to him or that the doc would be killed only days later? It was as if the money had fallen into his lap. Like his grandfather used to say, "When a baked duck flies into your mouth, don't ask questions. Eat it." Two separate women, two steady paydays—and neither one of them ever figured out it was crybaby Longfellow who had first put the wheels in motion.

Now he needed to put the screws to Leigh Ann one more time, but not for money.

She was obviously angry when she stepped from the station wagon, but she looked around cautiously, afraid to be recognized. There were other cars in the lot, but no visible occupants. The afternoon soccer and baseball games were already under way.

"You can't just call me on the weekend and demand that I drive out to the middle of nowhere at a second's notice. Luckily Daniel was at the office or—"

"Your husband needs to call his friends at the police department or the DA's Office or something for a get-out-of-jail-free card."

She looked at him with disdain. "Are you insane? That's something from a trashy crime novel. That's not how real life works."

If Brenner had been his usual self—a man always in control—he might have noticed that her voice wasn't tentative and nervous, as it always was when he spoke with her. Maybe he would have realized there was a reason for her newfound confidence today.

"That's *exactly* how it works. It happens all the time. Senator So and So's kid gets a DUI, and, oops, the paperwork goes missing. Congressman Whatshisname gets caught with drugs in his car, and the Baggie walks out of the property room. Strings get pulled, and now you and your big-shot husband need to pull them for me."

"I can't do that," she said. "Daniel doesn't even know about Martin. He still thinks he was just a man I knew through our parents. How in the world am I supposed to explain my connection to you?"

He almost started to laugh. She was so smart and yet so stupid. "Trust me, Leigh Ann, he knows who I am. He's the one who hired me, not Kendra. He knows about you and Martin. He's known all along."

He could tell she was thrown off by the information. "Well, he would never do what you're asking—even if it were possible. He's too principled."

"Exactly, which is why I need you to ask him to do it. He'll do it for you because he loves you and would do anything to keep you out of trouble. I know him. He'd take a bullet for you."

She looked down, and he could see her mulling over her options. She glanced around at the players on the nearby soccer and softball fields. She stared at the car partially obscured by the grove of trees.

"I'm worried about someone recognizing me. Let's talk in your car."

He double-clicked his key fob to unlock the doors and hopped into the driver's seat. When she was settled into the passenger's seat next to him, she said, "You were right about what you said. Danny does love me. And that's why I can't let you ruin everything for us."

She reached into her pocket and pulled out a gun.

60

Laurie watched through the binoculars as Leigh Ann opened the door and slid into the passenger's seat while Brenner got behind the wheel. Their car faced her. A foot-high barrier of railroad ties separated the parking area from the ball field.

Her thoughts were racing with pieces of the investigation. For the last twenty-four hours—since Alex first recognized Joe Brenner's photograph—she had been convinced that Brenner had killed Martin Bell in order to blackmail Kendra. But now she was replaying the words he had spoken earlier that day.

After all these years, I'd love to know the truth. You mean to tell me you didn't have anything to do with taking out your husband?

Laurie should have realized it then. Brenner wasn't hired to kill Martin, and he didn't do it on his own.

Continuing to peer through the binoculars, she said, "Dad, we need to do something. Brenner's not our killer. It's Leigh Ann."

She had typecast Brenner as the bad guy with the shaved head and the mean eyes. He was no angel, but that didn't make him a killer.

Leigh Ann Longfellow, on the other hand, had played the role of the innocent bystander, maligned as "the other woman" by a paranoid wife. And Laurie, along with everyone else, had fallen for it.

She was thinking so quickly, she could barely get the words out. "Dad, when the police verified Leigh Ann's alibi, it was all based on

Daniel. *He* was the one who was meeting with senators. *He* was the one with the hotel reservation. *He* was the one with his picture in the papers. And *he* was the one who confirmed his wife had made the trip with him."

She saw it as clearly as if the events were playing out in front of her in real time. An affair between two unhappy spouses: Martin because of his wife's depression, Leigh Ann because her husband's career had come to a halt in Albany. She pictured Leigh Ann's reaction to her husband's name on the lips of the governor. They could leave the state capital in the rearview mirror. He would hold federal office. They'd spend time in D.C. He'd be a strong contender for the White House.

But Martin Bell didn't want any of that. He wanted a stay-at-home wife and a future stepmother to his children.

Leigh Ann . . . Bell? No. It would never happen. Leigh Ann's children were her dogs. For her, Martin was a distraction when her picture-perfect marriage temporarily stalled.

And Martin wouldn't have taken no for an answer. He was the man who steered his wife away from a medical career. Who told others that she was insane. Who drugged her up rather than get her the care she needed when she had a mental health problem.

Just as Laurie had initially said about the idea of Martin and Leigh Ann as a couple: They were oil and water.

It was all so clear.

"Dad, we need to do something. I think Leigh Ann's going to kill Joe Brenner."

61

Brenner knew the truth the second he saw the gun in Leigh Ann Longfellow's hand.

"Of course it was you," he said coldly. "All this time, I thought it was Kendra."

"Just drive."

"Where to?"

"I'll tell you as we go."

He started the engine, put the car in reverse, and started backing up slowly. He tried to think of a way to signal for help. But where would help come from? He suspected the car behind the trees might have been tailing him, but that wouldn't do him any good if Leigh Ann shot him. If he needed to stand trial for extortion, so be it. Right now, all he wanted was to survive. He had to find a way to distract her.

"I saw you together," he said. "You and Martin. The two of you seemed . . . had the hots for each other. And he was no threat. Why would you kill him?"

Leigh Ann seemed less tense. She was still confident—the way *he* usually was—and seemed to regain control over the panic he had seen in her when she first pulled out the gun. He had no idea whether that was to his benefit or not. All he knew was that he needed to keep her talking. He was buying time. She didn't seem to notice he had stopped backing up.

"I thought he was harmless, too. That probably explains why I took up with him. I was bored out of my mind, and Martin made for a nice companion in Danny's absence. But in love? With him?" Clearly she found the idea ludicrous. "When he'd talk about his big plans for us to leave Kendra and Danny to be together, I'd pretend to go along with it, but I never thought he actually believed it. The last thing I wanted to be was some doctor's wife, let alone a stepmother. I don't even like children. And when Danny got word about the Senate seat, I knew the two of us would be okay again. I told Martin it was over. But he wouldn't accept it. He threatened to tell Danny about the affair if I cut things off with him. I told him, 'Do what you will. Daniel worships me.' He'd never leave me. If anything, he'd only work harder for my affection. But then Martin threatened to tell the media, right as Danny's career was taking off again. I couldn't let that happen."

Brenner knew right then and there that he was looking into the eyes of a woman who could justify anything. In her mind, Kendra and Daniel were to blame for the affair she and Martin chose to conduct, Martin was to blame for his own death, and, surely, Brenner was to blame for the bullet she planned to use on him.

"Does your husband know what you did?" he asked.

"Danny? Of course not. He doesn't even know I own a gun. I bought it to protect myself when he started spending so much time in Albany. I had to buy it on the street because heaven forbid that New York City voters find out their elected representative keeps a gun in his house. In fact, he was so convinced of my innocence that he didn't hesitate to tell the police I was with him in D.C. that night. I told him it was the easiest way to make sure the investigation focused on finding the real killer."

Brenner owned four different weapons, and they were all at home. That's how confident he had been about his sense of control. For five years, he believed that he owned both Kendra and Leigh Ann. Man, they had proven him wrong.

"I told you to drive." Leigh Ann's voice was now steely.

Brenner shifted from reverse to drive and turned toward the road that would be their exit from the park.

He pictured them on a remote industrial road. She'd leave him with a bullet in his head. She'd stage a suicide, placing her unregistered gun in his hand. He'd be blamed for Martin Bell's murder and buried in Potter's Field.

"I think one of us was followed here," he said, gesturing at the grove of trees in the distance to their left. It was the break he needed. For an instant Leigh Ann took her eyes off him. He jammed his foot on the accelerator and turned the wheel hard left. The 707-horsepower engine responded with a loud roar and skidded toward the railroad tie barrier. As Leigh Ann balanced herself and aimed the gun in his direction, the front wheels of Brenner's car hit the barrier. It sent the vehicle vaulting into the air. Leigh Ann pulled the trigger, but the shot passed Brenner and partially shattered the windshield on his side.

Brenner grabbed Leigh Ann's arm, trying to wrest the pistol from her hand. He had it for a second but lost his grip as the car bounced when it hit the ground. He got hold of Leigh Ann's wrist and tried to keep the gun pointed toward the dashboard. It fired again, shattering the navigation screen.

Brenner threw himself off his seat toward Leigh Ann. Holding her wrist with one hand, he was able to grab the barrel of the pistol with the other. With one quick jerk, he hoped to dislodge it from her hand. But then he heard a loud crash as he was thrown toward the dashboard and back, followed by what he thought was a gunshot. The car had come to rest after hitting the concrete support of the fence behind home plate. Both airbags had deployed, leaving Brenner and Leigh Ann stunned.

Leigh Ann opened her eyes and saw Brenner slumped sideways in his seat, his head down on his chest. When she moved her foot, she felt it hit something on the floor of the passenger's seat. Pushing aside the deflated airbag, she reached down and picked up the pistol.

62

Laurie was in the middle of a sentence with her father when they heard the roar of Brenner's engine. The black sedan hopped over the barrier and plowed onto the field.

"Call 911!" Leo shouted as he raced the car around the trees and sped onto the field. They watched helplessly as Brenner's car accelerated toward the backstop fence behind home plate.

I can still get away, Leigh Ann thought. Her shoulders ached from the effort of reaching down to retrieve the gun. She tried to think clearly. *I have my car. Maybe I can leave before anybody comes. Nobody knows I was here. If they find out, everyone will believe me when I say I did it in self-defense.*

Brenner moaned as he opened his eyes and tried to shift his body. Pointing the gun at his heart, Leigh Ann said, "Say hi to Martin for me."

As her finger began to put pressure on the trigger, a voice from behind her barked, "NYPD. Freeze. Drop the gun. Let me see your hands."

Leigh Ann turned her head and saw Leo in a firing position, his gun pointed at her head.

"I'm Leigh Ann Longfellow—" she said as she let the gun slip to the floor.

"I don't care who you are," Leo barked. "Keep your hands where I can see them."

Leo gestured to Laurie, who opened the passenger-side door. She picked up the gun.

With his gun still trained on Leigh Ann, Leo said, "Get out of the car and sit on the ground with your hands up."

As Leigh Ann complied, Leo glanced back and forth between her and Brenner, who was regaining consciousness.

"I'm not armed," Brenner said.

"Keep your hands where I can see them," Leo ordered as Laurie opened the driver's-side door. Brenner pulled himself out and walked unsteadily toward Leo. He sat down in the grass a few feet away from Leigh Ann.

Leigh Ann began shouting at Leo and Laurie, "Who the hell are you? Do you know who I am? Do you have any idea who my husband is? He's Senator Daniel Longfellow. When my husband, the senator, finds out what you're doing to me right now, you won't have a job tomorrow."

She gestured at Brenner. "He tried to kill me. He was holding me at gunpoint. He killed Martin Bell and has been blackmailing me. He just tried to kidnap me. Don't just stand there like an idiot. Do something!"

Brenner's hand reached for his jacket pocket, and Leo quickly shifted the gun toward him. "I said, keep 'em in the air. What were you reaching for?" Leo demanded.

"You'll see. Get it yourself if you don't believe me." With his hand still in the air, Brenner used his index finger to point to the pocket of his jacket.

Laurie looked toward Leo, who nodded his approval. She approached Brenner cautiously, slipping her hand into the pocket he'd indicated. She pulled out the same small digital recorder he'd had with him at Cooper Union. The red light was on.

"I've got her whole story on tape," Brenner said with a sly smile. "That's got to be worth something to the district attorney, don't you think?"

Brenner turned to Leigh Ann, who was glaring at him from her seated position. Smiling, he said, "I'll see you in thirty years if you're out by then. Oh, and give *my best* to the senator."

At the sound of the first siren, the driver of the white SUV started his engine and pulled forward. He would find a place to wait near the park exit, away from the police activity that was certainly going to follow the sounds of gunfire on Randall's Island.

He assumed she'd be leaving in that same little BMW. She wouldn't be able to get off the island without passing him on her way out.

63

A few minutes later, the loop surrounding Athletic Field 9 on Randall's Island was filled with emergency response vehicles. Leigh Ann Longfellow and Joe Brenner were both in handcuffs, secured in the back of separate police cars, and soon would be transported back to Manhattan for booking.

Laurie's cell phone rang for the third time in a row. It was another call from her Realtor, Rhoda Carmichael. She hit the call-decline button.

"She's just going to hit redial," Leo said. Sure enough, her phone buzzed again only seconds later. "Save yourself the headache and answer it."

The last thing she wanted to talk about now was real estate, but she followed Leo's advice. "Rhoda," Laurie said, "I can't talk right now."

Rhoda quickly interrupted. "Laurie, listen to me. You absolutely cannot lose this place. It's a new building on Eighty-fifth between Second and Third. The current owners have the entire sixteenth floor. It has four good-sized bedrooms, each with a private bath. They were about to move in when he accepted a job to run one of the big banks in England. They want to sell fast. The listing agent is a friend of mine. She agreed to let you go in and see it first before she puts in multiple listings tomorrow. It's very reasonably priced, and I know they're going to get full-price offers. You want to avoid a bidding war if you can. You and Alex have to get right over there today and see it. You'll probably beat me there, so I already gave the doorman your name and Alex's. It's empty and he's going to leave the apartment door unlocked for you."

Next to her, Leo was laughing, imagining the other side of the conversation. Laurie rolled her eyes. "We'll look at it tomorrow, okay?"

"No, I'm telling you: you've got to see it right now. Tomorrow's a Sunday at the height of the buying season. Any seller's agent with half a brain will have potential buyers lined up all day long."

"Now's not the best time," Laurie said, feeling herself giving in to Rhoda's high-pressure pitch.

"It's gotta be now," Rhoda insisted. "It's primo Upper East Side. You're a hop and skip away from the park and the Met. You're still near Dad and the school. It's exactly what you've been looking for, and it's in mint condition."

"That does sound pretty great."

Leo signaled that he had something to say. "You can go if you need to. This will take forever, and they're going to want you to go to the precinct to meet with detectives anyway."

"Are you sure?"

"I'm Leo Farley. Of course I'm sure. I'll text you the address for the precinct once they're ready for us, and you can meet us there. I'll ride back with one of the officers."

"All right. I'm sure Jerry will be happy to see his car in one piece." Returning to her call, Laurie told Rhoda she was on her way from Randall's Island.

"Great. I'm on my way in from the Hamptons—that's how sure I am about this place. Call Alex and tell him to meet us there. If you get there before me, the doorman will let you go up."

Once Laurie confirmed her plans with the lead detective, she got into Jerry's car and made her way past the line of police cars toward the park exit. She pulled up Alex on her list of favorites and hit enter. On the fourth ring, she realized that he was probably still at the Yankees game with his clerks. When the call went to voice mail, she left a message. "Hey there. Today went even better than expected. I've got so much to tell you, but I'm about to look at a place with Rhoda. Meet us there if you free up," she said, adding the address Rhoda had given her.

She turned on 1010WINS radio as she approached the park exit. The Yankees were ahead in the top of the ninth. With any luck, their timing might be perfect. She didn't notice the white SUV waiting for her as she left.

64

Behind the wheel of his white SUV, Willie Hayes was gleeful when he saw the little BMW approach the park exit with only one occupant: Laurie, finally all by herself.

Willie had been frustrated as he watched the scene unfold on Randall's Island. What he had thought was a stroke of good luck— Laurie going to an isolated area—turned out to be anything but. He had done his research. He knew her father was a big-deal cop. His suspicion that Daddy Leo still carried a gun was confirmed when he watched Leo and Laurie arrest the two people who'd crashed their car. Just when he thought the opportunity was lost, Laurie got in the car alone and drove off.

Once he began following her from Randall's Island, he thought about running her off the road on the way onto the Triborough Bridge, but it would take a serious accident to cause the kind of injuries he had in mind, and there were no guarantees in life—he knew that for sure. When she took the 96th Street exit, he assumed she was headed back to her apartment. He had never seen her drive a car on her own before. Did she park on the street or in a garage? Would he have a chance to force her into the SUV? He just needed to get her alone on the sidewalk and approach her from behind. He had a new gun in his jacket pocket that would do the trick. If only he'd owned it that night outside the piano bar. This would all be over by now.

His heart fell when she pulled over next to a fire hydrant, getting a wave from a tall, lanky guy waiting for her there. Willie recognized him as the friend who had sung that cloying song about marriage at her annoying little engagement party. Was he going to miss his chance yet again, after all the waiting he had done?

He was about to leave when Laurie tossed the BMW keys to her friend, who took her place at the wheel, giving her a cheerful horn honk before driving away. Willie inched his SUV forward, ready to make his move, but then she threw him for another loop by heading across the sidewalk to the entrance of an apartment building. Had they moved already? Based on the emails he had read on the laptop he'd stolen, he thought they were still searching.

A grocery delivery truck pulled away from its spot in the middle of the block. Willie inched forward to grab it, keeping his eyes on the rearview mirror as Laurie stopped to talk to the doorman. Willie hesitated for a moment on the sidewalk, arriving as she disappeared into the elevator. He assumed she was going to look at yet another apartment. His instinct told him that now was the time to make his move.

He walked up to the doorman, who was on the phone. "Excuse me, the woman who just passed—"

"Are you the husband?" the doorman asked.

"Uh, yes, I am."

"Sixteenth floor. Use the door opposite the elevator," he said as he went back to his phone call.

"Is my wife the only one there?"

"Yes, so far. The Realtor is on her way. She said to let you and your wife go up if you got here first."

Nodding, Willie passed him, went straight to the elevator, waited for the door to close, and pushed the button for 16. He laughed aloud as the elevator began to rise.

65

For once Rhoda was right, Laurie marveled as she stepped inside the apartment. The light was flooding through the arched ceiling over the foyer. On her left she could see the spacious living room with a fireplace. She walked into it and paused to admire the view.

"Hello, Laurie."

She jumped at the sound of his voice. "Hi. I thought no one was here," she said nervously. "Are you the owner?"

"Definitely not." He took great pleasure as her eyes widened at the sight of his gun.

Laurie knew she was staring at a complete stranger, but she was absolutely certain—on an instinctive level—that the man in front of her was the same person who had pushed her in front of a cab after her engagement party. Her best guess was that he was about fifty years old. He had the build of a man who used to be in good shape but had let himself go, the muscle turning to fat.

Her survival instincts told her to speak quietly as she held her hands up. "Whatever's going on here, we can talk about it," she said, trying to keep a tremor out of her voice. "You were outside the piano bar on Monday, right? Was that you?" She was grasping at straws, struggling to understand how he was connected to the Martin Bell case. "Do you work with Joe Brenner? He's in custody. He's well positioned to cut a deal with the DA. You could be part of that plea agreement, too. Or if Leigh Ann Longfellow hired you, you should know she's under arrest, too. You could get total immunity if you testified against her."

"I don't know what you're talking about," he said as he looked around in awe. "You bought this place? It's got to be a fortune."

"No," she said quickly. "I'm meeting a Realtor. Please, I have a young son. I have nothing to do with this apartment. This is my first time here. Let me go, and you can take whatever you want."

The man's gaze shifted between the kitchen and the living room. She could tell he had never been here before. He seemed impressed by his surroundings. This clearly wasn't a random encounter. The man had used her name. He was here because of her, not the property. Alex and Rhoda would be here soon. She knew she had to keep him talking.

"Did my television show pass on a case you're connected to?" she asked, struggling to find a reason someone would target her.

"A TV producer can't afford a spread like this," he said. "This is hot shot Alex Buckley, living the dream life once again. Big reputation. Fancy new job. Front page of the *New York Times* when he got through the Senate. And, to top it all off, a beautiful girlfriend he's about to marry. Too bad it's not going to happen."

The sound of Alex's name from his mouth was like an anvil falling from the sky. *What did Alex have to do with any of this?* Laurie knew that the very nature of her job put her in contact with people who had dangerous secrets they were determined to hide at all costs, but this was something different. She had no idea who this man was, but his desire to hurt her was palpable.

Ramon slowed to a stop in front of the building. The doorman was standing inside. Alex walked over to his station. "I'm Alex Buckley. I believe our Realtor Rhoda Carmichael spoke to you.

I'm meeting my fiancée and Rhoda to look at the sixteenth-floor apartment."

The doorman's expression changed. "A pretty young lady already went upstairs, and her husband a few minutes after."

"Her husband?" Alex asked. "Did the lady tell you her name?"

The doorman picked up a business card off his desk. "She gave me this. Her name's Laurie Moran."

"And another man went up to the apartment?" Alex asked, the concern rising in his voice.

"Yes, a guy who said he was her husband. I was surprised. He didn't look like her type."

Alex was already racing to the elevator. After pushing the button for the sixteenth floor, he dialed Leo. He prayed he would not lose the connection while in the elevator. "A guy who claimed to be me followed Laurie into the apartment. It's at 230 East Eighty-fifth, sixteenth floor. I'm on my way up now. Send help."

Leo disconnected without answering.

The elevator door opened to the sixteenth floor. Alex, grateful that the apartment door was not fully closed, moved it open very slowly. He could see into the living room where Laurie, her hands up, was talking to a man whose back was to him. He could overhear the conversation.

"You're running out of time, Laurie. Say your prayers."

In a second, Laurie saw snippets of a future she wouldn't be around to experience. The images were as real as if she had already lived them. Either Alex or Rhoda would arrive to find her body. Leo and Alex would probably tell Timmy together. Timmy would run to his room and cry on his bed, burying his face in his pillow so no one could hear.

Her current will appointed Leo as Timmy's legal guardian in the event of her death. Would Alex still be part of the picture when she was gone? She wanted to think so. He'd become an honorary uncle to her son instead of a stepfather.

Would her murder ever be solved? She imagined Ryan Nichols taking over *Under Suspicion*—maybe with Jerry at his side. Maybe her own case would be the show's first priority. But maybe not.

She pictured Timmy graduating from college. Getting married. Having a baby and maybe naming her Laurie.

All of it, she saw in an instant. And only then did she realize that she had seen a version of this story play out before. Greg had been shot in the head in the middle of the day by a killer known only as "Blue Eyes," based on the best description Timmy could provide as a toddler. For years, she believed the murderer was some dangerous man Greg had encountered as an emergency room doctor at Mount Sinai.

But Blue Eyes turned out to be a sociopath who had never even met Dr. Greg Moran. His long-harbored grudge was against someone else entirely—Deputy Police Commissioner Leo Farley. To ruin Leo's life, he planned to kill everyone close to him, starting with Greg. Laurie and Timmy were supposed to be next.

She looked directly into the eyes of the man pointing a gun at her and knew her instincts were right. He had nothing against her personally. This was all about Alex.

She had known Alex for less than two years, but they had no secrets. She took her best guess at the source of the grievance.

"This is about Carl Newman, isn't it?" she asked, referring to the investment banker who had run a Ponzi scheme on his clients to the tune of hundreds of millions of dollars. "Even Alex was surprised by the acquittal. Other defense attorneys would have strutted like peacocks on the cable news circuit. Not Alex."

"Stop saying his name!" the man said, straightening his gun arm out to bring the weapon closer to her.

"Please," she said. "I have a young son. His father is dead. He needs me."

"I had a family, too. I lost them!" he shouted at her. "I had a lot of money and I lost it. And the guy who did this to me got away with it because of your precious Alex Buckley."

Looking past him, Laurie could see the door of the apartment opening slowly. It was Alex.

"Newman stole your money?" she asked, struggling to remember the victims who were most vocal in their opposition to Alex's judicial nomination. She remembered Alex telling her that, despite the large financial amounts involved, most of the victims had lost a combination of inherited money and relatively small percentages of their overall wealth. Only a few people had been completely wiped out of everything they had worked for. Looking at the man in front of her, a name came to her: Willie Hayes, son of a handyman and a laundress, a wholly self-made contractor who rolled over all of his assets to Carl Newman after his baby was born, only to discover he had lost everything six years later.

"Are you Willie Hayes?" His face told her that she was right. "Please, tell me your story. I have a TV show. Carl Newman was acquitted in federal court, but the state could still bring charges. We could make that happen. A civil suit, too."

"None of that will rewind the clock," he said. "I used to have it all, and now it's gone. A loft in Tribeca, a country house upstate. A wife. A son. *Love*. I had to file for bankruptcy. The property, the bank accounts, the cars—all of it got taken. My wife and son, too. Alex Buckley doesn't deserve to be happy."

She pictured this man watching her engagement party at the piano bar. He had never been interested in her laptop and case notes. He was angry because she and her friends had been celebrating the life she was going to share with Alex.

"Please," she said, hearing her own voice begin to shake. "I have nothing to do with any of that. My work is literally dedicated to finding justice for people who are wronged. I have a son, too. How old is yours? I've been raising Timmy on my own since his father was murdered." She felt sick entrusting this sociopath with her past, but she was willing to do anything possible to live.

As she was talking, Alex was making his way quietly across the room toward them. The wail of a police siren in the distance helped drown out the faint sound of his shoes on the hardwood floor.

"Shut up!" Hayes yelled. "You . . . you mean nothing to me. If you want to blame anyone, blame Alex Buckley. He's the one who landed his dream job with courthouse security and U.S. Marshals installing high-tech alarms in his apartment. You're the only way I can get to him."

She opened her mouth to speak, not knowing what words to use. She wished there were some furniture, a couch to dive behind if he began shooting. There was nothing between the two of them as he began to walk closer, the gun at her chest.

66

"Now, Laurie Moran, you're gonna pay for what your boyfriend did."

Terrified, Laurie could hear the sound of her own breathing. She watched as his finger moved ever so slightly on the trigger of the pistol. The silence was broken by a noise from behind.

"Hey, Willie, I'm the one you want!" Alex shouted.

Startled, Willie turned in the direction of Alex's voice. As he did so, the gun moved slightly to his left and was no longer pointed at her. She recognized her opportunity and pounced.

Laurie sprinted toward Willie and grabbed his hand and wrist that held the gun. He struggled to turn it toward her. As they grappled for control of the weapon, a shot was fired and lodged in the ceiling. She heard Willie gasp as from behind Alex enveloped him in a bear hug, pinning his arms to his sides. Still holding onto his hand with the gun, Laurie slipped four of her fingers around Willie's index finger. She bent his finger back. He yelped in pain as he released his grip on the gun. It clattered to the floor. Laurie scrambled to pick it up. She assumed a classic triangular stance to level the weapon at Willie's torso, just as her father had taught her when she was in high school.

Alex was holding Willie's arms at his sides like a human straitjacket. "Why? Why, Willie?" he demanded. "This wasn't going to get your old life back. Now your son's going to have to visit you behind bars."

The moment of sympathy for his client's victim was only temporary. Alex ran to Laurie and held her around her waist from behind as she continued to aim the gun at Willie.

Laurie finally released her grip on the gun when a row of police officers rushed through the door of the apartment. Alex pulled her into a tight hug, turning her face away from Willie Hayes, who was glaring at them as he was handcuffed.

When Alex let go, he looked into her eyes with sadness. "I know how hard it was for you to accept me into your world, and now my work put you in danger. I would understand if it changed the way you feel."

She felt tears come to her eyes as she shook her head adamantly. "No, never. When I saw him standing there with that gun, all I could think about was the wonderful life we were going to have together. My love for you is even stronger, if that's possible."

"God, that's a relief. Oh, Laurie." He wrapped his arms around he. "I'll never let you go."

She murmured, "I'd marry you right here and now if I could."

Laurie began to feel the shock from what had happened and leaned closer to Alex for support.

Behind them, they heard a commotion from the foyer. They looked from the kitchen and caught a glimpse of Rhoda Carmichael trying to force her way past a police officer looping crime scene tape across the threshold.

Spotting them inside, Rhoda shouted, "What's going on? Sorry I'm late. The traffic on the LIE was *brutal*. But forget that. What's going on? What happened?"

Alex, still holding Laurie in his arms, called back to her. "What happened is that I want to get Laurie out of here. I'll call you tomorrow."

Laurie looked around, but didn't move. From the little she had seen, the apartment was beautiful. If they bought it, would they always be haunted by the memory of Willie Hayes pointing a gun at her? Maybe. Maybe not.

By now the police had let Rhoda in. She ran to them and tried to joke, "I didn't know someone would try to kill you to get this place!"

Neither Laurie nor Alex smiled.

67

Two Weeks Later

Laurie watched as Ryan Nichols looked into the camera with a somber expression. "Daniel and Leigh Ann Longfellow had been called the rulers of a New American Camelot—a beloved and beautiful political couple with the potential to heal a divided nation with their popular policy views, sterling credentials, and personal charms. But, tonight, we'll take a closer look at the shocking events that have left Leigh Ann in custody, facing a life sentence for murder, and Daniel fighting for the survival of his political career."

True to form, Brett Young had started publicizing the airdate of their next episode within twenty-four hours of Leigh Ann's arrest. When Laurie pointed out to him that they hadn't even begun to collect footage, he had winked and said, "Nothing like a deadline to motivate your team."

After working around the clock for two weeks straight, they were nearly finished with production. They had saved Ryan's introduction and closing comments for last to make sure they included the new facts that continued to trickle in daily.

For Brenner there would be no get-out-of-jail-free card. He was facing a multitude of charges for extorting and threatening both Leigh Ann Longfellow and Kendra Bell over a period of many years. Kendra was ready and willing to testify that her many withdrawals of large sums of cash and payments to him had been made in a desperate attempt to protect herself and her children. And, ironically, his recording of Leigh Ann on Randall's Island, which he had made to continue to blackmail her, would now be powerful evidence against him. The police had seized his recorder when they arrested him, and it was now stored in their evidence safe. There seemed to be little doubt that he would spend many years in prison.

Likewise, the case against Leigh Ann looked rock solid. They had Brenner's recording, plus ballistics tests showing that the 9 mm handgun she brought to Randall's Island was the same weapon used to kill Martin Bell. She had been so confident that she had gotten away with it, she hadn't even bothered to get rid of the gun. Leigh Ann, too, would probably spend most or all of the rest of her life in prison. The police were also looking into the role her law firm had played in funneling payments to Brenner.

In between all of the work on the production, Laurie had found the time to testify in front of the grand jury last week to support charges against Willie Hayes for robbery and attempted murder. Hayes told the police he was only trying to get Laurie to hear his side of the story in the hope that she would end her relationship with Alex. But the bullet hole in the apartment's ceiling told another story. They might never be able to prove that he was the one who attacked her outside of the piano bar, but he'd be going to prison for years.

Ryan looked at the studio door with annoyance when they heard a knock. The recording light was on in the hallway, indicating that no one should disturb them. A second later, the door opened. It was Jerry. "Sorry, but we're going to have to rewrite the copy anyway. Daniel Longfellow's giving a press statement in five minutes."

Grace, Jerry, Ryan, and Laurie gathered at the conference table in Laurie's office to watch Senator Longfellow step in front of the cameras. For fourteen days, he had managed to say nothing about his wife's arrest except for platitudes such as "continuing to focus on my work for the American people," "cooperating with law enforcement," and "trusting the greatest justice system in the world." Political pundits expressed dismay that, under the circumstances, he had not yet been arrested, let alone that he was still going to work.

Laurie hadn't seen Longfellow since Leigh Ann's arrest. He appeared to have lost ten pounds and aged a decade.

"Five years ago, I told the police that my wife, Leigh Ann, had traveled with me to Washington, D.C., while I was meeting with leaders there in anticipation of my appointment to a temporary vacancy in the U.S. Senate. That was a lie. I could tell you why I believed it was harmless at the time, but ultimately, none of that matters. It was a lie, plain and simple, and it was wrong. I never suspected my wife's involvement in the murder of Dr. Martin Bell. In fact, when the police contacted us, I assumed that *I* was the suspect they were investigating. The police spoke to Leigh Ann first, and she told them that she'd been with me in D.C. At that point, I had a choice to make: I could either repeat her version of events, or tell the police that the woman I loved had just given them a false statement in my defense. Because I was certain that *I* was innocent, and I had an ironclad alibi, I didn't see the harm in protecting my wife. I swear to you, the American public, that it never dawned on me that she was lying in order to create an alibi for herself. But none of that ultimately matters. We are a nation of laws, and I did not live up to one of the basic responsibilities we all share as citizens. I will work now to listen to friends, trusted advisors, and most importantly, you, my constituents, to decide my next steps. But, no matter what happens, I promise I will cooperate with the prosecution of my wife, Leigh Ann"—his voice caught—"and will never betray the public's trust again. Finally, I want to extend my deepest apologies to Martin Bell's parents, Cynthia and Robert; to his children, Bobby and Mindy; and to his widow, Kendra Bell, who lived for years under a shadow of suspicion that was wholly undeserved. I realize that my dishonesty and cowardice prevented you from knowing the truth about what happened to Martin, and the shame of that will live with me forever."

After he walked away from the microphones without taking questions, Jerry clicked off the television.

"It sounds like he's days, maybe hours, from resigning," Jerry said.

"Or not," Laurie noted. "I heard a panel of pundits this morning saying that he could ride it out. A lot of his supporters want him to stay in office."

Once Laurie was alone, she called Kendra Bell on her cell phone. She started by apologizing for interrupting her at work. "I wanted to make sure you knew about Longfellow's press conference."

"Are you kidding? Steven played it on the television in the waiting room. It's been a rough couple of weeks trying to explain to my kids why the wife of their senator wanted to hurt their father, but you don't know how good it feels to have my name finally cleared." She lowered her voice. "One of the old biddies who usually gives me the evil eye actually hugged me and apologized for having doubts about me. I feel like I finally have my life back. Steven's coming over tonight to celebrate. I've always been so grateful for his friendship, but I'm starting to realize that he was the one person who never doubted my innocence."

"Any chance you've heard from Robert and Cynthia?" Laurie had spoken to Martin's parents last week. She sensed their shame at having vilified Kendra for years, but admitting mistakes did not come naturally to the pair.

"We visited them last weekend at their country house, in fact. I was reluctant to accept the invitation, but Caroline persuaded me to give them a chance at being regular grandparents again instead of my adversaries. They were actually kind to me, if you can believe it. And more importantly, I can finally see how much they love Bobby and Mindy—in their own uptight way," she added with a small laugh. "Even Caroline seems . . . lighter. I wasn't the only one carrying the load of Martin's murder all these years. Anyway, a lot's changed for the whole family, and I have you to thank for that."

Something in Kendra's voice sounded warmer. Happier. It had taken Laurie six years after Greg's death before she could picture herself sharing her life with someone else. Kendra Bell was approaching that same landmark.

Laurie congratulated Kendra again and told her she'd call her once the production was finalized. She had just hung up when her cell phone buzzed. It was a text from Alex: *We're downstairs.*

Outside, a black car was waiting. Timmy bounded from the backseat, gave her a big hug, and then hopped into the front next to Ramon while Laurie climbed in back next to Alex.

"There had to be an easier way to do this," Laurie said. Ramon had picked up Timmy from school, driven down to the federal courthouse to pick up Alex, and was now in Midtown to gather up Laurie.

Timmy grinned at her from the front seat. "That's okay, Mom. Ramon likes having me in the car with him. We listen to jazz and I tell him about the different musicians."

"And then sometimes I make him listen to the hip-hop channels I like," Ramon said with a smile. "We could be in one of those movies where a young person and an old person switch bodies. Now where is our next destination?"

All Ramon and Timmy had been told was that they were all going somewhere together. Alex gave Ramon the address of a building on 85th Street between Second and Third.

When they got out, Timmy and Ramon followed them and Rhoda up the elevator to the sixteenth floor. Laurie was relieved to see that the crime scene tape had been removed from the apartment entrance, as promised.

"The owner will accept our offer," Alex said happily, "but before we make it official, we wanted to make sure you'll be comfortable here. If not, we keep looking."

Five minutes later, it was official. This would be their home.

"We'll definitely have the best 'how did you find your apartment?' story," Alex said as they signed the final paperwork for the offer at the kitchen island.

When Ramon and Timmy headed for the car, Laurie and Alex paused to take one final look, gazing up at the ornate crown molding on the thirteen-foot ceilings of the foyer. She took his hand in hers. "Think of all the memories we're going to make here together."

She was already thinking about the little person who might grow up in the sweet corner bedroom next to Timmy's.

Acknowledgments

Once again I am reminded what a wise decision it was when I chose to co-write with my fellow novelist, Alafair Burke. As a result of our joint efforts, yet another crime has been solved.

Marysue Rucci, editor-in-chief of Simon & Schuster, again provided valuable insight throughout the telling of this tale.

My home crew is still solidly in place. They are my spouse extraordinare, John Conheeney, and "Team Clark," family members who read and provide feedback the whole way through. They brighten this business of making words appear on the page.

And you, my dear readers. Again you are in my thoughts as I write. You are as special to me as the ones who bought my first suspense story back in 1975 and launched me on a lifetime journey.

Cheers and Blessings,
Mary

About the authors

The #1 *New York Times* bestselling author **Mary Higgins Clark** has written thirty-eight suspense novels, four collections of short stories, a historical novel, a memoir, and two children's books. With her daughter Carol Higgins Clark, she has co-authored five more suspense novels, and also wrote *The Cinderella Murder*, *All Dressed in White*, *The Sleeping Beauty Killer*, *Every Breath You Take* and *You Don't Own Me* with bestselling author Alafair Burke. More than one hundred million copies of her books are in print in the United Kingdom alone. Her books are international bestsellers.

Alafair Burke is the *New York Times* bestselling author of twelve novels, including *Long Gone*, *If You Were Here* and the latest in the Ellie Hatcher series, *All Day and a Night*.